C Vernieux

The Hermit of Motee Jhurna, or Pearl Spring

Also Indian Tales and Anecdotes, Moral and Instructive. Second Edition

C Vernieux

The Hermit of Motee Jhurna, or Pearl Spring
Also Indian Tales and Anecdotes, Moral and Instructive. Second Edition

ISBN/EAN: 9783337073732

Printed in Europe, USA, Canada, Australia, Japan

Cover: Foto ©Andreas Hilbeck / pixelio.de

More available books at **www.hansebooks.com**

THE

HERMIT OF MOTEE JHURNA,

OR

PEARL SPRING;

ALSO

INDIAN TALES AND ANECDOTES,

MORAL AND INSTRUCTIVE.

" *The cheerful sage when graver maxims fail,*
Conceals the moral in a pleasing Tale."

BY

C. VERNIEUX.

SECOND EDITION,

RECAST AND ENLARGED.

CALCUTTA:

PRINTED AT THE BAPTIST MISSION PRESS.
SOLD AT ALL THE LIBRARIES.
1873.

Price Rs. 1/8.

PREFACE.

More than sixteen years ago, the Hermit appeared in the "Calcutta Literary Gazette" which was conducted by Capt. Richardson.

It was originally published in nine chapters, but in the present issue, four additional chapters of interesting matter have been added, and the entire tale has undergone a complete revision.

The design of the tale is, to bring prominently into view, the character of our Moslem neighbours in the country; the incidents chosen, it is hoped, are calculated both to amuse and furnish the reader with interesting accounts of their personal qualities which, unfortunately, are not so well known as those of the Hindoos; the simple fact that books are more numerously written about the latter than the former, go to prove the assertion.

I have been faithful in delineating the customs, ceremonies, manners and habits of the Mahomedans, and their interior domestic life; not omitting, however, to present the reader with a picture of Indian life in general, with descriptive sketches of the gorgeous scenery of the country, and hints regarding its undeveloped natural resources.

The Indian Tales and Anecdotes were translated and published by me in 1864, and it has for some years past gone out of print.

The English reader has, by translations, been long acquainted with the gems of Oriental Literature. It has been my desire to furnish a collection of Indian Tales and Anecdotes not to be found in books.

They are legendary and oral, and current both in the Courts of Rajahs, Nawabs, and Princes; in mansions of opulence, as well as in the hamlets of the poor.

I doubt if there be any part in the world so abounding with this sort of light oral literature as the East. Being as they are, the inhabitants of an enervating climate, they generally beguile the tediousness of their unemployed time by listening to the recital of some stirring event, some pleasing fiction, some pathetic narrative, or some useful moral precept.

It has not been my design to collect written tales like those of the *Arabian Nights' Entertainments*, but from the many stories and anecdotes in Urdu, Hindi, and Bengali, I have had the opportunity of hearing, I have gathered such as possess some degree of merit either for the moral they convey, or the light according to which virtue and vice, deceit and integrity, are weighed in an Oriental balance.

Probably, too, it is by such short narratives and pithy sayings among such a people, that a very faint glimmering of the knowledge of good and bad, right and wrong, is diffused and propagated.

I have, in rendering them into English, discarded all embellishment with a view to preserve their originality and identity.

C. V.

CALCUTTA, *November*, 1873.

CONTENTS.

(vi)

THE HERMIT OF MOTEE-JHURNÁ.

OR PEARL SPRING.

CHAPTER I.

ON the right or western bank of the Ganges lies the village of Seebgunge, in whose vicinity are the ruins of Raj Girghy, so called under the ancient Hindoo Government, but subsequently dignified with the title of Akburnagur after Akbar, and lastly designated Raj-Mahul, by Raja Kanare Man Sing.

In the fifteenth century, when the Sultans made it the capital of their vice-royalty, it prided itself in possessing elegant buildings of a style of architecture remarkable for accurate proportions, beauty of design, and tasteful execution.

The portals and capitals of columns were adorned with numerous figures in basso-relievo, representing the celebration of festivals —gateways, large and handsome—the interior of buildings ornamented with wreathed mouldings—the palace of Nogeswarbag, Rungmahal, or painted hall—Jumna Musjid, Akbarabad Mosque, Sungge-dullan, or stone hall—the tomb of Bukht Homa, which contained the remains of Mirza Muhammed, Subah of Bengal, together with a well finished oratory, having its front lined with highly polished marble, and neatly inlaid with pious sentiments in black marble; these were edifices whose grandeur and superb architecture were inferior to none on the plains of India.

Raj-Mahul was once the residence of Futtehjung Khan, Sultan Shujah, houri-like begums, and polished *Shazadas*. But where now the monuments of their grandeur, where they whose laughter and merriment, bustle of occupation, anxiety and

1

hopes, which gave life and brilliance to the place of their residence? Alas! all the pomp and pageantry of dignity, the evanescent glitter of glory and ambition's rainbow hues which made earth and existence seem an imaginary paradise, and for time a desirable object of pursuit and acquisition—where are they now with their insatiate throb after painted pleasures, their fever of boundless ambition? They have passed away like summer clouds,—at times brilliant in their journey with the hues of sunshine, but for ever vanished into darkness and oblivion. All have been swept away by the irresistible tide of time. The best portions of those buildings themselves, which were more durable than their designers, have been undermined and imbedded with the sand of the Ganges, yet the few that remain, bear indications of their pristine magnificence, and may well support the designation of Raj-Mahul, or residence of princes. Sixteen miles from hence up the river, and two miles below the eminence called Sukreegully hill, was the beautiful and picturesque litte fall, which trickling like a pearl-spring, had derived its name—Motee-Jhurná.

In its neighbourhood, but at the distance of not more than two hundred yards, stands a venerable banian which spreads out its many lateral branches over an extensive area, beneath which the fibres descending at intervals, form themselves into sturdy columns to support each of the ponderous branches.

Some parasitical plants that adhere to its trunk, adorn the banian with their diversity of leaves and flowers of the most delicate hue, as well as gather little warblers who sip, poise on the tender twigs, and make the shade musical with their songs of innocent mirth. Beneath the umbrage of this wide spread canopy, dwelt a hermit whose fervent devotion, together with the extensive knowledge of medicine and the virtue of plants, which he pre-eminently possessed, spread his fame for many miles around, and attracted to his humble hut, the poor with their gift of flowers and humble donations, the opulent with more costly offerings and presents.

Ameerjan had the majestic and commanding air of one who well knew the sway he held over the minds of the ignorant and superstitious, and the fear and respect which his reputation for being in league with secret powers, had command over the great.

With all his pretensions, however, to occult science, he never made an ostentatious display of his talents, nor abused the influence thus acquired, but ever gentle and meek, the most timid would converse with him with perfect unreserve, and always leave him with an impression that though at times seemingly of a proud and haughty bearing, Ameerjan was the most kind and tender-hearted person in general deportment. In stature he was above the ordinary size, while his frame was muscular and well built. His dark hair which was parted in the centre of his head, waved clustering over his masculine shoulders in graceful ringlets, while his beard that descended two or three inches below the chin, was trimmed in shape like a crescent.

Constant exposure to the influence of several climes, gave to his complexion, which was otherwise fair, a tinge of olive. A pair of *junghyas* or trousers, was worn by him girded about his waist with a silk belt. The upper part of his person was covered with something like a waistcoat, over which, a tunic or cloak was used. A bag, pendant from one of his shoulders, contained different roots and drugs, as also a scrip and cruse with which he would venture forth from his hut on short journies to Raj-Mahul and its neighbouring villages. His only companion on such occasions, was a huge shaggy dog of Nepaul breed, led by a chain held on his left hand, while his right supported a cane formed of bamboo root, which at the extremity intended for the handle, was inverted, and had two side shoots clipped so as to resemble the head and antlers of a deer. Passing the gates of the Omrao of Raj-Mahul, his acquaintance with whom was extensive, and his society was highly appreciated by the *Amirs* on account, not only of his talents, but for his easy, graceful, and refined deportment, he after such recreative walks, would return to his little cottage which nestled under the shade of the banian.

Save the cheerful hum of birds, the gentle murmur of the Pearl-Spring, the sad tones of forlorn beings who repaired to his retirement to request his counsel, the sick and barren to obtain drugs in the concoction of which he was an adept, no human voice ever awoke an audible echo of sentiment from the anchoret. To relieve, however, the dull monotony of his daily occupations, his cottage contained scraps of the Koran, and verses of his favourite poets—Sadi, Hafez, and Furdosi. These constantly employed his leisure in their deep absorbing study, while the works of the famous Zurdhust, or Zoroaster, also occupied a portion of his time. There could exist no sympathy between the followers of Mahomed and the disciples of Zoroaster. The Hermit who was not a bigot, gleaned knowledge from whatever source he could, as he had no such weak prejudices. He admired the works of the great sage of Persia for the numerous valuable ethical doctrines enunciated in them, and did not therefore care a straw for objections which bigotry might raise against it, or in disfavour of any other learned productions of wise and good men, be they of whatever country, creed, or nation they might. He was familiar with the Arabic and Toorky languages, hence it was conjectured that he came from the beautiful city of Phars; but no more of his history was known than that he might be one of the sons of that brilliant clime.

From his cottage, through the openings of foliage, you might have a glimpse of the majestic play of the Ganges, sparkling and dancing in the sunbeam, and rolling onward unresisted in her course, bearing her tribute of waters to her parent the boundless ocean. Of an evening in spring, when the pale empress of night moves majestically over the blue ethereal sea, revealing by her pensive aspect the sorrows with which she too seems to be drenched, it was Ameerjan's habit to walk with his *setar* a few paces from that shade, to one of the projections of the hill near the Pearl-Spring. There would he touch its delicate cords into the sweetest thrill. Thus awoke into mellow whispers of pensive melody, it never failed to draw forth a response from his inmost soul. Accompanying the instrument at times with his rich sonorous voice, he would give vent to his smothered feelings in the following verses.

Tell me, Zeleikha! tell me why,
You glance me with your pensive eye;
Why at this distance doth it seem,
Your heart pours on me its holy beam?

Mem'ry! take back the image fair;
Of past events to think I dare;
Let chill oblivion wrap or blast,
I cannot look on what is past!

Smile Chandar! serenely smile,
And with thy influence soft beguile
My hours of pain, and I will be
Thy votr'y ever loving thee.

With the calm dews of night falling,
And thy bright rays softly bending,
Cool the fever of my throbbing breast
And steep my senses into rest.

A pleasing placid smile often sported about the lips of Ameerjan, though his looks wore indications of a deep settled melancholy which seemed to brood over his heart, and spread its gloom on his countenance, tinging the latter with a sort of serenity that was at times too painful to the contemplation of a tenderly susceptible heart. It was not difficult to discern through its medium, the volcanic eruptions from which the heart suffered, and like its expiring embers, threw out the flickering sparks of existence on the visage, by occasional smiles which were robed in gloom more than in cheerfulness.

CHAPTER II.

JUST at the hour when the young light of day peeps through the curtains of the East, gradually mantling the fair cheeks of fleecy clouds with roseate hues, and zephyrs wake from the lap of night and seek the perfumed breath of dew-gemmed flowers; or when the firmament glows with the farewell kiss of parting day, and mild evening with her cooling breeze fans the weary brow of industry, a young Ameer of a pleasing countenance and graceful appearance, would be seen mounted on a Toorky charger, richly caparisoned, prancing and curveting on the roads of Raj-Mahul.

Mobaruc Ulli, for it was he, was equipped in a costly *kinkhaub labada*, ornamented with gold buttons, and set with gems about the neck. A pair of canary colored silk trowsers waved beneath, displaying a pair of shagreen high heeled slippers, worn on the foot of the gay equestrian. His Cashmere shawl turban of emerald green, filigreed with a beautiful lacing of gold embroidery, crowned his head, below which fell a profusion of glossy curls in studied negligence.

Thus attired, the young noble (for he had not witnessed the revolution of more than two and twenty summers) would take his morning and evening ride, amusing himself and being admired by every idle saunterer about the bazar. They applauded the easy manner in which he curbed the restive steed, or praised the graceful attitude in which he seated himself on the spirited animal, by loud wah! wahs!

It was not often that the elegant Omrao shed the light of his countenance over the all-vivacious *chowk*.

On a road opposite the latter place, at the extremity of which the city terminated, a spacious edifice, somewhat out of repair, rose into view. From the corners and sides of its out-offices which were left to greater neglect, the destructive *asud*, with other tangled creepers, grew spontaneously. These buildings were enclosed by a high wall which surrounded more than twenty-five *biggahs* of land, laid out in promiscuous groves of leechees, mangoes, peaches, pomegranates, and other luscious fruits, the lavish product of a fertile clime.

The master of the mansion was an Amir of decayed fortune, though he had once amassed much silver and gold, and had kept a splendid establishment under the service of the predecessor of Sujah.

A host of asabardars, or mace bearers waited once on his pleasure; and several elephants and horses which formed his retinue, gave an air of dignity to the pageantry.

Where the garden wall swept round in another direction and was closed from the view of the public road promenaders, a small door opened towards a wide plain from whence at some distance, a few motley huts of husbandmen could be discerned covered with the broad foliage of plantains, with the delicately shaded green of the tamarind, and the dense leaves of patches of mangoe topes. Mobaruc, either to avoid the inquisitive gaze of idlers, or to pursue the even tenor of his calm undisturbed reflections, made this plain the frequent scene of his evening recreation.

The aged noble who lived so much secluded from society, gave little opportunity for people to whisper who were the inmates of that half dilapidated mansion. It was therefore, no doubt, like a vision from above, when Nujmoon Nissa, the fair inhabitant of that building, weary with the sameness of amusement and occupation which engaged her within the precincts of her retirement, sought the private gate with her companion, in order that from thence, they might contemplate the little world of life which the residents of the bungalows at a distance presented—and weave in their minds some brief but pleasing narrative of love, or grief, as the mood in which they lay at the time, might have suggested to beguile a few hours of listless occupation.

Mobaruc, in passing them, struck with an agreeable surprise at so unexpected a vision of beauty, curbed his prancing horse, and gazing intently, saluted thus; " Fair lady ! who could have dreamt a moment before that one so beautiful ever respired within those sepulchral walls, and had eclipsed her light and loveliness within their gloomy shadows, but even they which bore an aspect of cheerlessness before, seem now to me as luminous as the Ganges when the sun bathes in her his flood of golden light." As this compliment invited no response, and Nujmoon modestly drew the veil over her handsome face, he could not but reluctantly pursue the course of his usual ride. Nujmoon Nissa was a young lady of not more than sixteen years of age, consequently, so little as she was used to the converse of a person of the opposite sex, she had not sufficient firmness to look up at the stranger, submit herself to be studied with an eye of scrutiny, or bold enough to enlist herself in conversation.

Mobaruc had traversed the field, and as he turned his horse to repass them, Nujmoon who was watching his motion, took a hasty glance, then closing the gate, retired with her associate to her now cheerless apartment.

In the meantime he returned to his residence with reflections though not wholly free from sadness, yet that sadness was not unmixed with joy.

In that one vehement gaze, his heart had received a deep impress of her image; and his memory now brought back vividly to the view of his mental eye, her rich drapery of purple silk which composed her trowsers; her flowered Dacca *jaumdane* which covered her figure like a veil, and allowed her hair to be seen running down in graceful plats; her arms ornamented with armlets and bracelets, set with diamonds, emeralds and pearls; her tapering fingers decked with rings of value.

He had drank the melody of that musical voice which he heard when he first met her, and when she spoke to her attendant; "It is late, come let us retire." He sighed as he thought he still beheld her tender form of exquisite symmetry, reclining over her companion; and those orbs of light and life that then bent on him their rays of intelligence, as if still looking with pity and complaisance.

Musing thus on a balcony after his ride, he indulged in the following soliloquy: "Man seems to live and feel that he is a living being save when he comes into contact and communion with the fair sex. A thousand indescribable sensations of joy rush through his veins, and other emotions and sentiments grow into a sort of existence new and pleasing to himself, which might have otherwise remained in a state of dormancy for ever, or stagnated in the heart of a recluse, and bred apathy, moroseness, and misanthropy.

"I must see her again." Repeating the last words, he went to his dormitory and threw himself into the arms of Morpheus, to sleep and to dream.

Nujmoon, in the retirement of her chamber, indulged the image of the handsome stranger; and made many a conjecture as to who he might be, and if he would visit the field again? If her behaviour was repulsive, or such that it did not encourage his advances, was it of that nature which could not offend, but leave him hesitating which course to pursue, without totally checking him with despair?

A woman's feelings and judgment in these matters which are very acute, and give the most accurate interpretation, made her conscious that her person was not disagreeable to him; and that like herself, he might also desire an interview, and contract an intimacy which his first meeting evidently indicated he sought.

While in this mood of perplexity, her attendant, Goolchummon, entered her apartment. "Well, my ever kind mistress, you seem pleased with something, yet are sad. I hope nothing serious has transpired to make your pensiveness predominant, and your depression lasting." "You a woman, Goolchummun, and cannot read my heart." "To decipher your feelings I may, beautiful Nujmoon," she responded. "They are at present, if I have not already lost my penetration, absorbed with thoughts of the handsome Mobaruc, the admiration of all Raj Mahul, as you would be its perpetual praise, were your beauty suffered to be revealed to its light."

2

"You surprise me much, Goolchummun! how came you to learn particulars connected with him, so early?"

"That is far from difficult to answer. Discovering your loss of appetite, I went over last night to the *chawk* to bring you some dainty confection from our *hulchy*, when, describing the person of the stranger, his horse, and its rich housings, the pad and the gold-mohurs jingling at its neck, the confectioner instantly recognised the Omrao who, he said, was entertained high in the service of our mighty Sultan Sujah Bahadoor."

Thus conversing with her companion, Nujmoon pleasantly beguiled her monotonous hours of lassitude.

The anxiously anticipated evening, which had appeared advancing with leaden steps, arrived at last.

Nujmoon could no longer refrain from testifying her impatience to promenade about the garden, alleging as an excuse that the air about her rooms was too confined to respire freely.

Goolchummon smiling assent, joined her in the walk. After a few revolutions round beds of flower plants, they were attracted to one of the walks leading to the door which admitted an interesting prospect of the *maidan* and its distant villages.

Mobaruc was equally impatient to see her as she was, and had therefore come earlier than was his habit, and was exercising his horse in the wide plain.

Ever vigilant to learn whether Nujmoon had come to the gate, he constantly reverted his face towards that quarter, and when from that distance he thought he had spied something like a female form in shadowy outlines, he spurred the animal until the outline of that form became conspicuous, when drawing his horse to a gentle canter, and going up, he greeted her with his usual courtesy.

This civility was not, however, assumed as a mere matter of etiquette, a lifeless unmeaning phraseology, but a language intelligible alike to his feelings as to his heart—a sincere outpouring of his genuine sentiments.

"Gentle and ever beautiful lady! I trust this evening finds

you in health and felicity. Absence from you deprives me of peace, while your presence alone restores happiness."

"Stranger! your words, if sincere, flatter me much; but the lovely moon glows only with borrowed light, and we owe all our perfection to your company and conversation, which intercourse, had it not been mutual, would have lost all efficacy for imparting the least gratification."

"Fair lady! to live under the smile of your presence would be the highest boon of mortals. Would that I could lay me down where your cur is permitted to crouch with impunity."

Then presenting her with a bouquet assorted with emblematical flowers expressive of his sentiments, he continued : "Would you, fair lady, suffer me, like that envied animal, to dwell always before you; and like the frail flowers which now grace your person, and ere long will droop there, will you allow me, when weary of earthly toils, to lay my head and sigh there my last breath of existence?"

"Stranger," said Nujmoon Nissa, "the familiarity which exists between us and our domesticated animals, removes our aversion and engrafts esteem, so your intimacy with our sex, the weaker and dependent beings, suffers you to admit us as your friends and companions."

Of this tenor was the topic of conversation on this occasion, and at every succeeding interview, which was frequent, Mobaruc, who played his part so skilfully because so sincerely, gained much more admission into that heart than his first meeting could promise he would ever attain.

Chapter III.

THOUGH Nujmoon Nissa, by the inflexible custom of her country, and the rigid rules of her creed, was shut out from the outer world intercourse, and its multifarious amusements, she was not bereft of those which her little domain of female seclusion afforded her.

She had many kinds of recreation, and varied resources at her command, by which her hours were employed for purposes of not only mere pastime, but profitable occupation, or languid enjoyment.

The even tenor of Nujmoon Nissa's life was agreeably diversified by the occasional visit of some of her relations, who brought a stock of pleasant news, not gleaned, however, from the knowledge of the several incidents that had, one would suppose, transpired within their individual cognisance, but obtained from their husbands, or brothers, who had gathered them from the occurrences happening in the great city, or the different out-stations to which business, or pleasure, had taken them.

The female relations of Nujmoon Nissa, who were wont to visit her periodically, came as their custom was, in a palankeen borne by a set of four bearers, a couple of men running in advance of the conveyance, each holding a silver mace, and followed by a reserve relay of bearers, dressed in scarlet robes, edged with yellow braid.

The palankeen was similarly mantled with scarlet broadcloth, and it had two circular openings at each door, which were worked up with muslin to admit light and air, and to afford the inmate the means of gratifying her desire to see all objects, without being herself seen by anybody's prying eyes.

On the roof of the palankeen, at the centre, rose a graceful little silver dome, and there were four cones of the same metal, in the corners fixed to adorn the conveyance, and distinguish it from those belonging to the poorer classes.

When the palankeen had reached its destination, the bearers, after placing it beneath the portico, or vestibule of the house, retired from thence to a short distance, to permit the *Amir-zadi*, or noble lady, to enter the premises to which she had gone on a visit.

Not only by this means did the stock of her knowledge of the world augment, but Nujmoon's duenna, Goolchummon, who was a great gossip and an incessant gadabout, and whose insatiable thirst for knowing and meddling with the affairs of all persons, whether acquired by fair legitimate means, and obtained as they freely and spontaneously flowed from the history of the lives of honest simple-minded men who held conversation in the streets of Rajmahal, at the door of shops, or got them by pumping with insinuations and cunning questions, as well as by other tricks, in all which she had a protracted training, and evinced therefore, a tolerable amount of proficiency in the art of extracting news, though the mode by which she procured them, she did not care for.

That this was mean and dishonorable conduct, of this fact she was thoroughly oblivious. Considering the motive by which she was actuated to so sedulous a duty of collecting *gup*, that is, for the purpose of imparting some amusement to the child for whom she had, since her infancy, cherished the tenderest feelings of maternal solicitude, she exonerated herself from self-accusation and remorse, or any tender sentiment if she had actually a single spark of that feeling existing in her heart. Reflecting that her poor dove needed it, was sufficient reason to soothe her scruples, confined as she was within the bars of her cage, and from which she could neither soar aloft nor roam abroad, and bathe her lofty spirit in the circumambient light of heaven, sparkling herself with its reflection, and pouring out from her bosom a flood of joy, gladdened by the pleasant sights and sounds, and the thrilling emotions which are invariably engendered by such varied scenery the world in her changeful aspects presents to the eye and the thoughtful mind.

Children belonging to the houses of the wealthy and educated people, or men of high rank, have generally Moonshees and Maulvies employed to teach them Arabic and Persian at home.

In the case of boys, the instruction is prolonged for some time, while girls receive their mental culture up to their tenth or twelfth year, and as long as they are considered to be very young children.

Nujmoon Nissa had her share of such training. Verses of the Koran and Culnia were her first rudimentary lessons, to which other additions were made from time to time by the introduction of a few secular, elementary books, and by way of a finish to her studies, some ponderous books—considered ponderous with regard not only to their bulk, but subject—were placed in her hands.

Aristotle's Rhetoric, Life of Secunder Namah, or Alexander the Great, and Shah Namah, or the lives of Kings—works now nearly obsolete, or displaced by more modern books on the same subjects—were then in the full flush of their reputation, and therefore held in the highest esteem by the learned men of that time, and recommended by them as class books.

In feminine studies and accomplishments, Goolchummon was her mistress who taught her to ply the needle with dexterity in tamboor, braid, cassida, and embroidery works, and also in knitting gloves and socks. When weary of these occupations, and to while away some portion of her ample leisure, she had a few games of *sutrunj*, or chess, *punchisi*, *baugh-buckri*, and diversions of a similar kind.

On the northern extremity of the grounds belonging to the Omrao, the father of Nujmoon Nissa, is a spacious quadrangular tank that has a *ghát*, or landing-place on each side, having a flight of steps descending below to the surface of the water.

At each *ghat* is a square, formed of Chunar stones, the two entire sides of the square being built of a couch-like shape with masonry, where of a morning or evening in summer, the inmates went to sit, lounge, and converse, when the temperature within the house was too warm and close to be comfortable.

There is a good deal of poetry in the gorgeously glowing tints in their ever mutable hues, which robe the floating clouds; in the deep transparent azure of the sky, and the mild radiance of the stars and planets set in the firmament like rubies.

There is both magnificence and sublimity in the battle of clouds when they are surcharged with electricity, and intensely vivid flashes of lightning disclose their frowning aspect.

There is grandeur in the high soaring mountains with their vast undulations, waving across an extensive region, crowned with a mantle of eternal snow;—the many sea-like expansive rivers, and vast fields of primitive forests, densely garbed with foliage of many colours, and standing in the pride of their gigantic altitude.

All these sublimely great, or softly tender objects of nature, are cradled on the bosom of an Eastern clime in which the subjects of this tale have a local habitation.

Spring comes in with a fresh verdure and a voluptuous deliciousness in the balmy air, replete with the odour of lemon, babool, and other fragrant flowers of the season.

Flowers of many luscious fruit trees impregnate the air with sweet scents, whilst the highly odorous *Jahoria-champa*, the *Gundraj*, *Balá*, *chamali*, *Juen*, *Maluthi*, and *Kamni*, load the atmosphere of a garden with delicious fragrance, not only intensely cheering, soothing, and intoxicating in their influence, but inspiring one with feelings and sentiments of love for nature, and all that nature offers to the eye that is beautiful in form, pleasant to the taste, charming to the ear, and attractive to contemplation.

Birds of gorgeous plumage and melodious song, pleased and excited with the captivating powers of spring, burst forth into a torrent of harmony that spreads from grove to grove, and brings forth a rich flow of swelling music from other choristers in responsive song. While the gentle *dyel*, seated in melancholy solitude in the extreme verge of one of the boughs, apart from the joyous throng of merry-making birds, smitten with unrequited love as it were, utters his plaintive song in broken cadences, till tired of complaining, he falls from sheer exhaustion, into a state of forgetfulness in a doze.

*   *   *   *

One of the recreations in which Nujmoon delighted to indulge, was to bathe and swim in the tank during the sultry summer months, when persons take a natural pleasure in hot climates to imitate the amphibious denizens of the world, by being as often in water as in land.

Soon after dusk, when the stars are all visible to the eye, studding the heavens, Nujmoon divested herself of her gold anklets, that they might not be any impediment to her easy graceful cleaving of the liquid element, and sporting in the tank like one of the water nymphs.

She could swim across the tank, dive deep and pick up shells from the bottom, and rise like a river goddess with a liquid halo round her, while her luxuriant waving hair descended below her waist like a mantle, from which the blushing waters glided in numerous rippling streamlets, tinged with the moonbeam reflection, investing her fairy-like person with the charms of unearthly brilliance, and an ethereal beauty.

The ghat alluded to above, was very frequently the place where Nujmoon and her nurse spent many hours in so pleasant and absorbing conversation, that when the falling tide of evening deepened into the darkness of night, they were unconscious that the hours had so rapidly glided by with silken strides, instead of the leaden steps with which they desired that time would have marched.

When the radiant sun had dipped his burning brow below the western sky, and sleepy twilight was approaching with her softening influences, and the evening zephyrs waving their delicate pinions, the former mellowing the landscape, and the latter rendering the air voluptuous, Nujmoon and Goolchummon were seen to step out together from the house to stroll about the grounds, tastefully laid out with groves of luscious fruit trees, and beds of flowers of the richest perfume.

On these occasions, she was generally attired according to the season. In winter, she wore a green and yellow striped satin trowsers, a purple jacket, studded with gold buttons set with gems, and a Cashmere shawl having an elaborate border of gold and silk-work.

In spring, a pair of white cotton trowsers, a light canary colour jacket, and a muslin covering of the same hue, a colour which is universally adopted in the East, under a belief that it harmonises well with the season, greatly improves the complexion, and is most becoming at the time.

Sauntering under the shady topes of trees, now engaged in light sparkling conversation, now skipping about, and betimes stooping to pick up a fresh fruit, or berry, shaken down by the fanning breeze from the boughs of trees, bent under the weight of their full maturity, too heavy, and possessing a slight hold on the branches to be supported any longer by them, they dropped pattering on the ground.

Sated with diversions of this sort, and after she had exhausted herself with such gambols, Nissa and her nurse rested themselves on the pucka masonry couch at one of the banks of the tank.

Depression of spirit is often the parent of much mirth, whether real or assumed, though the source of either is so deep and hidden, that to the eye of the strictest observer of physiognomical indications, the cause of certain emotions will always remain a mystery, save that, when it is assumed, the buoyancy of spirit has but an evanescent existence, while the real state of feeling invariably asserts its own power, and is indicated by its predominating influence.

In consonance with these observations, Nissa, when seated at the ghat, entered into conversation with her nurse, the general tendency of which was of a gloomy complexion.

" The thought very frequently obtrudes itself in my mind, Chummon," observed Nissa, addressing her nurse, " that the laws of nature and of Allá are all reversed to favour the claims of men, and that women having nothing to do with them, are

3

excluded from all participation. The sunshine and air of heaven, and the beauties of creation, were, it would seem, all created for the sole use and enjoyment of man, and for him only. All animate existence enjoys as their birthright, the freedom which Mowlah had intended for them, and yet we poor creatures are shut out from sharing them, as if we, above all things, were beneath the dignity of rational beings, nay, even below the irrational also."

"My darling child!" replied Chummon, "how could you permit such sharp thoughts to come across your little head, and embitter your life? Is not my Nissa, the sweetest flower that grows in the garden of her father? Is she not surrounded with every enjoyment and pleasure that an indulgent parent has with a lavish hand provided, sparing neither trouble, pains, money, nor influence in procuring them for her happiness, and by a parent too who dotes on his child with a depth of affection that can hardly be fathomed?"

"That is all very true, Chummon," added Nissa in a subdued tone, seeing the solicitude depicted in the countenance of her nurse, "but does not our very nature revolt at the idea, that whilst the animals of the forest, and the birds of the air, enjoy the thrilling delights of freedom, we who are equal with men, and are suitable companions, should be cribbed and confined like the turtle to its shell, is a thing that will always be abhorrent to our feelings."

"My little bird," responded Chummon, "has taken very capricious fancies into her head this evening, and that very suddenly too. What does my Nissa desire? She who has known no other world, and has been acquainted with no other freedom from her infancy, save the world of her father's house, and the full liberty of roaming within her own extensive residence, why should she aspire after things of which she has no knowledge, and therefore not safe to be longing for the unknown."

"Oh! Chummon," cried Nissa, "is not accurate knowledge

of persons and **things** obtained by **personal** experience, **and** from seeing, hearing, **and** judging **for myself?** Does not know-**ledge** expand by **freely** mixing with **society, enquiring for the** reasons of things, **and** finding out the **cause, and** ascertaining the effect, **as also by** several other **means?"**

" **If there be some** advantage," **said Chummon,** " which men **derive from** unshackled intercourse **with the world, believe me,** my darling, there exists a great **amount of evil in society, from** the contamination **of which, my pretty child has been spared,** in consequence **of her** retirement from their destructive and **baneful** influence."

" I would rather be acquainted with both the good and the evil," continued Nissa, " **which exist in the world, that** by com-**paring the one with the other, the good might shine with a** **brighter lustre, and the evil appear still more hideous. Besides** **which, there is no true merit in a person who is locked up in** **seclusion;** who exercises **no moral influence, and whatever be** the virtuous conduct **she might be applauded for by others, she** who has never **had to battle with temptation, subdue her pro-**pensities when **they are reprehensible, and restrain her passions,** **when they are powerfully evoked by circumstance, and every** **opportunity to break out by** fresh incitements which **she could** have resisted, deserves not the praise that is bestowed on her."

" We who are so weak and helpless," interrupted Chummon : " **so infirm** in our resolutions, **and so tender in our susceptibili-**ties, **was it not wise and far-sighted in our Sages and Sires, to** **adopt such prudent, social rules for our** benefit, knowing that **in our contest with the rough** world **to** which all **our** powers are **inadequate, and being** certain that **it would** result **not** only **in mortifying defeat, but in our dishonorable conquest;** I say, **was it not prudent not to** permit the brittle **earthen** vessels to float **down the stream of time** along with **the hard** utensils of brass."

" **As** water **is the natural** element **of** fishes in which they **must live and** thrive," **exclaimed Nissa with** some degree of im-.patience, " **so** men and **women are intended** to live in the world and receive the training in the school prepared for the sons and daughters of Adam by an all-wise Providence. There is an imperative necessity for the good and bad to grow up together, and whatever might be the incidents which are transpiring around us, they are all intended to teach us some lesson, useful to us now or hereafter. Our acquired experience and knowledge of things and affairs will set them up as beacons on the pathway of life, to warn us, pilgrims, of the dangers that beset our walks, and to direct our wandering and unsteady steps to safe roads in our journey in this world.

"Does it not strike you, Chummon," said Nissa, "that the lords of the world rank us with the inferior animals of creation ; if not, why are we not receiving education of a higher standard, and why are we prevented from joining in so reasonable a service as going to pray at the musjeed, when the matin and vesper muezzin calls all believers to join in the praises of Allah ?

"Has the beneficent Being made man with a different nature and constitution, and bestowed on him a more exalted soul than he has given to woman, owing to which that man is made worthy to hold intellectual communion with his Maker, and render Him spiritual service, which we cannot, being incapable and falling as it were beneath His notice ?"

"O, Nissa, you make me very sad with such dark thoughts in which of late you are too often indulging. This spirit of discontent with the existing state of things about you, will, I fear, not pass unnoticed, but by its frequency invite the attention of your loving father ; it would result in an inquisitive enquiry as to who the person was who had put such novel ideas into the head of his beautiful child, and by it was marring her enjoyments, and making her life burthensome.

"I cannot solve your doubts, nor answer any of your many questions, but I would advise you to be very cautious before whom you ventilate your numerous surmises, so uncongenial as they are to the manner, modes of thought, and habits of action, belonging to the creed of your fathers."

It was verging on to midnight when Chummon coaxed the petted child to retire from the ghat, and forget her sad reflections in the arms of sleep.

Nissa moved away mechanically from the spot, being led by her nurse to the house and to her apartment, where she threw herself on her couch, and with eyes bedewed with tears, she fell asleep, and oblivion spread her mantle over her agony of the past day.

Chapter IV

THE hermit's solitary cell to which Mobaruc frequently resorted either to divert his leisure in pleasing and edifying converse, or in the better amusement of acquiring a knowledge of skifully handling the *setar*, now on his visit after his late interviews with Nujmoon Nissa, began to evince a moody gloom, which, being an unusual symptom in his general deportment, did not pass unobserved by the attentive and feeling-hearted Ameerjan. "A cloud," observed the hermit, "that seldom flitted across the brow of my vivacious friend, hangs darkling with its heavy gloom his ever cheerful aspect.

"If ever Ameerjan has shared thy joys, or partaken of thy sorrows, impart, my friend, the secret of thy pensive looks, and the cause of thy studied taciturnity, for they too deeply affect me with unpleasant dejection."

"Pardon me, Ameerjan, for I know too well the tender sensibility of your heart which never fails to offer sympathy to the afflicted, balm to the lacerated spirit, and the benefit of your experience and valuable counsel to the helpless and the unhappy.

"It was my purpose in coming here to ask your aid, and obtain your advice in a matter that deeply affects my peace.

"I would not have hesitated to disclose to you the racking uneasiness of thoughts with which I came burthened, had I known the best method of divulging the sad story. But since you have advanced the point to an issue, nothing remains but a disclosure of the subject.

"When my evenings were not given to you, my friend, or to your captivating minstrelsy, I passed them generally in riding over the extensive plains contiguous to a half dilapidated mansion, near the suburbs of Raj Mahul, where unnoticed, I could muse on the frailty of glory, the emptiness of earthly glitter, and the links of indomitable fate which bind our actions to a course from which it can scarcely be diverted.

" But to begin the narration. So unexpected as it was, conceive my surprise when I beheld at the little private garden gate, a being so transcendant, sylph-like, and shrouded in the graces of so much unearthly loveliness. Nujmoon Nissa, or ' Light of the Morning Star,' is the name by which the fair inhabitant of that mansion is designated. Her melting eyes fringed with dark long lashes ; her cheeks suffused with the glow of health, the airy-like form, with innumerable other bewitching graces, conspired to raise in me a feeling of deep respect and love, not to be easily subdued. Her lovely image, her looks, her very movements be-came objects of my solicitude ; and like our own shadows, they pursue and disturb the repose of my mind.

" I was ill at ease unless I saw her daily, nay every moment of the day if it were possible.

" I met Nujmoon Nissa frequently and have exchanged vows of eternal fidelity. I feel a secret satisfaction in saying that the proffer of my hand, heart, and fortune, were not rejected by the ' Light of the Star,' or I should rather say, Light of my Soul.

" I feel also that without her, my life would be a barren gloomy existence not worth cherishing. You, my friend, have now learnt my unhappy predicament, and will readily excuse the gloom that gave you uneasiness."

" Your case is not hopeless, Mobaruc, for I am admitted into the private *divan* of the Ex-Nabob, on the praise of whose amiable daughter you have been justly lavish ; and if it be your pleasure, I will be your *mosata*, or bearer of marriage over-tures."

" Though I could not propose the task to you, yet as you my friend, voluntarily tender your assistance in your usual kind manner, you could not lay me under greater obligation, or render me a better service."

" Say no more, Mobaruc. Before the crescent moon fills her disk, I hope to be the messenger of glad tidings to you, my friend, and though adverse fate has persecuted me, and unrelentingly doomed me to be the most unhappy of mortals, it has not converted me as yet into a morose misanthropist. I am on the contrary, ever devoted to the service of humanity from which alone I reap abundant satisfaction. It is the only antidote to my lacerated heart, to be useful to others. To relieve and ameliorate the condition of my fellow-sufferers in the weary pilgrimage of life, is the only source of joy which I can derive from existence."

" This, Ameerjan, reminds me of your repeated promises of narrating the history of your incidental life, and it will not only be a proof of your confidence, but a kind return to my un-hesitating candour."

" To you I owe my unreserved sentiments, and at a more befitting time when I can make you happy, and see you more cheerful, I will not fail to communicate them, though in doing so, I cannot fail to smart by opening the wound afresh."

The young Ameer, bidding a cordial adieu to his friend, the hermit, descended from the hills. He gained the road which ran its mazy course over cultivated fields, laden with a rich crop of mustard, linseed, and rice. The new moon glittered like a silver bow on the azure canopy. It was studded with innumerable stars that shed their lustre on the silent repose of creation. The night breeze had also sprung up in slight whis-pers; it came pregnant with the odour of the scented lime, *babool*, and *champa*.

The breeze gently dallied with the pendant curls of Mobaruc, ruffled the mane of his Arabian, and passed away on their downy wings over ears of corn, agitating them with a soft rustling undulation.

These were the thoughts which the time and scenery awoke in the mind of the otherwise gay equestrian. " What serenity ! What harmony dwells in the firmament above ! What profound soothing repose ! The moon and the stars are wrapped in a heavenly beam of refulgence, and their aspects present for ever an undisturbed tranquillity ! Though their eyes nightly witness a thousand revolting scenes, fraught with rapine, murder, treachery, ingratitude, still they remain unaffected, and no tears drench their brow, nor passions agitate the calm of their bosom. Flowers which beautifully adorn the face of nature, bloom cheerfully and emit a constant fragrant incense to heaven, while their expiring breath is a sweet sigh of gratitude. Man is the only vile being who degrades his birth by becoming a dupe to his passions, instead of making them and every thing else, subservient to his rising in the scale of beings and by indefatigable devotion to all laudable undertakings rising to an atmosphere of purity. Why have we the will to do, if the faculty, the power of execution is not at our command? Surely there is a wreck of innate goodness which was a primitive boon with our creation.

Nature is a divine volume replete with instructions, and he who attentively peruses her pages, will learn much of himself, and much of that mighty Being who presides over the glorious fabric he has created and vivifies with his constant presence. Oh! for the wings of a seraph, that I might soar to regions where eternal calm, unvarying harmony, and unchanging love, abandoning the earth on which perpetual tumult and sedition dwell, have taken up their constant habitation in a region of eternal peace and love."

CHAPTER V.

IN the neighbourhood of Raj Mahul there are dense jungles which wildly luxuriate in their pristine glens, sheltering venomous reptiles and other animals, as also the more ferocious tenants as the monarchs of the woods. From hence the undaunted tiger freely roams abroad, visiting the adjacent villages in his prowls, and occasionally making sad ravages among men, women, children, and the domesticated breed. *Shecaries* who earn their livelihood by giving intimation, and serving as guides to sportsmen, are ever vigilant in learning the rendezvous of the tiger. Though they *often* go and craftily perch on some trees from whence they direct their envenomed shaft at the breast of such foes, yet when a better remuneration is expected by announcing it to the *omraò*, they will not fail to secure that reward.

Tigers, either to shake off the drowsy sensation of repletion, or as exercise to digest their meal, are in the habit of stretching their length and scratching the bark of trees, and by it the traces of the animal are discovered. *Shecaries* by this means easily capture them and possessing the jaws, nails, coats of leopards and tigers, they dispose of them for a small amount to such as would pass for a sheerkha, who collect them as trophies of their reckless valour. Selling also to such other credulous old people as believe in the medicinal virtue of hair, tooth, and claws.

Prince Sujah to whom the *shecaries* conveyed intelligence of some recent depredation made by tigers, circulated a proclamation to the Ameers of his court, to be ready before dawn, to join him on a hunting excursion. When the morning began to peep through the east, one or another of the Ameers began to throng the court-yard of the palace. Prince Sujah descended the flight of steps, and gracefully received the salutation and good wishes of the nobles, then mounted his huge elephant.

The stately animal was painted on the body, and covered with a rich crimson velvet, ornamented with gold work. The *howdah* was surmounted with silver, and the instrument with which the *mahoot* guided him, was of the same metal, but solid. The throng slowly moved through one of the roads of Raj Mahul, which led to a field situate at the distance of five miles. From thence they proposed setting out after games. When a prince intends making a move in any direction, news circulates as fast as the wind. Distant villages through which he would have to pass, were long awake before the cavalcade had stirred from the palace, and were all impatient with expectation.

Some ran to and fro, some walked out to the distance of a mile to meet him, others through imbecility of age, were content to remain at their doors, smoking away their impatience, and chatting with the idle saunterers. Children clapped their little hands with rapture, and shouted with exultation, though far from knowing the nature or extent of fun and frolic they anticipated. Young men and virgins posted themselves before their doors, slightly kept ajar, or stood before venetians partially lifted.

Peerbux, a decrepid old man, who was placed on the pension establishment of the Prince, and who had devoted the prime of his life to the service of his beneficent master as an industrious, faithful adherent, also left his warm comfortable bed, and sat himself by his gate with his old partner, who, by her gossip and garrulity, kept him from dozing under the somnific influence of the cool morning breeze.

" Well, Peerbux," said the woman to her husband, " this is enough to try the patience of our holy Prophet. It is an hour since the bustle began on the road by the vagabonds, still nothing is in sight. It has deprived us of our rest two hours before our usual time to stir out, yet the Prince and his retinue are not in sight."

" Why, Golaub, since we are awake, it matters not if we pass our time in gazing at the procession of the Prince, or at the animated bustle of men. The unrestrained conversation of the latter, with its merriments, might be more amusing."

A fresh simultaneous shout of lads, and the appearance of some *assaburdars* and *sotaburdars*, announced the approach of the Prince. The stately elephants of Sujah, soon after, burst into view, refulgent with the dazzle of gold and silver. Next followed the no less showy animals of the Ameers, and lastly a number of men bearing glittering spears.

All the while that the men were passing in procession, the loquacious old wife of Peerbux remained silently gazing with awe and wonderment, but so soon as they had gone to some distance, she resumed her chat. " How is it, Peerbux, that those handsome and opulent young men do not know how to spend their time better than in risking their sweet lives in hunting wild animals, as if they had no servants or *shecaries* to send out to destroy them ?"

" The children of the great," observed the husband, " whose future lives will some time or another be exposed to the hardships of warfare, are brought up to these manly sports, in order to exercise their valour and skill in attack and defence. These sports prepare them in some measure to contend with the more inveterate foes of their country. It is to their valour and intrepidity that we owe the peaceful enjoyment of our hearths and lives. They are the best bulwarks of our city; in times of need and emergency, they withstand the furious rush of our enemies, and repel every unjust foreign aggression."

Prince Sujah, during the course of his journey, addressed his followers with the following conversation in his usual affable manner :—

" An opportunity for attending these diversions is seldom lost by Shufteralli. Are his wounds so thoroughly healed as to make him forget his recent encounter ?"

" It is the presence of my Prince," replied the sturdy Shufteralli, " that invigorates his servant, and makes him willing to endure every trouble and face danger, provided that he has the pleasure of being nigh his protection."

" Are you also with us, Mobaruc, leaving the merry tones of you *setar* to silent neglect, and exchanging it for the dissonant growl and roar of wild beasts ?"

" My Prince has a prior claim on my devotion, and when better employments do not engage my time, trifles may relieve *ennui*, though my Prince may remember that on the last scuffle with our enemies, I played more music with my *shumshere* then my *setar*."

" I acknowledge thy merit, thy zeal, Mobaruc ; may the continuance of thy fidelity ever earn for thee as hitherto, the grateful acknowledgment of thy friend and protector."

The riders had arrived at the *jungle. Shecaries* and spearmen filed off, a portion to the right, and another to the left, forming an extensive crescent within which it was intended to drive the game.

On entering the forest which was dense, dark, and tangled, each individual felt a queer dread at the awful silence and solemnity of the place. It was so much so, that were a pin to drop, it could be heard distinctly ; the sense of hearing became exceedingly acute from apprehension. It was all ear and eye.

Trees of a slender make which opposed the progress of the gigantic animals, were easily broken down.

Elephants are very sagacious, and they have an instinctive dread of their formidable opponents, and this was evinced by their knowledge of their presence, indicated by a dead halt at places where the tiger had rested.

There they paw the ground, strike their trunks, and blow through their proboscis a sound not unlike the blast of a horn.

A *nullah* overrun with sedges and matted with lilies, lotus, and other aquatic plants, was soon crossed over, and on the opposite bank, three immense wild büffaloes were seen to wallow in the shallow stream.

They arose irritated at the interruption to their amusement, and with a loud bellow, a wild toss of their horns tangled with weeds, they made a furious rush at the elephants. These withstood the charge, while from their backs, from the arms of the Ameers, flew a dozen well aimed spears. Soon followed a few whistling bullets which were lodged in their foreheads. The brutes staggered a few paces, and fell one after another with a great splash. The elephants, who were not mere idle spectators, trampled and put a period to their existence.

A few deer, which the well exercised archery of the nobles added to their game, concluded the first day's sport.

The party came up on the following morning, to an open space overgrown with high *cassia* grass. The hunters spied in it two noble tigers, feasting on some carcass which lay near them. The ferocious beast which was about sixty yards off, erecting himself in the power of his might, and placing his paws over the work of destruction, sent forth a hideous growl which resounded fearfully through the circumambient forest:—his eyes were glowing like balls of fire; his ears standing erect, and his looks threatening defiance to the unwelcome intruders.

"Here is sport my men," said the Prince, "such as we seldom come across. Keep the space clear on the front—fall back with your animals a little more to the right and left, so as to prevent their escape. Meer Sufteralli, your elephant is too near the heels of mine; pray keep back a little for the play of each animal."

The Prince advanced a few paces—his glittering barb whistled in the air for a moment and then was buried deep on the back of his brindled enemy. The infuriated brute gave a dreadful howl that reverberated through the forest, and not heeding the fragile reed quivering at his side, came bouncing onward. After a momentary halt, he made a spring on the Prince, before the Prince could have time to aim another winged shaft of death. Mobaruc, who was all the while a silent but impatient spectator of the scene, aimed his ready arrow at the glaring eye of the tiger, where it remained transfixed. The wounded beast fell back with a howl, bit the arrow at his side to fragments, and snapped the other in two.

Foiled in his purpose, and furious with rage and pain, he rushed with a mad, yet instinctive fury, at the Prince's elephant from whence he had received the first attack. There he fixed his claws and made a deep wound. The lacerated animal who could not easily shake off the tiger, nor extricate himself from the jaws and claws of his desperate foe, was in jeopardy, as the Prince felt himself placed in the same predicament, being unable to use his weapon with effect, from the rolling of the animals which threatened every moment to dislodge him.

Mobaruc leaped down instantly from his *howdah* with his true Persian sabre of approved steel, grasped in one hand, while the other held a well charged pistol. With the former he made a deep cut in the spine, and the ball of the latter which had penetrated the heart of the monster, laid him dead at the feet of Mobaruc. All this was performed within a short time. The other tiger was despatched with greater ease and facility.

During the afternoon, they met with another tiger, besides three leopards. They gave them some sport, as the Ameers' elephants, and the Omras themselves took back tokens of their fury.

The scars were not soon effaced nor forgotten. It afforded a subject for conversation and matter for congratulation for a long time to the individuals who had taken a prominent part in the adventurous exploit. The rage for the chase being appeased on the third day, they returned to Raj Mahul laden with trophies. The Prince distinguished Mobaruc with fresh marks of favour. The other Ameers were also noticed with tokens of satisfaction, for the display of valour and intrepid conduct of which the hunt gave abundant proofs.

CHAPTER VI.

WHILE the animated bustle of the chase occupied the time of Mobaruc, his faithful and devoted friend, the Hermit, failed not to obtain an interview with the venerable nobleman.

On entering his *díwán-khána* the parent of the lovely Nujmoon Nissa lay reclined on a Persian carpet, with one arm resting on a velvet pillow, holding to his mouth the point of the snake of his *hookah* which was made of pure silver, ornamented with flowers of gold leaves and buds formed of emeralds and rubies. He was inhaling from the tube a delicious smoke, which curled above in circling .volumes, perfuming the whole apartment with the richly scented tobacco of Persia.

"I salute thee, Ameer," said the Hermit, "with peace and length of days to thee and thine."

"Ah! is that Ameerjan that my eyes behold! He is as rarely to be seen as the flowers of our fig tree, and therefore do I doubt the accuracy of my vision. But whither have thy steps so long wandered, and from whence comest thou?"

"Be assured, Ameer, that I am present with my body, and that I come from my humble cell from whence I had never ceased remembering thee in my daily orisons."

"Thanks to thee, Ameerjan; thy acts are always in union with thy appellation. If no generous deeds had marked thy conduct, thou wouldst not have been distinguished with the favourable designation of the "noble heart." But to what chance do I owe the pleasure of thy kind and agreeable visit?"

"One lovely flower which blooms in the seclusion of your garden, and will some time or other require the society of a man who can duly appreciate her value, and would cherish and protect her with fond solicitude, such a man, while your eyes are open, will be your highest prudence to select."

"Alas! Ameerjan, those are the very thoughts which seriously occupy my anxious mind; but seldom or never do I go out

now and mix with society ; I have therefore little opportunity
for learning the temper and qualities that constitute a good
character in a husband, so as to make choice of one."

" Of all the gay youths of the Court of our Prince (may his
shadow never decrease, nor his star decline), I can point out one
who is the brightest of them all, and will answer your highest
expectation. The name, Mobaruc, with whose fame all Raj-
Mahul is ringing, might have reached your ear ere this.

" In the field, in chase, in archery, or in musical talents, few
will excel him. He is elegant in person, as he is mild in disposition. His attachment to the person of the Prince, and his
general merit, have raised him to a post of distinction, aspired
at by most, but attained by few. His affability, candour, and
benevolent spirit, have won him the good opinion of all, and
the friendship of many. Educated under the tuition of learned
moulvies, he is versed in the Persian, Arabic, and Toorky
languages, and from a natural taste for ornamental studies,
he has acquired many refined accomplishments.

" He has recently come into possession of a large property
bequeathed to him by his parent. Not given to an extravagant
waste, either in sinking debauchery, or any of the frivolous indulgences which young people are in the habit of, a portion is ap-
propriated to the wants of the indigent, the education and enligh-
tenment of the poor classes, and in works of public utility. The
source from whence those bounties flow, is, however, modestly
concealed under the appellation of, " a friend to the poor !" Such
then is the man whom I strongly recommend to your favourable
notice."

" The person," observed the nobleman, " who possesses those
exalted virtues, lofty endowments, and is at the same time the
object of the encomium of Ameerjaun, cannot be a man on whom
my choice could be misplaced."

The hermit saluting him courteously, retired, pleased with
himself at having succeeded to his satisfaction in bringing together the fortunes of two of the most deserving beings, whom

5

perhaps the caprice of fate, or the unreasonable severity of parents, migh have separated for ever.

He was pleased that he could now be the messenger of happy news, and be enabled to witness the rapture that would brighten the countenance of his much esteemed Mobaruc.

It would be as a drop of sweet in his bitter cup of woes, an emerald isle, a silver stream in the Sahara of his life, sustaining his fainting spirit with the reviving draught of the one, and giving repose to his weary limbs on the other. Such satisfaction, and ecstacy of joy, an approving conscience invariably bestows on virtuous acts and works of benevolence.

His hermitage presented now a more cheerful aspect of comfort than it did before.

As he was wiping off the dust from the *sitar* which lay suspended at a corner of the cot, intending to handle and once more draw forth its melody which was chained up so long in silence, Mobaruc greeted him with an affectionate filial embrace.

" I hesitate," said Mobaruc, " to interrogate you regarding the result of your visit to the nobleman, for by one breath, you might kill or bid me live."

" Nay, impatient Mobaruc, you are an ill decipherer of physiognomy. Do you behold aught in my countenance that portends a withering blast ? Not to keep you in suspense, know then that the father of your beloved Nujmoon is disposed to bestow her fair hand to a kind, gentle, and virtuous man, and if such you believe yourself to be, then you are the person to whom the promise has been given."

" How can I thank you adequately, or express the unutterable emotions of gratitude. I will owe you the best part of my happiness. You have delivered me from utter ruin to which the torment, the agony of feelings, would have inevitably consigned me."

" In serving you Mobaruc, in promoting your welfare, I am as much a gainer as yourself, for I have always participated in all your sorrows, and hope now to share your joys."

The preliminaries being adjusted to the satisfaction of all parties concerned in the interesting transaction, the first moon of the following month was selected, as being the most propitious time for the celebration of the nuptials of Mobaruc and Nujmoon Nissa.

Chapter VII.

THE intended celebration of the wedding being generally known, it gave work and occupation to the hands of the bazar men for several days. All classes of artisans had sufficient employment during the revolution of a month. The old *hulwhy* had to tax his ingenuity in the invention of sweetmeats of all colours, shapes, and niceness. *Goolsazes* were busy in painting transparencies for the gates, garden, and *naobútkhana*, to suspend coloured lights arranged with fanciful design.

During the *lugun*, a time of merriment, the mansion of the Ameer rang for several days with songs of mirth and bustle of occupation.

From different quarters of the city, the Ameers who came daily to pay their *devoirs*, were received courteously and with cordial welcome. Itur and rosewater were brought into requisition as often as a new guest entered the *diran*. Beetel leaves folded in triangular forms and spiced and scented, were offered to each visitor on rich golden salvers, while cool, fragrant *shurbets* were handed to such of them as ceased to masticate the former. Some were taken up in a mere idle manner in extracting a luxurious treat from costly tuberous *penchwans*. Ameers were entertained with a delectable repast of *polao, cullia, cofta*, and a libation from goblets glittering with the famed wine of Sheraz; while, for several days, thousands of the poor bore away their moiety of *khitchery* and pice.

Some *tyfaas* of celebrated dancing girls, of exquisite symmetry and grace, were engaged to afford a change of amusement to the Omraos, by the fascinating witchery of their evolutions. As one or another was touched with the dulcet melody of their voice, or the admirable execution of some difficult parts of the dance, they flung pieces of *asshurfees*, shawls, and rings, as tokens of their approbation, or with a view to evince the bounty, generosity, or affluence of the respective donors.

Naobút-khanahs, which glittered with ornamental works, contributed in no small degree to exhilarate the languor of satiety by pouring occasionally a deafening noise from the *nuccárra, tasha, murpha, robab, duf, roshunchowcky;* but of all the instruments, the latter only gave a faint idea of melody, though the rest were barbarous dissonance, yet harmony to ears attuned to their jarring discord.

The happy day at last arrived. The road was lined with men on either side, who bore over their heads artificial flower gardens, or held on their hands, imitation chandeliers. Camels and elephants carried bands of gaily dressed musicians.

Next to them were two elephants on which were seated a couple of respectable looking men, of tried integrity, who had the duty of distributing charity on this occasion of universal joy.

They did so by thrusting their hands into spacious bags, and lifting up a handful of rupees, scattered them on the way for a free scramble among beggars.

The bridegroom was sumptuously attired and mounted on his favourite charger. Over it was held a large beautiful silk umbrella, having a silver handle, and pearls pendant from the top.

Elephants and horses, differently accoutred with ornaments, manifested the opulence, or dignity of the several equestrians who escorted the bridegroom.

After these, appeared the very rich palkee of the bride, half concealed by a velvet covering to prevent the inquisitive gaze of idle strollers, and escorted by *assaburdars, chobdars,* and *solahburdars.*

She was attended by vehicles which conveyed her friends and relatives. The rear was occupied by the dependants of the Ameers, and by a promiscuous crowd attracted by the rich and diversified pageantry which a great man's wedding invariably promises, also by the curious procession of grandeur and comicality which are the inseparable accompaniments of ceremonies of the kind.

On entering the premises, **Mobaruc** was surprised to see his friend **Ameerjan** dressed in the *habille* of a Cazi, and ready with other *mullas* to solemnize the ceremony by reading passages from the Koran adapted for the occasion, and articles of marriage written in the Culma. The Cazi on learning that the parties mutually consented to the union, celebrated their nuptials with due formality.

Thus having finished what the anxious **heart** of the Hermit most desired, he partook unceremoniously of refreshments, and accepted other marks of civility with which Mobaruc loaded **him. A cheerfulness mantled the** face of his friend, to witness **which was gratifying to Mobaruc.**

The stream of time **bore away days and months rapidly, but** they were passed by them with delight, **enhanced by the agree-**able society of each **other** who entertained reciprocal esteem. As **Nujmoon** was above the ordinary class of society, the culti-vation of her mind was not **neglected.** She could therefore converse with intelligence on most **topics, and give** fresh interest and **pathos by the delicate language in** which she dressed **her thoughts.**

Every day augmented the felicity of Mobaruc, as he ex-**perienced** the many blessings which attended the steps of con-**nubial** life. He found in **it many secret sources** through which **copious streams of joy, not to be** found in any other condition so **complete and so full, ran refreshing his** inmost soul.

If his mind **was** agitated by any disturbing passion, or his heart throbbed with anxiety, **her** company and conversation had power to lull **or** dispel them.

Before her enlivening **smiles,** every gloomy thought fled that **marred** the brightness of **his countenance ;** and in the sunshine **of her** cheerfulness and vivacity, he could not but enjoy what he **imbibed—the gay** humour of her buoyant spirit. Every idle **pastime abroad was** totally abandoned for **the more** rational and pure delights of **a home enlivened by** the engaging deportment of her who presided over his domestic comforts, as their sole sacred guardian : and to her it was that he owed his entire reformation from every irregularity of youth.

Within the space of two years she gave him as many children, the pledges of love and faithful affection. The boy bore some resemblance to the mother, the girl had a striking appearance that reflected the father's image, yet both were as beautiful and lovely as cherubs.

The Hermit frequently visited Mobaruc, finding great pleasure in his society and that of the little innocent children. Their early lispings, and endearing manners, afforded him a calm delight, and inspired the faded heart of Ameerjan with a sweet sensation of joy and benevolence.

As the children were growing up, he took great interest in their education and welfare. He paid great attention to the growth of their young ideas, entered into their infantile sports with as much hilarity as if he were one of them, and participated in their evanescent grief with much sympathy. His melancholy face glowed with pride and joy, when, as the beautiful infants climbed up his knees to snatch a kiss, their parent taught them to respect and love him as their second *bapjan*. Now that the garden of Mobaruc was trimmed and kept under greater care than before, flowers of a variety of species and genus bloomed in their freshness ; while every plant dressed in its vivid green, made it a desirable spot for the scene of their evening recreation.

Here the *setar* was resorted to when topics of exhilarating conversation lagged, and in its whispers of melody, the hearts of Mobaruc and Ameerjaun were steeped in a melancholy joy, more easily felt than described.

Mobaruc took this opportunity of addressing his friend on the subject of the history of his life.

"I have," observed Mobaruc, " no thought, no wish which you are not made acquainted with ; no schemes laid, no plans proposed without first consulting you ; in justice then to my perfect unreserve, you should oblige me with a recital of your adventures without further hesitation."

" To the want of sufficient confidence, I hope you, my friend, will not attribute my not having sooner made you the depository of my secret ; and give no unfair interpretation to my studied silence on that subject for so long a period.

" As the season has, however, arrived in which I purposed to narrate to you the particulars of my sad history, I will no longer delay indulging you with the narration, leaving you to judge whether I could at all times take a ready pleasure in its publication.

" If I now do so, it is only because I can better support the agony of their reminiscence, surrounded as I am with the smiles of your children, your own happy looks, and the sympathy of your tender heart.

" The evening being far advanced, and as I should not be able to bring the theme to a conclusion, you will kindly have a little more patience in waiting till I pay you my next visit, which I will endeavour to make earlier than usual, in order to gratify your curiosity, or rather your friendly solicitude."

Chapter VIII.

I WAS born in that land where the sky is almost always unclouded; where the sun sets in unrivalled glory, imbuing the firmament with a rich variety of tints; where birds of gold and emerald plumage, both adorn her groves, and make her vallies resound to their songs of joy, and the most rare and delicious fruits and plants vegetate in lavish profusion, without much care of tillage, or a laborious irrigation.

It was the lovely city of Phars, whose fragrant air my infant breath first drew; whose clime matured my feelings, and moulded them to an intense degree of tender sensibility.

A brother and myself, were the only surviving children of my father, who was *mosaheb*, or aide-de-camp to Sultan Nadir Shah.

Nadir vindicated the independence of his country, but his conquering arm which gave no respite to his subjects, involved them in frequent broils, and allowed them no leisure to taste the advantages of peace.

My brother and I were the admiration of our country for our graceful horsemanship, and expert use of the bow.

My brother was reckoned one of the best poets of the place.

So great was the love of my father for truth, probity, and candour, that all the intercession of my brother and mother, could not at one time divert him from his inexorable purpose of giving me a sound correction for denying that I had broken one of his valuable pipes, although I have often been guilty of greater damages done to most costly mirrors and vases, and have escaped punishment by merely acknowledging my fault.

A proud, haughty, and opulent nobleman, who had a daughter of exquisite beauty, lived near my father's residence.

We as children were suffered to play for years together without interruption. She was about my age, or a year or two younger. I could not have been more than seven or eight years old at that time.

6

I found an undefinable pleasure in her company. We ran together after the gayest butterflies in the garden, and however difficult the task may have been, or whatever impediment thwarted my eager pursuit, I was sure to surmount it in order to entrap the gay flutterer for my playmate.

I culled the prettiest and most fragrant flowers and presented them to my Zeleikha, who was always delighted with my early assiduity to please her; one instance of which, a rather hazardous one, I must relate:

A pretty lotus was seen floating on the surface of a tank in the garden. She clapped her hands with innocent exultation, pointing to me the gay flower bedewed with crystal drops of rain and blushing as if through tears.

I plunged after it, though ignorant of the art of swimming, but had I even been skilled in the art, it could not have been of any service to me, entangled as I was with weeds.

The opportune help of the nurse, however, saved me from being drowned, yet not before I had enjoyed enough of soaking, and drinking more water than I had a thirst for.

I found my play-fellow after my immersion, looking pale and trembling with fear and agitation. Seeing me, however, safe again, tears of joy rolled down her blooming cheeks. She was ever, after this accident, fearful of expressing her admiration of anything in a dangerous place, lest she might involve me a second time in difficulties, but I, who could decipher her wish by the expressive intelligence of her eyes, always gratified her desires as far as they were practicable.

We reluctantly separated after play-hours, she to retire to her apartment, I to my father's house, thoughtful and unhappy that she and I were not together for ever.

The hope of seeing her every evening and the pleasure which that would infuse, in a manner reconciled us to every-day separation. We could not long remain as children, nor be allowed to indulge in recreations, however harmless and innocent in their tendency, without infringing the rules and violating the laws of decorum or custom ; besides, her father, who was absent for some years, returning about that time, exercised the authority with which nature had invested him as a parent, by prohibiting our interviews.

In conformity with the strict injunctions of her master, her duenna became vigilant in watching my fair Zeleikha.

Frequently did I visit the garden, whose flowers she out-rivalled, and where she chained my devotion to herself, but, alas! the Eve of that Paradise was now doomed to pine in the seclusion of her retirement.

I had a glimpse of her once as she stood before one of the windows waving her hand and looking like an angel from the distant world of spirits to bless my ever-longing eyes.

She looked pale and wasted, and I could not help shedding many a tear at the visible change I noticed in her appearance. Though her form became indistinct from the dark advance of night, still my eyes were fixed in its direction, and I fancied I had an occasional glimpse of her emerging through the surrounding gloom.

I know not how long I might have remained thus in a sweet delusion, had not the gardener announced the lateness of the hour, and his intention of closing the gate.

Every other attempt that I made to see or hear of her, proved unsuccessful for some time, and during that period of suspense, you might imagine what must have been the degree of torture I was fated to endure.

In the mean time, my parent, who had observed a radical change in my demeanour, and was likewise apprised of the attachment which existed between myself and the Ameer's daughter, to divert my mind from the object, procured me a post under Kurreem Khan, one of Nadir's lieutenants, an able chief who triumphed over all his adversaries, and substantiated his claims to the *musnud* by strength of arms.

I was deeply engaged for several months in repressing the forays of the rude banditti who shelter themselves in the mountain chain which runs through the kingdom from Armenia to the Persian Gulf.

Thence sally the marauders who spoil rich plains and attack valuable caravans.

When their depredations were in some measure suppressed by our troops, I returned to my parent, but not at all cured of my passion, as he had intended and expected, for that on the contrary broke forth with more violence from absence and restraint.

I devised every means of effecting an interview, and on this occasion was less unfortunate than I had been for sometime before.

Gold had power to remove the scruples of the Ameer's dependants, as it had sufficient efficacy in withdrawing bolts and bars.

One happy evening,—but why do I recal it?—it was my last day of joy on earth—I was admitted into the garden, and to our favourite seat.

I waited and Zeleikha appeared. She ran to my arms and fainted with mingled emotions of joy, fear, and grief. Oh! how time had added to her charms! If she was beautiful when young, how much more lovely when all her graces were developed and matured by years, and increasing refinements of the mind had expanded. Would I not have been content and happy with that precious burthen in my arms, and have been ready to sacrifice life's best treasure to call her mine?

She communicated to me the secret instructions her parent had given to two ruffian Toorks in his employ, to destroy me, in the event of their finding me within the walls.

I drew out my sabre, observing, that the last drop of my blood would be shed to protect her, and that the arm which felled the foes of my country to the ground, would not lie idle to punish the villains who would dare raise their coward weapon against an innocent and harmless man. I said everything else to allay her fear, or soothe her grief, but so great was her apprehension for my safety, that nothing could comfort and compose her mind.

She lay her sorrowing face on my bosom, and in that posture, with her mild eyes turned upwards, addressed me in her usual mild accent: "Dear Mobaruc, this moment repays me for all my past privation and suffering which I have endured in my rigid confinement. Your prudent circumspection may, at some future period, afford us the means of enjoying each other's society. My parent may relent at witnessing the protracted suffering, the torture he unnecessarily dooms us to without receiving a single token of violation of our fidelity to each other. Promise me, Mobaruc, that for my sake you will not thus expose your life to the mercy of menials, and I will contentedly support any affliction my cruel parent may invent with which to inflict me. The night is far spent, and if I should be missed, it would only aggravate the misery of our situation. I cannot, I must not, delay any longer, if not on my own account, at least on yours; so remember my entreaties, dear Mobaruc, adieu!" Saying which she gave me an affectionate salute, and extricating herself from my arms, rushed into the building and was seen no more.

I was led by my conductor to the outer gate from whence my steps led me mechanically to my own residence. I endeavoured on the morning to meet an influential friend who was on terms of intimacy with the proud, haughty Ameer, and who like myself was an officer in the Khan's Cavalry. I disclosed to him the attachment which had been cemented from early youth between myself and my neighbour's daughter; that the attachment grew and was strengthened with our years; that she had become to me as part of myself, and therefore without her, existence would be a desolate waste. I asked him the favour of conveying to her parent the honorable intentions I entertained towards Zeleikha.

He laid my views before the noble, and urged my suit with all the warmth that friendship and esteem could prompt, but he found him inexorable, and inflexibly bent on his determination, urging as a plea, "that a private gate," alluding to our secret assignation, "was not the most eligible path to obtain access to his daughter, nor an honorable way to win her consent, and that he, who could be guilty of such impropriety, was not worthy of his daughter." His ire rose not from this circumstance alone, for, pointing to a scar across his forehead, he said, "as long as this mark remains indelible, so long will the memory of what has transpired between the father of that youth and myself, remain unforgotten. Bid the young man seek his happiness elsewhere, and if you value my friendship and good opinion, seek not to make any further allusion to the subject which is sufficiently odious to me for more than one reason."

CHAPTER IX.

"" I HAD gleaned the secret by enquiring of my father's old acquaintances and friends, and learnt that during the early youth of my father, his valour and intrepidity in every daring enterprise, while it procured him complete success in all his undertakings, and his merits which secured the admiration of his colleagues, provoked the ungenerous envy of his friend to so intense a degree of malice, that he could not rest in peace unless he daily framed and circulated some foul report to asperse and tarnish the unsullied reputation of my father. My father, meeting him in one of his walks in the city, accosted him with resentment, and charged him with spreading invidious insinuations, a base practice unbecoming the dignity of the son of an Omrao. This gave him umbrage, and he placed his hand on the hilt of his sword. My father drew out his sabre. His antagonist stoutly defended himself for a time, but as his strength and skill in the use of the sword, was not equal to that of his adversary, he received a deep cut across his forehead, and was in a moment disarmed, and at the mercy of my father, who, wishing to take no further advantage of his victory, left him to resume his walk, after tendering, however, his services to bind his wound, which he disdainfully rejected.

Alas! that the man who was himself the cause of the ill usage he had received, should carry his inveteracy so stubbornly, and so far, as to make us the innocent unhappy victims of his malice! How bad must that heart be that can feed an evil vindictive temper for so protracted a period without forgiving or forgetting, or feeling its malignity abate from the influence of time. Two, to us, dreadful long years had revolved, and within their tardy course, the nobleman made several unsuccessful attempts to marry his daughter to some Omrao, but one uniform refusal she gave every time when such proposals were made.

As the fame of her beauty was the theme of all Persia, she had a long train of flattering suitors, among whom was a chief in sway of one of the *pachalics*, dependant on Sultan Nadir Shah.

Zeleikha made the following answer, as was communicated to me by one of her confidants:—' I am flattered with the notice the chief deigns to take of me, but regret much I cannot make him happy as he merits to be for his temper, disposition, and the many good qualities he is said to possess. My heart has cherished from infancy the image of but one, and to that man my feelings and affections are already wedded, and to give my hand to him, he would marry but a lifeless statue. The Chief, who is known to be as generous as he is humane and discreet, will, as his most prudent action, cease to harass me with his solicitations, for it will be not only useless, as I do not vacillate in my resolution, but will diminish the good opinion I already entertain of him, and the respect I am disposed to evince.

Acting in studied opposition to the fond wishes of her parent, he became so exasperated at her stubborn non-compliance that his kindness was wholly withdrawn from her. She was refused every gratification how simple soever, for the sole purpose of breaking down that resolution which she so rigidly maintained.

She began to pine under her father's obstinate displeasure, the constant persecution of her suitors, and her hopeless situation. Cheered no longer with a bright prospect of the future, when every day gathered fresh masses of dense dark clouds over the horizon of her once serene existence, her tender spirit shook before the raging blast as the leaf of the *cudma*.

About this time I was again far away to the south of Shiraz on an expedition, and while seated one evening in my tent wearied with my occupations, I had received a message, intimating that her indisposition was so severe, that several skilful *hakims*, or doctors, despaired of her recovery, and that she was on the verge of dissolution. I was paralyzed with this sudden unexpected tidings, and I did not know how to act.

"On recovering the proper use of my bewildered faculties, I ran straight to the commanding officer, and obtained his sanction to go back to the city on very urgent affairs that demanded my immediate presence. The General sanctioned my request, and being mounted, I spurred my animal to a full speed, as if he could in one uninterrupted run traverse the distance from Shiraz, where I was posted on duty at the time.

"After running some miles, my horse was so completely exhausted, that I feared to lose his service in the early part of a long journey. I was forced to dismount and lead him by the reins till we reached one of the inns on the road, as daylight began to spread over the east. Some provender was all I was anxious to secure for my horse, and having done this, I was again ready to start. Thus with scarcely any rest or refreshment, I reached my destination within five days. Though expeditious as I could possibly be, I was fated to behold my Zeleikha no more on earth. The morning of the day of my arrival saw her remains laid in a beautiful marble mausoleum, resting unmolested by the ashes of her ancestors.

"I was left during the frenzy of my grief to hover undisturbed around her remains, watering her tomb with my tears, praying over it, watching, and resting when weary of everything else. It was the only place where my grief flowed copiously and relieved the fever of my brain. I planted cypress and willows round the monument, that they might mourn with me her early unhappy fate.

"My brother, who was deeply attached to me, won me with his kind persuasive language to visit the roof of my parent. He led me and I returned, but alas! with what altered feelings. I no longer took an interest in pleasure, mirth, friends, relatives, wealth, or property. My father's eyes were bedewed

7

with tears at the sight of me as I stood a wreck of all I was before. He spoke to me many a consoling word in the language of sincere affection, and were it possible to heal the wounded spirit, or calm the tumult of my breast, his kindness, if nothing else, ought to have ameliorated my bitter condition. Little did he know of the extent of desolation that had spread itself round my withered heart, and undermined the source of every joy. For months I took pleasure in nothing but visiting the monument of her who was my all. Her tomb was the grave of everything dear to me in life, and with her I lost all relish of existence. As time glided away, a deep settled melancholy took possession of my spirit; and as I could not endure the sight of all those scenes and places which were dear to me in her society, I left my father's home with a resolution to visit foreign lands.

"In my rambles, I sojourned at Mysore, Bengal, Oude, and Upper Hindoostan, and volunteered my services to such Mahomedan princes as were harassed with foreign invasion, or the unjust aggression of predatory foes.

"I fought under Azeem-ul-Omra against the Maharatta power. The marauding Jaats, Bheels, and Thugs, have severally felt the weight of my weapon, nor have Chettoo and Kurreem, chiefs of Pindaree freebooters, escaped receiving a lesson from troops that I had joined, and was one of their leaders. I had received, while at the Court of Mysore, the news of the demise of my father, and of his leaving me and my brother a large bulk of his wealth, reserving the rest for the erection of a superb mosque. But what would the possession of such dross be to me? Could it bring back one moment of banished joy, a single ray of faded hope, or even a momentary participation of that peace I once enjoyed?

"I had not the smallest desire to go back to my country; and of the amusements of war I was weary. As I came out in disguise, I assumed different characters, but the termination of all assumptions is, as you now find, the garb and character of a lowly hermit, who is fast verging on to the confines of another world."

Thus far the hermit continued his narration, when feeling tears fast gathering round his eyes, he lifted his hands to his brow and thus addressed his betrothed : —

"O, Zeleikha! now that thou art lost to me for ever, what have I to console or comfort me? Where shall I lay my racking head and weary limbs, and where find repose for the heart withered and rent by grief and sufferings beyond endurance? Still as thou art always present to me in thy ever adored and indelible image, O enshrine thyself in my soul which is held sacred to thee from the pollutions of life, that living as thou hast lived in innocence and purity, thy soul may commune with mine, and when the last sleep of life shall have passed away, I may wake to a full vision of thyself, and to the never ceasing joys of Paradise! Until then adieu, peace, joy, and repose!"

CHAPTER X

MOBARUC was reluctant to disturb the full flow of the feelings of his friend, but when he had after a time recovered his composure, he tenderly held him by the hand, and with affectionate anxiety observed : " Yours is indeed a severe affliction, and well may we weep over a tale so fraught with incidents of no common severity and suffering.

" Your bleeding heart can receive no cure, no consolation from any earthly balm, but faith and hope may yield some fruits of peace. Since regret is unavailing, resign yourself to the fate which *Allah* has in his wise providence assigned you. Comfort yourself, my friend, for in me you will find a brother, and in these little ones behold your children. On you now devolves the care of rearing them in the path of virtue; and to us you will not grudge to give the experience of your age, your agreeable conversation, and prudent counsel. Useful in the sphere allotted to you for your actions, you will look back with no disappointment on a life spent in piety to God, and benevolence to mankind."

" The human mind," said the Hermit, " is so happily constituted by an all-wise Creator, that it can adapt itself to every exigency, and support every trial to which life is exposed. Would our calamities, nay our very joys, if to an excessive degree stimulated, be supportable, if objects which on every hand arrest our attention, and thoughts to which abstract ideas give existence, had they not diverted our cogitations from one channel into another, and interposed to ameliorate the poignancy of the one, and lessen the excitement of the other? Could we bear the spectacle of human wreck, seen as it is in the revolting degradation to which it is reduced at death,—a seeming disappointment of our high aspirations, a frustration of our sanguine hopes, a mockery of our towering thoughts—had not a ray of hope shone forth from the invisible world to cheer the dreary path, and reveal to the eye of reason, the immortality of our existence, and the eternity of future bliss?

" Human life would be indeed a galling burthen if there were no future existence, and no future rewards to recompense expectations that have grown with our growth.

" This alone supports us under every conflict, and reconciles us to every disappointment, the having the assurance that a few revolutions of the sun will usher us to a state of being, vastly different from that we have quitted, and unite us once more and for ever to friends and relatives from whom we were parted but for a season.

" Teach these little ones who are parts of yourself, to weave lofty sentiments in the most glowing, elegant, and refined language, that, according to their noble descent, their education may appear to be of a dignified order of culture, reflecting the brightest glory and the fairest renown on the possessor, and be a pleasing satisfaction to the hearts of the parents.

" But above all, assist them to raise their virgin thought from the lower objects of the present life. In the contemplation of vast objects, pursued through the ocean of unfathomable space, the insignificancy of the visible and the transient will be made apparent."

The Hermit occasionally spent some of his remaining days with Mobaruc, and the lovely little cherubs of his friend, whose innocent mirth ever beamed in their eyes ; from whose tongue the sweet word, *father*, thrilled the heart of the Hermit with a new pulsation of tender solicitude, and lighted up his cloudy brow at times.

But for them and Mobaruc, his life would have been a condition of unmitigated sorrow. To draw him from the solitude of his hermitage, was an attempt on the part of Mobaruc as fruitless as extricating a living turtle from its shell.

He delighted to reside there and indulge himself in contemplating the beauties of nature, and in cherishing the habit of calm spiritual devotion

It is generally believed, that a person whose life has been spent in a course of uniform austerity, and in total devotion of self at the temple of duty and benevolence; that he who disregards personal ease and employs his best energy in penances and mortifications, obtains no small share of the favour of heaven; and the very tendency of the employment of his mind and body to holy purposes and pursuits, inherits, it is believed, a degree of purity and perfection bordering on the superhuman, which the vulgar and the ignorant deify, and to which the intelligent pay respectful homage.

Thus, Ameerjan's character and habits which strictly corresponded with the above requisition constituting a sacred personage in the estimation of the simple, was looked upon with uncommon reverence at first, but after a lapse of years, time that beautifies the dead, gilded his memory with a halo, and enshrined him among the saints, or *peers*, to be venerated in after ages as the sequel will show.

CHAPTER XI

THE Hermit, seeing one day a number of men and women setting out on a pilgrimage from the neighbourhood of Raj-mahul and the adjacent country, his curiosity was powerfully excited to join them, and thereby satisfy his insatiable desire to see *Allah's* wonderful works of creative power, and loving benevolence. He doubted not they would be amply displayed by travelling to the south through the wild countries which he would have to traverse in going to the shrine at Deoghur, or Buddinath, to which the Hindu devotees were at the time bending their anxious steps.

It was not an unusual occurrence that a good number of Mahomedans, whether a hermit, fakir, or tradesman, should be seen at one of the Hindu festivals : nor did it produce any remark from parties belonging to either the one, or the other profession.

Throughout Hindustan and Bengal, a Mahomedan or Hindu festival generally collects a large concourse of men of all castes and creeds, who sally out to witness the *tamasha* held by the one, or the other sect.

Attracted to such places of public gathering, not only for gratifying personal curiosity, or whiling away time with the many gay amusements which such bustling places afford, but a *mela*, or fair, being invariably held at such times, men of all countries and classes meet for trade and commerce, if not absolutely for purposes of devotion.

The Hermit had set out on his journey on a clear pleasant morning in October, in company with two men as his attendants, one of whom carried a carpet and deer skin, a pillow and blanket, with other indispensable requisites for the journey, while a groom followed the horse on which the Hermit was mounted.

In those days when no roads were laid to connect one district with another, and no sure footpath, or, if any had existed which was made by the tramp of travellers through the forest in the past year of their pilgrimage, it was soon effaced by the rapid growth of tropical vegetation, a journey was therefore undertaken, by taking the bearing, or direction in which the temple from the starting point lay.

On this account, the distance to Buddinath lengthened out considerably, persons being under the necessity of going zig-zag through the woods, avoiding a pile of huge boulders in one place, a stream in another quarter, and a rugged difficult ravine in some direction or another.

These impediments on the path of the mere pleasure-seekers were sources of inpatient annoyance and frequent complaint, and their murmuring voice was heard by the Hermit with some degree of curiosity which craved to know the reason why people started in a journey without calculating the cost, while to his taste and habits, it had diversified sources of absorbing interest, profitable occupation, and pleasurable pastime.

As Ameerjan usually followed on the wake of the pilgrims, or leisurely moved on the outskirts of the crowd of men, he had ample time to drink deeply of the ever varying beauties of nature, which his poetic mind presented to his fancy in rich fervid colours, and in tints mellowed into supernal softness.

There have always been a few men among the Mahomedans notably fond of the study of alchemy, mineralogy, and chemistry, and the Hermit, by the curious collection of stones of every description seen in his grotto, gave convincing evidence of his being a lover, if not a master, of those sciences.

Attracted by the curious appearance which stones in certain localities bore, some cropping out of the soil, he would dismount and loiter for some time, examining, exploring, or searching after something in their neighbourhood, an employment which his groom, who had not the same talent and appreciation for such insignificant trifles as he designated them, very generously attributed to occupations of this nature his master's deficiency of brain, and a want of mental equilibrium, repeating to himself, that he must assuredly be a *diwana admi*, or madman.

His master, however, had he even known it, would not have cared a straw for what opinion his groom had entertained in his own stolid head; so long as his propensities were gratified, and his enjoyments were all his own creation, he could afford to be indifferent to what other people might think of him or his pursuits. He returned after such explorations with exultation when they were successful, and as his knowledge was extensive, and his penetration deep, it was often that he returned from such rambles with an air of profound gratification, exhibiting a bag full of fantastic stones, some stratified, some granular, but most of them thickly impregnated with silver, gold, copper, or led. The country through which he was passing, indicated by igneous eruptions and certain rocks, the presence of metalliferous substances, and that the streams possess auriferous deposits. In his extensive wanderings, he had collected a small store of nuggets and gold dust.

Whenever the pilgrims halted for the night, the scene became extremely picturesque, lively, and bustling.

A thousand extempore ovens, dug in the ground, would blaze with faggots, and look like a grand illumination, while the vessels clattered, and the hissing and bubbling of pans made a sort of music in all directions, rather pleasing to the hungry travellers.

After the fatigues of the march, the opulent had their carpets spread on the ground on which they reclined themselves, smoking and chatting so long as their dinner was getting ready; not so their poorer neighbours, who had to betake themselves to the jungle to collect fuel for culinary purposes, and to keep fire to scare away the wild animals at night. These were seen mounted on branches of trees, some picking sticks on the ground, but all by turns craking the dry branches as they were broken or snapped from the trees.

8

It happened sometimes that a few *jatrees*, or pilgrims, went astray from their companions far into the woods, and were attacked by some wild animals who bore the shrieking victim into darker and denser parts of the tangled forest, while the cry of the poor man caused a hasty retreat of the rest, followed by a wild burst of uproar among those who became aware of the depressing tragedy which had happened.

Almost all men who travel through the territories inhabited by wild animals, provide themselves generally with some weapon of defence, such as either a spear, sword, gun, pistol, or even an axe, the latter being an inseporable companion with the poorest; it being so, and while one or two men were now and then taken away by a tiger, it also happened that the axe of the woodcutter, with two or three ponderous strokes, inspired by agony of feeling, and the instinct of self preservation, had stunned a bear, a wolf, or a hyena, which was borne to the camp, and the man who had performed the daring feat, more by accident than his own skill, was made for sometime a hero in the camp of the pilgrims. The forest through which the Hermit journeyed, was not an unprofitable jungle which yielded nothing that commerce needed, for it was replete with valuable timber for building purposes; different kinds of woods for cabinet ware; rich with nuts that produced oil; trees from which shellac, lac-dye, and catechu, were manufactured; and fruits from which native wine was extracted.

Here and there, at long intervals, small villages of the wild aboriginal tribes, emerged into sight through luxuriant patches of cane and Indian corn cultivation, and topes of mangoe and jack, under whose shadow hamlets lay embosomed in tranquil repose.

Troops of Sontals would at times burst into view as they were returning from their usual hunting excursion. Some with a deer tied to a pole, others with hares suspended to a stick, borne on their shoulders, but all equipped with bows and arrows, swords and axes, followed by a pack of hungry, half-starved hounds, whose value lay not so much in their appearance, as the possession of strong hunting instincts, acquired by a course of early and constant training.

The sixth day of the journey proved to be close, hot, and stifling, and the burning rays of the vertical sun almost scorching ; the forest therefore became so still, that the slightest stir of a leaf, agitated by the spring of a bird from twig to twig, was audible with a distinctness.

The sun had scarcely drawn away his retiring glories from the eastern sky, when tokens of a northwester appeared in the western horizon, in which direction cumulative clouds sprang up in rapid succession, one over another in ever widening circles ; sounds of awe came in the meantime rumbling deeply with the low sullen murmurs of the elements,—the sure presages of a coming storm.

Eagles and vultures were seen with rapid wings to mount the sky in a spiral flight, as if endeavouring to cleave the heavens, and rise above the conflict of the elements ; and as heralds of the gale, gusts of wind came rushing over the forest in fitful pulses, bending the summits of trees by their violent blasts, and rocking them like huge, angry billows with deep, awful moanings.

To this war of the clouds and wind, succeeded the awe-inspiring sounds which assailed the ear, coming from all quarters of the forest in deep moans and frightful roars of the terror-stricken animals, as they bounded forward with glaring eyes, and mane erect, to avoid the impending danger.

The rain descended in a torrent, and the wind which had acquired its utmost intensity, snapped the branches, and hurled them down to the ground with a crash, while the roll of thunder, and flashes of lightning, rent the air with their incessant glimmer.

As if these were not enough of awe-inspiring images, snakes and reptiles, instinctively sought shelter in more elevated localities, rendering the situation of the travellers, not only hazardous, but extremely unpleasant from the repulsive feelings which it called into existence.

With a brow fearless and calm, the Hermit stood contemplating the changeful aspect of grandeur and sublimity, seen in the murky sky, or the fitful gloom of the **forest**; the electric flash in **the clouds, and its** deafening peals.

Though desolation and **destruction** surrounded him on all sides, his thoughts, full of consciousness **of the** immortality of its spiritual nature, felt its energy rising proportionate to the emergency of the occasion, so that he could bear to look unmoved at the threatened annihilation which he knew could not reach the **soul, but only the temporal tenement which he** was inhabiting.

The morning sky **succeeding the night of the storm, was** peculiarly **charming and delicious.** It was felt to be cold **and** refreshing **to the** body, and cheerful to the mind from the combined effect producted by the sweet fragrance of the scented wild **flowers; the** fleecy **clouds** sailing like the ripples of a tranquil **lake on whose brow the earliest kiss** of the sun reposed, evoking a soft ruddy blush over them as they floated onward in modest silence. The pilgrims were now approaching the out**skirts of the** place in which the celebrated temples of Boddheo**nath rose in all the pomp in which the** bigotry and superstition **of a** people who knew no **better, had invested them.**

The buzzing of **the** multitude of the *jatrees* **who were** assembled at the place, came floating on the breeze like the distant murmurs of the sea, and it was heard by the Hermit while he was yet at the distance of a few miles.

The cupolas **of the** temples, bursting into view above the groves of mangoe **and tamarind trees** that surrounded them, excited the **pilgrims with emotions of joy at** the prospect of an early termination to their **hardships and** privations, and they broke forth into reiterated exclamations of *Horibole, Horibole.*

Owing to **the** undulatory formation of the country, interspersed with numerous mounds, streams of the pilgrims could be seen from the camp to which the Hermit belonged, converging towards the *mela* from all directions of the wild country, and swelling the circumference and density of the sea of human heads.

After the lapse of a few hours, the pilgrims from the direction of Rajmahal, had not only arrived, but were in the very vortex of the fair to which all were drawn.

The sun shining on the minarets and galleries of the temples, reflected them in a blaze of refulgence, while a strange looking stone image within, drew crowds of deluded men and women who prostrated themselves in unprofitable servility before the impotent deity, where offerings of several kinds were being laid before the shrine, to appease the wrath of Boddheonath, obtain his blessing, or make him propitious to their prayer.

. All the votive offerings of the numerous devotees that augmented the revenue of the pagodas, also increased the wealth and prosperity of the avaricious priests who presided as their guardians, and the spiritual guides of ignorant men.

The seductions of vice and error are more potent in their influence than the attractions of truth and virtue ; the Hermit therefore looked with heartfelt regret on the infatuated votaries who appeared absorbed with the idle ceremonies of the place, and who were bewitched with ritualistic observances which had nothing rational about them to commend themselves to their reason, but that they yet had absolute power over their warm imagination, and the senses which always solicited for their gratification things in perfect harmony with the material part of their nature ; while their lethargic and apathetic minds shrunk from the labour of investigating the truth, or yielding to its wholesome and beneficial influence when it became known.

He was grieved to witness the simplicity of man, or rather the weakness of those who without question, quietly submitted themselves, as well as their reason and judgment, to the control of not only false illusions, but the demeaning sway of men as fallible as themselves, and who were in some instances not superior in their mental endowments to the infatuated men who stooped to the dust in their presence.

But he had not come to moralize and to preach, but to see and know all things, and obtain the knowledge that exists in other places, and among other people, though he could not, from the dogmas of his own creed, help looking with supreme horror and abhorrence on all idolatrous practices.

There was everything about the fair, well calculated to excite a person to a high degree of distraction, bordering upon absolute bewilderment.

There were jugglers and mountebanks, snake charmers and tight-rope dancers, with their inexhaustible tricks and gabble ; and there were sets of dancing boys, singing amorous ditties lustily, and dancing ravingly to the accompaniment of deafening music : at a short distance from these, were to be seen bear and monkey dance in full activity.

There was a large gathering of Brahmins and Khettrees, followers of the Musnavi Sect, Byragees, Sunyasees, Mohunts, Jogees, and even the low despised Domes, who were busy in carrying on a brisk trade in bamboo-basket, and other kindred works.

But there was also a few select *tyfas*, or troupe of dancing girls, with small silver bells fastened to their arms and ankles, which made music, their hands and feet in motion, keeping correct time with the instruments, and dancing with the grace of slow measured steps, and soft oscillations, heightened into excitement, or mellowed into langour as the occasion required by the style in which the *tamboor*, *tabla*, *saringa*, and other soft-toned instruments were played upon.

Booths and tents, with other temporary sheds, made of the branches of trees, formed a spacious bazar, having a walk between lines of shops, numbering more than six hundred, extending in sections over the whole of a large field, beaten down smooth and even by the tramp of the multitude of pilgrims who were attracted to the shrine and *mela*.

The shops were well-stocked with large quantities of wares of all kinds, and articles of every description, from a trifle, to a rare curiosity, or things of indispensable utility.

There were many shops in which several bales of English piece goods, cloths, whether silk, tusser, or cotton fabric of Indian manufacture, were laid out; next to which, in another shop, large quantities of spicery, and then another that exhibited brass utensils intended as water vessels, pots, pans, and lamps, all blazing with a yellow lustre, furnished as they had been for the occasion.

Confectionary of every shape and of divers colours were arranged in heavy masses on trays of brass; they looked tempting and inviting, and crowds of merry children stood admiring and casting longing looks, first at one, and then at another of the trays, seemingly undecided which to chose from, but on the whole, they patronized the confection and the Benares toys more largely than any other.

Great numbers of traders from Calcutta, and from many large towns of India, came with their goods for disposal by sale or exchange, while there were others, men of limited resources, who purchased wares and goods intending to dispose of them in remote parts of the country, and the interior of districts, where they purposed to open out retail business which promised to be very profitable, and of undoubted success, from the mere circumstance that competition in such quarters did not exist.

Each shop was decorated with some fanciful ensign, or ornamented according to the taste or opulence of the proprietor, intended also as marks to distinguish them from each other, and to guide to the locality those persons who lost themselves in the dense crowd, and recognition of places became a matter of doubt and uncertainty.

Crowds of religious mendicants were to be seen pushing their way and demanding rather than begging for charity.

The dialects of most countries of India were spoken, and the jargon and confusion of voices was excessive and from a distance, the buz was like that which proceeds from a thickly studded wasp hive.

In the motley crowd, men dressed in every variety of costume, from the rags of a beggar, to the resplendent robes of a native nobleman, served to lend their individual singularity to increase the grotesqueness of the spectacle.

The Hermit had the good fortune to fall in company with a few travellers who had come on a long journey from the far North, and who appeared to be jaded, weary, and exhausted from protracted travel.

He was delighted to find that they were men from the border countries of Iran, in Persia; and that they were of the same faith as that which he professed, was easy to discover by a single glance.

Of these three men who had fallen on his way, one of them, the youngest, was peculiarly delicate in the general outline of his figure, form, and profile; and appeared to be a young man over whose head not more than twenty-six years had revolved. Though the years of his life were not numerous, yet that they were not altogether pleasant and joyous, but had rather been pregnant with care, anxiety, and gloom, could be easily discerned by a cloud of sadness which was visible on his youthful countenance, and stamped it with the impression that it was the seat of some secret sorrow.

He differed from his two associates in several points; they were tall, robust, and somewhat dark from long exposure; their eyes were black and deep set, yet they shone with intelligence, unwavering resolution, and a fixedness of purpose from which as if nothing could divert the men.

The young man though also slightly tinged with a few shades of brown caused by travelling, was on the whole of a light colour. His hair, which fell in soft ringlets over his shoulders, was dark, and his eyes were light-brown, full in their orbs, and they possessed an ever varying expression that heightened their lustre and their beauty.

These men on being questioned by the Hermit as to what object they had in view that could have induced them to undertake so long, laborious, and perilous a journey, replied that it was not only their curiosity to see other countries which compelled them to leave their home to enlist themselves in the service of the emperor of Delhi, or any one of the princes of Hindustan, where their valour and talent, finding proper scope for their exercise, they could distinguish themselves, and by that means secure respectable posts and lucrative employment suitable to their rank and education.

Some merchants were returning from the *mela* to Upper Hindustan, and the two elder travellers joined their company with a view to carry out their intention to visit the Court of the emperor.

The youngest traveller, whose name was Ismail, charmed by the sobriety of the Hermit's character, the extent of his wisdom, the gentleness and affability of his manners, and the prudence of his actions, resolved to follow him as a *shágird*, or scholar, while the Hermit bore the appellation of *ustad*, or teacher.

The sojourn of a week at the fair had so satiated the Hermit and made him feel so thoroughly tired of the puerilities, the deafening uproar, and the shallow enjoyments of the place, that he began to look back towards Raj-Mahal, and long for the quietude of his retirement at the Pearl Spring, so he started one morning long before dawn, with those only who were his personal attendants, and his newly acquired companion.

The return trip, now that the path was known familiarly, was comparatively of a shorter duration than before, and the road was enlivened by meeting occasionally with merry groups of men, women, and children, who had preceded them in the walk, so the journey terminated after the expiration of a week, the Hermit being glad to be back to the serenity of his grotto, and its unruffled enjoyment.

9

THE Hermit, now that his residence was enlivened by the congenial society of a countryman, did not find time hang so heavily as it did before ; and by frequently conversing with Ismail on topics that had an intimate connection with the city in which he was born, the pent up associations of years were stirred into lively activity by the chords of memory being touched upon which awakened them, and he began to feel as if his youthful days were renewed, and that he was living again in the midst of bright and familiar scenes in which life to him had been a prolonged sunshine, and every sensation a throb of joy.

After the expiration of a few weeks, when a good deal of the natural shyness and reserve which had existed at the beginning of their acquaintance, had worn out by an increased familiarity, the Hermit sought further information.

"I desire very anxiously to know, Ismail," said the Hermit, "something of the class of free* thinkers, or sceptics, in Persia, who lived, and their sentiments were rapidly spreading through the country when I was about to leave it, if they still exist and are as popular now as they were at that time."

"Yes, *ustad*, I remember the class of men to whom you allude," answered Ismail, but he did so with some diffidence, as if not thoroughly conversant with the subject, and afraid that he might therefore commit some blunder.

"I remember the sect very well, as their peculiar dogmas, and the novel views they held, were often made the subject of serious coversation, and were largely commented upon by many persons.

"They are neither attached to the Soonni, nor Shea sect, and they do not place implicit belief in the doctrines enunciated in the Koran. They not only exist, but most people are tainted

* A class of religious sect called Sufi or Sofi.

with their sentiments, whether they avow it publicly or not. Do you not think it to be very wicked conduct in those men who are so zealous in subverting the established faith of the country, and marring the tranquillity of the people with their new speculations ?"

"I do not think, Ismail, that, as rational beings, we are not bound to investigate the merit of every subject, whether it be secular, or religious. When we cease to do so, we lock up the exercise of our own reason and judgment, and yield a blind, and not an intelligent assent to what we profess to believe.

"Religion is so deeply important to each individual, as on it depends his eternal welfare, or his endless misery, that it becomes an imperative duty therefore, not to accept one's religion from his forefathers, but to investigate and choose for himself, inasmuch as he, as a moral agent, will be personally responsible for his actions.

"Allow me to say in conclusion that Allah, who has made the glorious morning and the evening, with the soft moon and the stars that sparkle like gems on the brow of night, made our sentient bodies also, and gave to our minds an immortal flame, that our spirits linked hereafter with the Eternal Spirit who vivifies the whole universe, we might also live for ever in his presence.

"A Being so wise, so powerful, so good, and having such benevolent designs towards us, could never have left his rational creatures to grope their way in darkness and mortifying uncertainty.

"God is the moral Governor of the world, and He has therefore furnished his subjects, with moral and divine laws for regulating their conduct. Man though a rational and intelligent being, is not infallible, and under this circumstance, if he is not provided with definite injunctions, he would be erring perpetually, and from the absence of definite laws, he would plead ignorance for his justification, and make excuses for his guilt.

"I differ, then, from those men in Persia on this point, and would say that we have the strongest reason to expect that God did give to man a written law, and made him amenable to its injunctions. If some doubt its genuineness and authenticity, and the Koran be not the book, yet a revelation must of necessity exist somewhere. He who repudiates the existence of such written laws, indicates the grossness of his desire to live perfectly disengaged from all restraints, and to enjoy an unlimited freedom of action.

"But I might pain you with my present reflections, and would on that account change the subject by asking, how was it that you did not of your own free accord tell me the reason which brought you to this distant country, while your other companions related to me their reason for doing so with perfect unreserve."

"I would have done the same, good *ustad*," observed Ismail, somewhat abashed, not only for the implied want of confidence, but with regard to the quality of the disclosure, "had my reason for leaving my country been of the same complexion as that of my two companions. That which I would have to reveal, was a subject too painful for me to dwell upon, nay, it was intensified agony to think about; I would yet, that I might not appear unthankful for your kindness and generosity, reveal the secret which lay hid in the depths of my heart for many long weary years.

"Twelve years ago I was secretly betrothed to a very worthy individual," commenced Ismail with his narrative, in relating which, there was much pathos in the tone, and a perceptible modesty and tenderness in the manner of his delivery, which could not but enlist the sympathy of his friend, the Hermit.

"The growth of that pure and honest affection, on which God who is the essence of love, and who could never look with disdain, man in his blind arrogance, cruel revenge, and influenced by a sordid spirit, condemned.

"We were so well known to each other, and our regard which

was mutual, was deep and sincere, because it was based on the thorough appreciation of our respective merits, that no idle rumour, or spiteful detraction, however sedulous to cause a breach, could alienate our affection.

" A wily plan was adopted, too long to relate at present, and that succeeded in separating us, though nothing else could; to be brief, I abandoned the place for its being full of duplicity and ᵗrickery, and because I could not endure the bitter reflections which had sprung up in my mind, and the numerous sufferings and persecutions to which I was subjected.

" All that I possessed of worldly wealth and grandeur, I left behind, esteeming them as dross, that I might be as free as the air to wander over more congenial countries, enjoy peace and quietude elsewhere, and meet with men who might be more humane, and in whom I might trace some resemblance to the moral image of their Maker.

" But go where I might, I cannot divest myself of that which forms an element of my own nature. I bear my own thoughts and feelings wherever I go; hence if any circumstance should for a brief time divert them, the momentary restraint gives them a greater momentum, and redoubles their power."

The Hermit, whilst listening to this touching disclosure, seemed wrapped with wild and conflicting thoughts; his head drooped and he stood in all the magnificence of a faithful figure of despair.

He who of late years appeared to his friends to bear the calmest exterior, for no trace of human passion disfigured his intellectual brow, or furrowed his tranquil countenance on which rested the serenity that conscious rectitude always produces, was moved to blinding tears, and shaken to the core of his heart, for memory that bore a faithful record of past events, was active in tracing a close and sad resemblance in their destinies.

" I accord to you, good Ismail, my deepest sympathy, and offer you my sincerest condolence," replied the Hermit, with feelings of earnest pity and compassion, seeing a person so much younger than himself, yet who had borne the strokes of torturing thoughts, commensurate with his own galling experience.

To offer in a small measure some consolation, poor and inefficacious as it might be, yet which might, he thought, serve to divert him from his brooding cares, and ameliorate the poignancy of his feeling, he spoke thus, addressing Ismail.

"The good Being who has formed us of clay, while He has given us strong minds, and created us with frail bodies, to compensate us for the deficiency, He has provided with counterbalancing agencies both in nature and in our capacities, making up as it were for the existing difference.

"Not only that the most severe pain subverts its own power by its intensity, but the very frequency of suffering, which habituates and familiarises us to its infliction, softens the stroke.

"Not only so, but observe how, as in the physical and social, so in the mental world, all things are subject to the law of reaction. The river has its rising tide, as well as its receding ebb—a depressive tendency succeeds the tension of the nervous system—the wildest conflict of the elements subsides into perfect calm, and to the most vehement grief, there is a certain limit, regulated by constitutional capacity, up to which it will rise, and then a reaction must supervene.

"Under this altered circumstance and state of feeling, even a child who is prematurely brought to feel the weight of affliction, is by his suffering and privation, forced to think and act for himself, and to devise plans for his relief, or build glittering castles in the air to soothe the woes of his young heart, and by these circumstances, though a child in years, he becomes mature in mind and feeling, and old for his age in thoughtful actions.

"But a man of maturer years, who manifests the reverse side of the tension point, rises up to the highest tide of grief and watchful care, but descends to total heedlessness, and to absolute self-abandonment, luxuriating in fun and frolic, commensurate with the pressure of his former depression.

" If these be not the indications of his reactionary mood, it is often seen, that the person who suffers most for a certain thing, makes up for the amount of previous suffering by indulging in very opposite propensities ; he loses an angel, but from that thorough abandonment, he does not care afterwards to hug a monster."

" I admit that time blunts the edge of sorrow, but it never thoroughly eradicates the complaint. According to the worth of the character of a person, so is the memory of the good cherished as a valuable gem in a rich and durable casket," observed Ismail, with a pensive expression which indicated, as if nothing could soothe, or which would be a crime for him to study to efface from the page of memory.

Finding that to border on tender subjects, however remotely, was not calculated to heal but to irritate the wound, the Hermit willingly dropped it and made no further remarks, but drew away his young friend to read some books which they were in the habit of looking over together.

The works of the Persian poets engaged their attention more frequently than a production in metaphysical subjects did. The latter was taken up occasionally, but the former oftener, and as it was at the present time.

In this occupation, as it was his wont, he commented on the merits and demerits of some of the compositions of the poets, adding the following remarks, after the observations which preceded it had closed.

" Most of our poets are very elaborate in singing the praises of all the gay and brilliant things that adorn the features of nature, or transpire in the chequered scenes of life, but we have veryfew muses of a pensive cast in our Parnassus.

" The gay things of the world have a sparkling lustre and an attractive charm that admit of no question, but the sad things of life possess a melancholy beauty too, which, if garbed in the rich and delicate drapery of poesy, would appear most pleasing and captivating by their touching sentimentality.

" But I forgot that there are one or two isolated instances in which our sweet melodious versifiers, have indulged in pleasing fancies on the topic of grief, but which, however, are happily not mere soarings into the regions of fiction and unreality, but fall within the actualities of life.

" One for instance, illustrates the character of a good man, by representing him as a towering rock, standing above the sea; the wind and wave of affliction strike in vain against him, and the cloud and tempest spend their fury to no purpose : his brow is ever calm, bright, and tranquil, above the angry surge, and the cloudy observations below !"

CHAPTER XIII.

FROM the very beginning of their acquaintance, there was a mysterious something which seemed to envelope the character of Ismail, the Hermit was awakened by it into a new and delicious existence, half on earth, half in dreamland, yet though he sat trying hard to unriddle the enigma, it was far beyond his power to come to a satisfactory solution as to who he was.

He sent his vigilant thoughts rambling in every direction of surmise, and still he was as remote from the fact as ever.

There was a softness in Ismail's voice, a gentleness in his manners, a tenderness in his demeanour, all which were a puzzle to him, but what added still more to his perplexity was, that the tone, mildness, with the expression which flashed forth at times from his countenance and eyes, were as things that came dawning in slight glimmering lights to his mind as remembrances of some sweet, but hallowed music that had gladdened his heart in earlier, happier days.

Could he, the Hermit thought, have been a school fellow of his, in whose congenial society he had spent the years of his youth in very pleasant companionship? But as soon as such reflections visited his mind, he was obliged to abandon them, for he could not think of any school fellow between whom and himself there had existed any marked disparity of years, and such intimate companions, as he had the good fortune to possess, were generally young men of his own age, or older than he, but scarcely any one who was twelve or sixteen years younger.

These tokens of mystery began to multiply as time advanced in its steady onward course, but though they were fraught with much matter for trying speculations, yet they served to keep the attention of the recluse engaged, and diverted the monotonous life he had lived in unrelieved sameness, before the advent of his countryman, situated as he was in the solitude of a place seldom frequented by tourists.

It could not but strike the Hermit as remarkably singular, that Ismail invariably avoided, and never once accompanied him, when he went to the Pearl Spring for his daily ablutions, though he did so in his absence.

There was scarcely anybody in the vicinity of the spring, for it was not only a secluded spot, but was well screened by brushwood growing in its neighbourhood, and a network of tangled creepers that thoroughly concealed its locality, therefore, if Ismail, with his singular tastes and habits, had any objection on the point of its being exposed, it could afford him no excuse.

The Hermit had the misfortune to receive a severe hurt one day, as after his usual bath he was returning from the *Jhurna*, his right foot, which had trod on one of the many fragments of quartz scattered profusely about the place, slipped, and his ankle had by that accident, received a severe sprain, and was cut with their sharp edge.

At first there was neither a swelling, nor any sensible pain, but before night had set in, a painful inflammation came on, accompanied with a burning fever and excessive thirst.

The recluse had studied the medicinal properties of the plants abounding in the jungle, and had communicated to his friend their virtue and efficacy, and these came very opportunely into valuable service on the present occasion, for it helped to soften the severity of his indisposition.

Ismail who was powerfully agitated by seeing him suffer, ran with all anxiety to the nearest wood, and collected some roots of the *kurhur* as a febrifuge, and some *neem* leaves for an embrocation, returning with them with much haste, he boiled the former to make a decoction, and bruised the latter, and prepared with it a warm poultice.

No woman could have attended on the patient with greater solicitude, and with so much mild, soothing care; with a forestalling of his wants and wishes, and with so deep, sincere, and earnest expression of concern, as was depicted in eloquent language in the sorrowing eyes, and melancholy countenance of Ismail.

He was, with scarcely any relaxation, seated constantly at the foot of his bed, ministering to his wants, and with his assumed cheerful conversation, soothing his physical pain, and diffusing a healing balm over his mental sufferings.

For three days and nights, the Hermit was occasionally delirious, and between a state of half consciousness and partial sleep, he was heard to pronounce, though very softly, the name Zuleikha, at intervals.

There was surely a spell in that name, or why should it have moved Ismail so profoundly.

Could it have been that he too had associated with that dear appellation all that was beautiful in form, pleasing in manners, and lovely in the graces of virtue, and to whom he had resigned his heart? or was it that he grew petulant at the reflection that his friend and benefactor did not sufficiently appreciate his ministrations, but was at that time thinking of softer hands to smooth his pillows, and with far more winning ways, tend on his ruffled temper, now rendered capricious through the power of irritating disease?

Ismail sat bathed in tears on hearing that name fall from his lips, fall with the softness of the dew and its reviving influence, as after its descent it reposes on the fragrant bosom of some decaying flower, which, but for that timely refreshing visit of heaven's distillation, might have faded for ever under neglect.

What could have touched the fountain of his heart, and bid those tears drench his pallid cheeks? Were they tears of sorrow or joy, or did they partake of both?

A strong constitution, combined with careful, intelligent, affectionate nursing, subdued the early symptoms of his indisposition; and when in a state of convalescence, he was resting, his countenance looked as peaceful as that of a sleeping child troubled with no disturbing causes, expressing a serenity that revealed the tranquillity which the mind of the Hermit was partaking of at the time.

When the Hermit, who was in a short nap, awoke, he felt a deep concern, for he saw that some strong emotion had disturbed the mind of his good nurse, as that had become too visible in the disorder of Ismail's looks, to pass unobserved by him.

He beheld tears, and listened to sighs, deep but subdued, thoroughly unconscious that he was the adored object for whom they dropped, and for whom they breathed.

His heart pulsated with a wild throb, new to his curbed feelings, and novel to his experience of past years. His mind was beginning to be swayed by tender reflections, and his heart was being ruled by softer feelings. Shadowy recollections began to dawn in his mind gradually as the twilight ushers the full day refulgence.

He began to wonder less at Ismail's lively but delicate modesty, a reserve that was pleasing and attractive, and which eminently distinguished him and was his peculiar characteristic.

His conviction amounted almost to a certainty, that the person whom he for months had sheltered in his residence, could be no other than a female in disguise.

" My good and kind friend," said the Hermit, " pray restrain your tears, and moderate your grief, for they affect me too painfully.

" Instead of promoting my health, they would prostrate me again, and all the good you have been doing by your affectionate attentions, would be defeated by your present immoderate indulgence of sorrow."

This allusion to Ismail's loving sympathy had not the effect of checking his feelings, but served rather to cause a fresh overflow of tears, and under the vehemence of his conflicting emotions, Ismail sank down his head at the foot of the cot where he was seated.

In doing so, his cloak fell down from his shoulders, and revealed to the astonished eyes of the Hermit, a red mole of a singular formation, having a striking resemblance to a *sháhdána*, or cherry, and it was bright from the contrast of a clear, smooth, and fair complexion on which it was set.

It was now his turn to be intensely overcome at the revelation, and borne down by its violence, he fell with tears and sobs on the neck of his friend.

When they had both risen from the paroxysm of their grief, and their feelings had moderated, the Hermit said.

"My fair celestial visitant, have you left your bright spirit-land above, and come down to be my guardian angel in this desolate place ?"

"Oh, dear Ameerjan, could you have been so sadly deceived by the lying reports spread to achieve a villainous purpose ? How tardy you have been in recognising me, but a woman's instincts which are stronger than a man's perceptions, made me months ago familiar with your real character. I was gratified yet tortured in seeing you grateful and kind to my memory, but suffering from a wrong impression of my supposed death."

"That, dearest Zuleikha! was occasioned chiefly by my implicit belief that you were no longer an inhabitant of this world, but a bright happy resident of the skies."

The Hermit now in some measure could understand the reason how even without the sanction of his will, he was drawn spontaneously towards his friend with a gushing affection over which he had no control.

Zuleikha now related to him, that on hearing that Ameerjan was deceived by the deception practised upon him by her parents, who caused the erection of a tomb which, however, contained nothing besides bricks and mortar, that he might under the delusion, abandon his projects, and persist no longer to sue for his daughter's hand ; that being informed of this wicked trick played upon him, and that it was the cause of his forsaking his country, she shortly after, being no longer under the control of her parent, for he had died three months before, matured her plans for coming out in his search, and finding him, might contradict the report, and defeat the most unnatural, and unjust designs, and the cruel treatment of her relatives.

She was well informed of the number of persons who, not

finding employment at home, usually emigrated towards Hindustan in quest of lucrative and respectable engagements, and of positions of trust and honor, according to the talent and capacity they took to the courts of the several princes of the land.

She had started with these emigrants in the disguise he saw her, the number thinning constantly as they separated on the journey, some taking a different course, but with the two travellers who were bound for Raj-Mahal, with them she cast in her lot.

The rest of the incidents being known to the Hermit, it needed no further explanation.

It was necessary, as he very justly thought, that he ought to send for a Mulla, and he did send for one from Azimabad, who read the service, and united them privately in marriage, it being not the wish of the Hermit to give publicity to the affair, as they fully made up their mind to return to their country, and take possession of the property to which they were entitled.

One evening, after the sun had set with his retiring glories, the air had been balmy, and the scene softly enchanting, the Hermit went and had a private interview with his true friend Mobaruc, to whom he communicated about his meeting with some travellers from his country at the fair, who gave him the information, that the daughter of a certain Omrao of his country was still alive and not dead, as it was believed, and that this news necessitated him to quit the neighbourhood of Raj-Mahul, and go back to Persia, but should *Moulah* spare his life, he would visit the place, and see him once more.

The friends who were locked in each other's embrace, parted with tears of sincere regret, and wishing Heaven's choicest blessing to descend on each other, the Hermit retired from the house in which he had partaken of much peace, comfort, and happiness.

Two days after this painful interview with Mobaruc, a *bahay-lee*, drawn by a pair of stately, sturdy oxen, round whose necks several bells jingled merrily, was seen with labouring steps to ascend one of the acclivities of the undulatory country.

Two travellers were seated on the *bahaylee*, Zuleikha still retaining the use of her disguise in the journey, and now and then the Hermit cast a longing and regretful look behind at the peaceful hermitage he was leaving for ever, abandoned and soon to be in full possession of rank vegetation, and the wild animals of the forest in its vicinity.

" Dear Zuleikha! I leave the place with some regret, for driven away as I have been from my home, I sought its shelter and quietude, and found there the enjoyment of a life of undisturbed peace and tranquillity. Save the bitter thoughts of my having lost you, I had no regrets to suffer from, and I indulged in no other aspirations."

" Having now obtained our hearts' fond desire, we can afford to forgive the treachery of others, and in our present happiness, study to forget the saddening recollections of our past trials, and be thankful for the enjoyment of this change in our destiny."

Conversing thus, the *bahaylee* was lost to sight in the next downward course of the path through the waving country, but it still proceeded onwards, steadily to a distant land.

Age that undermines all things, had at an advanced period shaken the strength of the Hermit's robust frame, and laid him down gently to his final rest in the lovely country of Iran, but this was not known to the residents of Raj-Mahal; the disappearance of the recluse from that locality was a secret which was known only to his friend Mobaruc.

Out of respect to the memory of so good a person as the Hermit, the residents, as a tribute of respect, erected a stone momument after the lapse of a year.

The sudden and unexpected appearance of the tomb was supposed to have been a miraculous erection, as a memento of his holy life on earth, and as the shrine at which to kindle the expiring flame of devotion ; while the ignorant and superstitious entertained a belief that his body was lifted up and veiled among the clouds on his ascent to *firdaus*, or paradise.

Thus the tomb acquired a degree of sanctity in the eyes of men, and especially in that of love-stricken maidens.

With the offerings of flowers and sweets, the shrine was frequently visited to make the Hermit propitious to their prayers.

The overwhelming surge of time has now swept away those votaries who resorted to the spot, and fragments of scattered stones in the vicinity of the rocks, covered with wild flowering creepers, are pointed to by the ignorant as *Peer-Ke-Durga*, or the tomb of the saint, but which in reality is no other than the supposed tomb of the Hermit of Motee-Jhurná.

———◆———

A BRAHMIN AND HIS PUPIL.

———

A BRAHMIN was in the habit of visiting several towns and villages, for the purpose of procuring for himself the means of subsistence, by the gifts and alms of those who considered charity to a person of his holy life and pious character, a high meritorious act. In these pedestrian tours, his pupil was invariably his companion. Going to a certain country, he gave some pice to his scholar to make bazar for their use. The youth going to the market, discovered that all things in it were being sold at one uniform rate and value. He had obtained 1 seer of rice for 1 pice, and a seer doll also for 1 pice ; wood, sugar, ghee, all these, and every thing else, at the same rate. Highly pleased with this idea, and going home to the Brahmin, he told him how fine a country it was, recommended him never to leave it on any account, but said that if he did so, his own resolution was made up never to depart from a country so cheap and luxurious. " My son !" replied the Brahmin, " you have no experience of the world. All that glitters like gold is not that bright and valuable metal. There is no fair and equitable administration of law in this country, and there can be no impartial redress, as it is evident, or the value of wood would not have been estimated on a par with sugar, ghee, and rice." Saying this, and finding that his pupil's resolution could not be

11

shaken, he took his leave and departed from the country, warning him that he would surely come some day into trouble.

After the lapse of five or six months, there was a storm in the country, which brought down part of the wall of a house, and it fell on a person and killed him. A woman of the village, in which this sad event happened, went to the king, and complained about the wall which caused the death of her husband. The king ordered the man to be brought whose wall had fallen. On his being presented at the durbar, his majesty rebuked him severely for not mending the wall, or not building it strongly, so that it would not have fallen and destroyed one of his subjects, he therefore ordered the man to be suspended on a gibbet. The poor man answered with fear, that it was no fault of his, but of the mason who had erected it with bad materials, though paid by him handsomely for the work. His majesty judged it to be unfair to punish him and not the architect, and so he ordered the mason to appear. The mason, knowing that the king's decision was fickle, heard his sentence pronounced with no emotion of fear, but took courage thereby to frame a plausible story, saying that it was not his fault, but the fault of the ironsmith who made the spade, which was bad and crooked, and he could not work with that to his satisfaction. To the king the story appeared to be true. It was not, he thought, the mason on whom blame could be fixed with justice, but the smith who had furnished the implement, so the ironsmith was in due time summoned, and the King ordered him to the scaffold; but he too palliated his fault by urging, that if the spade was made badly, it was not on account of his negligence or want of skill, but the wet coal supplied by the collier. The king again commanded the collier to be brought into his presence to answer for the harm he had been instrumental in producing. His majesty scolded and abused him for supplying bad coal, saying that if he had not done so, a human life would not have been destroyed, therefore that he must expiate the crime with his life. It was the turn of the collier to justify himself by saying that it was not his fault. He was bringing coal in bags laden on bullocks one morning, when a village woman was seen going at the time to fetch water, and he could not help looking at her. While doing so, the bullock had strayed from the path, and had descended into a stream to slake its thirst, and so the bags of coal had got wet, all owing to the woman coming out on the road at that time. The king, whose gullibility was not small, was led to believe that blame was to be attached to the woman. He commanded her to be brought up on trial, but the father-in-law of that woman, thinking that her presence at the public durbar would entail disgrace on the family, willingly presented himself, requesting that he was ready to suffer for the crime of his daughter-in-law. The king, accordingly, ordered him to be taken to the gallows, but the executioner respectfully urged, that the man was lean and sickly, and not quite so well suited for the halter, as a stout man would be. Hereupon the king consented that a plump person should be produced. After a diligent search, the executioner's choice fell on the youth who had been the companion of the Brahmin, and who had so much admired the country with its wonderful cheap market, and who, on that account, could not be persuaded to quit the country which the judicious Brahmin perceived was dangerous to inhabit, where the administrations of the Government were so capricious and inequitable. The youth who had spent his time in enjoying the good things of the market, had grown smooth, oily, and corpulent, and for that reason, was the very person the executioner selected for the halter. He was ordered to the gibbet, and when at the place of execution, he called to mind the words of his master, and sighed deeply that he had not attended to his good admonition. The report ran through the whole country, that a young man, who was the companion of a Brahmin, and was seen travelling through the country some months ago, was on a certain day to be executed. The rumour reaching the ear of the Brahmin, deeply affected his feelings with grief for the youth. He travelled with great expedition, and when come to the country, he ran up to the king, fell at his feet, and said, while he went and firmly embraced the post with both his hands—" O good and wise king, I have travelled from a great distance to obtain this supeme felicity, suffer me not to be disappointed. I will mount this scaffold most joyfully, and will not permit this insignificant youth to ascend it, for he who goes up this scaffold to-day will surely mount to the paradise above." The king thought within himself, that this celebrated Brahmin must have communicated what was true, and, if so, then why not put his decrepid, old, sick, suffering father out of all his trials, sufferings, and troubles, and send him at once to the region of enjoyment. Arriving at this superlatively wise conclusion, he orderd his father to the gallows. The aged man was executed, not however with sorrow and regret, but with joy on the part of those whose ignorant zeal urged them to accomplish what they deemed a holy act. Relieved from danger, the youth, with demonstrations of gratitude, joined the Brahmin in his journey, never more to quit his side, or neglect his wholesome advice.

THE STORY OF SIX BROTHERS.

THERE lived six brothers in a certain country, five of whom had good sight, but the sixth had defective vision, and could, therefore, see but imperfectly. His brothers separated him from their society, giving him a small dilapidated hut, as his portion, in the distribution of their paternal property, with a few other very insignificant or defective things. There stood a large tree near the hut of the blind brother. Some dacoits were in the habit of going under that tree, and dividing their plunder among themselves. One night, the blind man overheard the dacoits saying, as they were sharing the money, "He who did not make a just division, God's thunder would descend rattling on his head." To take advantage of this accident, he cunningly devised a plan to work on their superstitious fear, by slaughtering a bullock which he had, drying the hide in the sun, and with that stiff rustling hide, he ascended the tree in the evening, patiently waiting the arrival of the thieves. As was their habit, they came with their booty under the tree, and as they were sharing their plunder with a view to insure a just distribution, repeating, "That God's thunder would descend on the head of the person who dealt dishonestly," just at that moment the blind brother let down the dry hide, which descended with a thundering rattle on their heads. This appalled them so excessively that they jumped up in great consternation, leaving all the money behind. The blind man descended from the tree, picked up all he could collect, and with that retired into his humble hut. He desired his mother on the following morning to call on his brothers, and ask for the loan of their *coonkee*—measuring-basket—that he might weigh out all the money he had taken home. In returning his brothers their *coonkee*, he took care to put in two or

three rupees between the rattan ties. The brothers were not a
little surprised to discover several rupees sticking to the *coonkee*,
and therefore with anxiety asked their mother where their brother could have got so much money, that in weighing out, some
had stuck which was not missing. She replied that he had
brought home that morning a good deal of money, but from
whence he had obtained it, she was perfectly ignorant. She
desired them to go and enquire of their brother. They lost no
time in visiting him, jealous as they were of his good fortune.
They enquired how he came to possess so much riches. The
blind brother answered thus : " It is my bad fate that I do not
possess several other bullocks. The hide of the old, starved
animal, which I had from you, was the means of my obtaining
the money. Had I as many cows as you have, I could make
ten times as much money." On hearing this, the envious brothers went and slaughtered all the valuable cows they had,
tanned their hides, and went to the market to dispose of them.
They found to their grief that no purchaser would offer more
than a few annas for each hide. They were sadly disappointed, and returning to their homes with sorrow and vexation,
they exclaimed—" Our brother has given us evil advice with an
intention to injure us, let us therefore go this evening and set
fire to his house." They did as they had planned, but the
blind brother, on the following morning, very carefully gathered charcoal from the burnt house, filled two sacks, and hiring
a bullock went to effect a sale. While he was going with the
coal, he fell in with a company of merchants near sunset.
They had their oxen laden with bags containing gold, silver,
and precious gems; the blind man therefore encamped near
them, asking permission to be allowed to keep his bags in the
same protected spot, urging that he had similar articles for sale,
and would rather be in their company than depart at that hour
and be plundered in the way by going unguarded. Just before 3 or 4 o'clock in the morning, before the hour for starting,
he crept stealthily from his place, and placing his bags of coal

with theirs, dragged a pair of their bags near his bullock, when he woke them and asked the merchants to be so kind as to help him to lift the bags on his animial, saying that he had a long journey to go, and on that account he intended to begin early. They pitied the blind man, and helped him to load his animal.

The blind brother started on his journey with alacrity, and going but a short way in another direction, shaped his course towards his own house, whither he drove his bullock as fast as it could trot. Getting home he requested his mother, as before, to go to his brothers and ask for the loan of their *coonkee*, or measuring-basket. This he did, not with any desire really to weigh out his bags of gold and silver, and gems, but to find an opportunity to put in some small pieces of the treasure, that the spite and envy of his brothers might be mortified, and thereby that they might be rebuked and punished for their wicked designs against him. The brothers seeing some valuable metal adhering to their *coonkee* when it was returned, asked the mother again with greater solicitude, how the blind brother had come to the possession of such valuables. The mother replied, that all she knew was that she saw him collecting all the charcoal from his burnt house and going to sell it. They ran to their brother eagerly to enquire. The blind brother said: "Alas! what a misfortune that I had not several houses. My poor hut was burnt down, and with the charcoal procured from the conflagration, I have earned so much wealth. Had I several houses, what a princely fortune I could acquire." The envious brothers therefore went and set fire to their respective spacious houses, in hopes of obtaining great wealth. Going with the charcoal to the market for disposal, but finding no one to offer more than 1 or 2 annas for each bag, they returned home with much vexation and sorrow. They consulted together, and were determined to punish their brother very severely for bringing so much distress on them by his wicked counsel. They went therefore, and tying his hands and feet, put him into a sack and let him down in a tank. As soon as this diabolical work was accomplished, they, to elude detection, decamped from the spot with all haste. At that time some cowherds who were watching the herds grazing in the field, and who had silently witnessed the whole of the atrocious transaction, ran quickly to the tank and rescued the blind brother from a watery grave, after which they went away to break their fast. As soon as the brother had recovered from the stupor, he drove the herd to his own house, not intending finally to make it his own property, but with the view of punishing his brothers. They were not a little surprised to see him not only safe, but bringing with him a considerable herd of cows. They asked him again about his good fortune and preservation. He answered: "O brothers! how shall I describe to you what happened; when I was thrown into the tank, on opening my eyes, I beheld innumerable cows; all I had to do was to pull them by the tail and drag them up. I had been but a short time in it and got this large herd. Had I continued longer, I could scarcely have driven them home by myself." They became anxious to know how they could get them. The blind brother said: "Allow me to bind your hands and feet, and fling you into the tank; I have no doubt that you will meet with better success than I have had by my individual exertion." The deluded brothers suffered him to tie their hands and feet, allowed themselves to be put into sacks, and then let down into the tank. The consequence was that their folly, envy, injustice, and wickedness, produced their own punishment. The blind brother was avenged for all the wrong and injustice they did him.

A MERCHANT AND HIS SON.

A WEALTHY merchant, while lying on his bed indisposed by sickness, and the infirmities of age, invited his son to his room one day, and spoke to him in these words—" My son, from this sickness I may not recover. Should I die, I fear you would squander all my hard earned wealth by dissipation and idleness. You know that in my vocation as a merchant, I have prospered and enjoyed all the blessings of this life. I fear you will not be able to conduct the business with care and discretion, yet I would recommend your following the profession of your father. In doing so I lay no restraint upon your visiting every land under the sun, but I strongly dissuade you from ever venturing into the Himalayan regions." The son was desirous of knowing the reason why his father prohibited him from going with his merchandise, if he ever traded, in the Himalayan mountains. " My son," observed the father, " my long experience of the world, my knowledge of all countries and their denizens, enables me to form a just and accurate estimate of the characters of men. The inhabitants of that region have been found invariably to be very artful and dishonest. They will not only rob a man of his purse, but if they can find an opportunity, or a single excuse, they will without remorse strip him naked and appropriate his clothes. Should you ever forget this my parting advice, and go into that country, and fall into any disaster, remember to call on Golab Sing, the chief of the country, who is a friend of mine ; mention my name to him, seek redress from his justice, and he will enable you to remain there in the peaceful prosecution of your trade."

The merchant died shortly after as was expected, and the son, whose curiosity was excited by the merchant's prohibition, resolved upon visiting the lofty hills. To carry out this object,

12

he procured a large stock of valuable goods, and such as were not only in general demand in the country, but highly valued by the mountaineers. With this merchandize he loaded fifty camels, and set out on a fine morning on this perilous and uncertain journey. Having arrived in the country after two months' tedious travel through interminable forests and fields, the merchant's son thought it to be appropriate to announce his arrival in the usual manner by firing a salute; but instead of wasting his powder in merely making a report, he deemed it more prudent, that, while the salute was fired, he might as well aim his musket at a heron which he saw seated quietly near the verge of a spacious tank, and thus accomplish two objects at once. Having shot the bird he went to pick up his game, but in doing so, he saw a washerman occupied in scouring clothes, who spoke to him thus: "What have you done? Have you not a grain of common sense? The heron was my father who had transmigrated into the body of that bird, and he was very useful to me, watching and encouraging me in my operations, and guarding the clothes which are spread out to the sun for bleaching purpose. Now, pray, resuscitate my father and give him back to me, or lay down four hundred rupees, or you do not go away so easily from hence." While this conversation was being held by the two individuals, another man who had approached the spot, and was silently listening to the conversation, and who was blind of one eye, thus accosted the young merchant—"Your father, peace be to his spirit, was a just and liberal man, who traded in all kinds of things, and dealt in eyes. He took a fancy to my eyes and purchased one of them for six hundred rupees, with a promise of paying me that sum on his next visit to this country. Though I am suffering from the loss of one eye, I have not been paid yet for my loss and suffering. I forego the interest on that sum due to me these several years, and as you are his son, I expect that you will discharge that debt willingly, or we must proceed to court. Give me the amount or restore the eye to me." In this altercation between the parties, there was a third person listening to the discourse. She was a woman with a child in her lap, she came forward and saluted the young merchant in a bland soothing manner. "It is my good fortune to meet you in this country, and how happy I am to see you of whom I have heard so favourably from your parent. How well you answer his description, just those eyes, and those arched brows, and that soft outline of lineament; I am his poor wife, and this unhappy boy is his last son by a second marriage. At the time of his going away for a short period, he told me to borrow such sums as would defray our expenses, and that on his return he would refund the money with interest. I trust you will help me to pay off the debts incurred during two years and six months, and, as you are like my own son, that you would support me and take me under your protection, that no disgrace may be cast on the honorable name of your worthy father."

The young merchant became so confounded with these novel and unexpected attacks and unceremonious demands, that he regretted he had not listened to the salutary advice of his father, the consequence of which was, that he was so soon after his arrival in the country, experiencing so much annoyance, and was plunged into so much trouble. It occurred to him, however, in this distress of mind, that in the event of his suffering from any adverse circumstance, his father had advised him to call on Golab Sing, the chief of the country. With this object in view he told the people who were pulling him on each side and almost quartering him, to go with him before the Rajah, to whose decision he would submit, and be guided by his counsel. Before the merchant could arrive at Golab Sing's residence, these dexterous rogues ran and presented themselves before him to offer their respective complaints, crying out, "help *Maharaj !* help *Maharaj !*" Soon after taking their deposition, the merchant also arrived, and was interrogated by the Prince as to the country from whence he had come, and what his name was. On discovering that he was the son of his friend, the old merchant, the Prince was moved with emotions of unfeigned grief at the news of his father's death. The rogues seeing the friendly terms on which the merchant stood with the Prince, lost all courage and would have decamped from the court rather than advance the prosecution. But it was too late to recede; they therefore screwed up their resolution to stand the investigation. The Prince, knowing too well the tricks and stratagems of his subjects, took the merchant aside and advised him what to do in this affair. He said, " When the washerman comes and makes his claims against you, you make this counter charge against him,—'When your father became a heron, my father was a small fish in the river, who swimming and jumping in the shallow water, was journeying home, up the stream, when your father, the heron, pecked at him, and getting him in his bill, swallowed him. Produce my father first, and then I will restore yours to you.' To the second claimant say—'My father, it is true, traded in all sorts of things, and also speculated in eyes, but as there are so many eyes in my possession, and I do not know which is yours, give me the other eye, weighing which in the scales, I could ascertain the exact weight and restore the precise eye to you.' To the third say thus, 'I admit the truth of your allegation, for I have heard my father mention to me frequently that he was married in this country, and had a young son; he told me therefore to bring his wooden sandal, and to give you that to wear and mount the funeral pyre. Do that and I will believe that you are really his second wife.' "

Being thus advised and prepared by the Prince, those persons, while endeavouring by all artful means to substantiate their claims, were defeated and confounded by as cogent counterstatements from the young merchant as those which they tendered. The merchant being dismissed with marks of regard by the Prince, followed his professional occupation in the country without any further molestation, while the wicked rogues were sent into prison to chew the bitter cud of reflection, and to work on the roads under the weight of heavy chains.

THE STORY OF AN INDOLENT MAN.

THERE was a certain man who was excessively indolent; his wife therefore said to him one day, " Since you do not work to support me, and have not brought me a single rupee since the day of our marriage, it is far better that you should consent to my leaving you and working for my own subsistence." On hearing this, the husband consented to go out in quest of some employment; the wife, knowing that he always did so, but sauntered idly about the streets, and came home always with some frivolous excuse about his bad fortune in getting no employment congenial to his taste, prepared some cakes with poison which she tied up in a napkin for him to eat on the journey, thinking that by this contrivance, she would get rid of a useless, idle fellow. The indolent man took the cakes and went out joyously one morning with the intention of enjoying them on the road, and then returning with a well-framed, plausible story to appease her displeasure. He had rambled through a good part of the country, when he began to get weary and feel a keen appetite for the cakes. Seeing a tank before him with a majestic tree in its neighbourhood, he placed the napkin containing the cakes, together with his walking cane, beneath the tree, and descended the flight of steps for the purpose of washing himself. Being so occupied, it happened that in that quarter of the country, a wild ferocious elephant was creating much havoc in cultivated lands, as well as destroying life. The Rajah of the district had notified by beat of drum, that whoever would kill the elephant, would be entitled to a handsome reward, and be provided with a lucrative employment. It so happened that this elephant in passing the tree, took up the napkin, shook out its contents, and devoured the cakes. In a short time he fell dead on the spot. The indolent

man coming up from the tank and finding an elephant lying
dead, cut off a piece of the trunk with the intention of taking
it home as a trophy of his valour. The people of the village
soon gathered themselves round the elephant like vultures
about a carcase. Some took with them the tusks, and some
bore away the tail. With these they presented themselves before the Rajah with the expectation of receiving the promised
reward; but the Rajah asked them where the trunk was, for
he who had the trunk was the person who had slain the animal.
Not being able to furnish a satisfactory answer to this query,
they were discovered to be mere pretenders. The indolent
man, hearing the particulars of the elephant story, presented
himself in due time before the Rajah with the missing trunk.
The Rajah asked if he had slain the elephant. He said
emphatically that he was the author of its destruction. On
being questioned how he had effected the death of the monster,
he answered boastfully that he did it by merely squeezing the
animal, and could, with the greatest ease and facility, dispatch
half a dozen others. The Rajah being highly gratified with
his courage and skill, presented him with a purse of two hundred
rupees, and gave him an employment by which he could earn a
hundred rupees per month. From this circumstance he was
designated the Squeezing Giant.

This Prince had frequent territorial disputes with a
neighbouring Zemindar, in which the parties had several
skirmishes, but in most of them the men of the Prince were
defeated. On the present occasion, however, instigated by
the retainers of the Prince, the Squeezing Giant was advised
to go and exhibit his prowess before the enemy. As he could
not refuse to go, he assented, thinking to himself that when
once mounted on the horse for battle, he would get away from
the country and go far beyond the reach of the Prince. With
this resolution he desired to be furnished with a good charger.
Mounting the animal with all the airs of a general, he desired
the men to fasten him to the horse, that in the heat of battle,

he might not, by any accident, fall and get himself unhorsed. Proceeding in a canter until he got out of sight of the palace, it was his desire to turn the head of his horse in the direction of his country, but the spirited animal, trained to battle, and hearing the beat of drums and the notes of a bugle, began to paw the ground and prance, and much against the disposition of the rider, to shape his course toward that quarter where the men of the Zemindar were assembled in battle array to dispute the rights of the Prince. In this dilemma, and while the horse was bounding forward, he grasped at the branch of a tree with all his might, either to check his progress towards the scene of danger, or by getting up the tree to escape from his unpleasant predicament; but neither object being gained, the heavy branch rested in his grasp and on his shoulder. With this strange weapon he was seen advancing towards the field. The men of the Zemindar having heard before of the Squeezing Giant and his supernatural powers, and seeing too his approach with a tree uprooted as they believed, and thinking that with a single swing of that tree, he might lay thirty or forty men prostrate, broke up the camp in haste and disappeared. The Squeezing Giant thought no more of returning to his country; he came back to the Prince with proud looks and buoyant hopes, telling him that he had no occasion to unsheathe his sword, the mere appearance of his person in the field had driven away the enemies of the Rajah with terror and amazement. The Rajah was well pleased with his valuable service, and as a token of his approbation, he conferred on him titles of distinction, augmented his salary, and continued to entertain him in his post of honor and responsibility.

After the lapse of a year or two, a powerful tiger was reported to have come into the country, and was daily destroying men and cattle, and there was found no one capable of checking his devastations. Several *shicarees*, or sportsmen, belonging to the Rajah, had gone out to destroy him, but they came back baffled in their attempts. The Rajah then thought of his "Squeezing Giant." He called him to the durbar, or court, and informed him that none of his retainers had succeeded in killing the tiger which was doing so much harm to his country. The "Squeezing Giant," with a show of courage, promptly answered that he would willingly go and slay the tiger, as it was but an insignificant work, but at the same time he was getting icy cold with fear, knowing that the elephant and the battle were very fortunate affairs, and merely accidental occurrences. The thought of this enterprize made him lose his appetite for several days, but deeply cunning as he was, he made minute enquiries of the sportsmen where the tiger was to be found, and the place which was his chief haunt. On learning that the tiger generally slept under a tamarind tree after it had fed itself, the "Squeezing Giant" told the sportsmen to furnish him with all sorts of weapons, to lift and fasten him tightly to the tamarind tree, and that at a convenient time he would show the tiger who he was. This being done according to his instructions, and to his own satisfaction, the sportsmen left him with a secret wish that he might fall a prey to the fierce animal, because, since his entertainment in the Rajah's service, their emoluments were meagre, and their reputation had suffered in the estimation of their employer on account of his extraordinary exploits. Soon after the glaring sun had set, the tiger, as was his habit, came near the tamarind tree, and snuffing the air, discovered that there was a human being in that locality. He cast his glowing eyes hither and thither in search of the man, when they fell on the "Squeezing Giant" in the tree. Fixing his gaze intently for a time, he gave a terrific howl, and then sprang towards the branch on which the man was. He began to quake with great fear. His trembling hands had no power to hold the weapons with which he had been furnished. They therefore fell from that lofty branch with a force that caused them to penetrate deep into the body, eyes, and neck of the animal. It soon lay weltering in its own blood. When the man came to find the disabled state of the tiger, he

struggled wildly to get free from the cords which confined him to
the tree. He succeeded in snapping them, when coming down
from the tree, he bawled out lustily for the villagers, and as he
saw them stirring about from their huts, and approaching him,
he commenced with a volubility of abusive language to beat
the back of the expiring animal with a ponderous branch. Having, after such an achievement, marvellous in the eyes of the
village rustics, commanded them authoritatively to bear away
the tiger to the Rajah, he walked slowly behind, musing
on the thought that at some future period he was sure, if he
continued in his present employment, to come into disagreeable
contact with much greater perplexities. The wisest course therefore for him to take, he concluded, would be, to leave the Rajah
with all his honors thick upon him, and his reputation for courage
and strength unmarred. On seeing the Rajah, therefore, he
asked permission, after so many years' service, to visit his
family and country. His sanction having been obtained, he
asked the Rajah for the use of a horse from his large stud. The
horse which he had thus obtained, he mounted after the eastern
quixotic fashion, commencing his journey with exultant reflections as to what stories he would spin out, and what wonderful
things he would do, and how he would make the people stare
their eyes out in the recital of his wonderful deeds, when he
was in his own house and country. Thus beguiling the tediousness of his solitary journey, the bright sun began to decline
with his gorgeous light, and evening's sombre shadows to mantle
the landscape, when he came to a hut on the way. Here he
alighted with an intention to repose and rest himself for the
night. It happened to be the residence of a gang of six brothers,
in which their six wives and sisters were dwelling with their
mother-in-law. The aged woman gladly admitted this traveller.
She provided him with all the requisites for supper, giving him,
however, wet wood that he might be long engaged in kindling a
fire and dressing his dinner, lest he might, after his refreshment,
think of pursuing his journey, by which her sons would lose

13

their opportunity of stripping him of his property. One of the young wives of the robbers, knowing of the treachery and wickedness of her mother-in-law, and knowing too that the robbers not only divested a man of his money, but that it was their invariable practice to murder those they robbed, felt sympathy for the fate of the innocent traveller. She endeavoured secretly to apprise the man of the danger which awaited him, should he remain till the robbers came back from their excursion. The traveller rose up in alarm, collected his baggage, and came out with the intention of starting on his journey; but the old wily hag, meeting him at the threshold, tried to dissuade him from his purpose, telling him that he ought to refresh himself before undertaking a laborious journey, and that she would provide him with more ghee, dall, and sweets, if he were not satisfied with that which she had previously provided him. His terror made the power of her soft eloquence of no effect. He gave her to understand that he felt no desire for food, feeling not quite well in health, and that on that account he would not lose his time unnecessarily.

The old woman finding the she could not prevail on him to remain, went and tied a purse full of mustard seed to the tail of his horse, that traces of the road he travelled through might be discovered by her sons on their return. When the free-booters came home, the mother expressed her deep regret that they had lost a good prize by the departure of a wealthy traveller, but said that it was possible to find him by the mustard seed, which they would find strewed in the path by which he was advancing, "Don't you, however," she said, " go by yourselves, but take one of your sisters. Should you overtake him on the road near some secluded spot, you may despatch him in your usual way by strangling, but in the event of your meeting with him at any populous place or town, mention within the hearing of others, that he had married your sister yesterday, had left her behind, and was running away from her." The robbers not having found the man on the road, followed him up to a town. The traveller turning round and finding that he was pursued, enquired of the inhabitants if there lived any Rajah in the town. Learning that there was such a personage, he urged his horse forward, reached the *rajbaree*, or palace, and sought shelter and protection from the Rajah. To him he disclosed all the events of his last journey, and the danger from which he had escaped, requesting his protection from the wicked design of the robbers who were in pursuit of him and were just in sight. Soon after this disclosure, the robbers also presented themselves before the Rajah, bowing submissively in his presence, and crying out, " Help, *Maharaj !* help *Maharaj !* This man married our sister only yesterday, and instead of taking her along with him, he is running away from her secretly, wishing to leave his wife a burden upon us." The Rajah desired the robbers and the traveller to rest and refresh themselves, and that on the morrow he would hear their petition. When night had approached, the Rajah ordered the robbers a separate dwelling, and the traveller a different apartment with his supposed wife. He instructed one of his own men to remain concealed in one of the rooms next to the traveller's, and to listen to any conversation held between him and the woman during the night. Late at night the woman was heard by the spy to tell the traveller to give up his money, or that she would kill him. He replied, saying, that it would be useless for her to deprive him of life, for by that atrocious act she could not succeed to his property. The affair was known to the Rajah, and the crime of his murder and theft would be visited with condign punishment from the retributive justice of the Prince. A small dagger was seen concealed beneath the folds of her ample garment, and to carry out her determination, she was feeling for the weapon, and insisting on his making over the purse, or bearing the consequence of his refusal. The traveller still persisted in saying, that though she killed him, still the money would never be her property. " But before you kill me," he said, " listen first to a story which I have to relate, and when that will be concluded, od what you please with me." She assented, and the story was begun as follows :—

"There was a merchant who had brought up a parrot, and who, being about to go on a long trading voyage, left strict injunctions with his dependants, that whatever the parrot ordered them to execute, they should obey cheerfully. The parrot accordingly, on the departure of the merchant, commanded a certain parcel of ground which measured twenty biggahs to be properly ploughed and richly manured. The servant announced the execution of his order, and wanted to know what other commands he had for them. The parrot ordered them to cultivate the field with pumpkin creepers. After a month or so, the field was coverd with an abundance of succulent pumpkins of an extraordinary size, and fit for being gathered up. The servants desired to know if they should gather and take them to the market for sale, or dispose them to some speculating farmer. The parrot instructed them to go to the field, and then to irrigate the land with a copious supply of water, so as to immerse the plants and the pumpkins. Having done according to the parrot's bidding, the servants came to the parrot to censure his insane proceedings; telling him that if the produce were taken into market and sold, and not destroyed so ruthlessly, it would have realized for their master more than three hundred rupees. The parrot answered, 'What does that concern you, go now and drain the field, after which when the field becomes dry and is adapted for ploughing, plough and manure it as before, then plant out cuttings of sugar-cane.' After a short time the canes sprung up with a growth of vigorous luxuriance, lofty in height, thick in circumference, and redundant of saccarine matter. The servants came to inform the parrot that the canes had acquired perfect maturity and were fit to be cut; if allowed to stand longer their productive sap would diminish. The parrot recommended them to go and cut down the canes, after which to lay them in a heap and set fire to the stack. The laborers replied with amazement : 'What are you going to do with our

master's property ?' ' What is that to you, go and do as you are
bid,' was the parrot's further injunction. Having done so, the
laborers were told to sweep the place and collect the ashes from
the conflagration into a bungalow. ' When this was accomplished, the time for the merchant's return approached. As
soon as he had come home, the servants recounted all the impru-
dences of the parrot; the merchant being at that time in bad
temper on account of the disorders into which some of his other
affairs were thrown, got fiercely angry with the parrot, and,
without reflection took him out of the cage and dashed him to
the ground.

" After the lapse of a few days, the merchant thought of examining the ashes which had been gathered and stored up in a
golah or godown. Doing so, he discovered to his surprise that
it had, by some secret, mysterious process conducted in the cru-
cible of nature rather than art, acquired medicinal properties
which made it of considerable value; he lamented, therefore,
deeply, his rashness in destroying his faithful bird."

The story was heard by the sister of the robbers in silence,
but as soon as it was concluded, she repeated her former demand
for the traveller's purse, saying that the night had nearly passed
by and the dawn was fast approaching. The traveller told her
that she would not succeed in obtaining the money; but, said he,
" Listen to another short tale, the relation of which I hope may
instil into you some portion of common sense :—

"There lived a father and mother whose family was composed
of several childen. The mother placing a bowl of water before her
little boy, with which he might play and amuse himself, went for
a short while to winnow the corn. Just at that spot she tied a
weasel. A venomous snake seeing the child playing with
water, with no one at that time in the house, made bold to
come out from his secret dwelling in the crevices of the old wall
to slake his thirst from the water of the basin. The poor child
not knowing what it was, put forth his innocent hands to catch
and play with that which he might have taken for a pretty amu-

sing toy. He played for some time, the snake coiling and disentangling himself from his arm, till by some accident the boy, unwittingly hurt the snake, and the ill-tempered reptile stung him, and he lay lifeless, but in all the beauty of innocent childhood. Witnessing the sudden catastrophe, the weasel cut his string with his teeth, and going into the neighbouring fields, came back to the house with a root which was an antidote for snake poison. At this time the mother who had come back from her occupation, and seeing the child in that state, stood petrified with sorrow and anguish, then she fell on the body of her child and wept bitterly. After she had given full vent to her grief, she stood up to go and announce the mournful occurrence to her husband, when seeing the weasel loose from the tie and approaching her, she thought that it was by his absence and remissness that her poor boy was lost, and therefore, in a fit of vexation and rage, she grasped the weasel and threw him on the floor with all her might. As the weasel lay dead, a curious root was discovered in his mouth, which extricating from his clenched teeth, she took in her hand, and thought that it might possess some medicinal virtue which the instinct of the animal had procured. The mother in her agony would leave no means untried, and so she ground the root and administered it to the child. To her great joy the lad began gradually to give indications of returning consciousness. With the child's recovery the faithful weasel's death was a constant source of grief and compunction to the mother."

The spy who had listened to their discourse thus far, and had taken it down on paper, proceeded to the door of the apartment, and violently knocked. It was dawn, and the traveller and the woman were taken out and conducted before the Rajah. The incidents, as transcribed by the spy, being read before the court, the wily woman was sentenced to be transported, after her person had been disfigured with a brand on the forehead, and her flowing hair had been shorn.

The six artful ruffians finding the light of day dawning, decamped from the town, knowing too well that if frustrated in their deep artifices, the further investigation of the case by a court of justice, would but entangle them in their own net of treachery, and bring a heavy judgment against them, disastrous to their lives of infamy.

The traveller was set at liberty to pursue his journey, which he did without meeting with any further accident or disaster. By slow stages he came back to the land of his nativity, but in reaching it, the first blow to his joy and his anticipations, was the news which he heard of his wife having taken another husband, thinking that he had long been numbered with his ancestors.

He accused himself severely as the cause of all the misfortune and disaster which had been brought upon himself by want of energy and occupation. The experience which he had acquired in his travels, made him more sober-minded, led him to appreciate habits of useful industry, and to reflections conducive to right conduct in life, and a proper discharge of social duties. Having a small capital of his own, he resolved to apply a portion of it to purposes of trade, to purchase a small farm, to marry a virtuous wife, and live in occupations of usefulness and acts of charity.

A BADSHAW AND HIS SEVEN DAUGHTERS.

THERE was a *Badshaw* who had seven daughters. He called them before him one morning, and asked, "My children, by whose luck are you supported?" The six eldest answered that they were dependent on their parent for support, but the youngest replied that she was supported by her own fate. The *Badshaw* addressed his youngest daughter thus:

" Whatever individual I meet with on the morrow, I will make you over to him, you ungrateful child!" A wood-cutter was the first man whom the *Badshaw* saw in the morning. He told the woodman that he would marry his daughter to him, because he had resolved upon it in his own mind for the purpose of punishing her. The wood-cutter apologised, and begged that the *Badshaw* would forgive him if he had inadvertently given him offence, since it was only for some such reason, he said, that he was being bantered with. The *Badshaw* told him he was quite serious on the subject. The wood-cutter persisted in saying that he was a poor man who depended for a precarious subsistence on cutting wood, by which he hardly earned enough for his own support, and how, then, could he take a wife and plunge her into trouble and suffering. The youngest daughter, who happened to be present at the conference, told the man not to be discouraged but to consent, as she would do everything for her own maintenance, and would not prove a burden to him.

Thus they were married, and the man took his wife to his hut, and leaving her there, said; " You remain here, and let me go to my work, for it is late. By a whole day's hard labour, I can cut but a basket-full of wood, and obtain for that only one hundred and twelve shells. I must therefore be up and doing, or we must starve." His wife inquired: " What, do you always sell your wood at one uniform price, and never sell under or above that rate? Show me your wood before you go to sell it." Receiving this instruction, he went forth to his daily occupation, bringing in at the close of the day, a basket of chips. The wife, finding the wood to be no other than sandal wood chips, told the simpleton to make a demand of five rupees for them, and if any one declined to purchase for that amount, to bring them back. As taught, so he asked five rupees, but a buyer laughed and inquired if he had lost his wits during the night, and what had come to pass that he made such an exorbitant demand as five rupees, after having received only a hundred and twenty cowries at first. The man would not give in, but stuck to his resolution. The tradesman was obliged to take it on the terms of the woodman, and in paying the five rupees into his hands, cautioned him to take the wood no where else, since he would purchase it every day at his own enhanced price. On receiving the five rupees, the wife went and purchased a large stock of all necessaries, after which, she asked the woodman of the size of the tree he was cutting. He told her that it was a very large dry tree, which after the manner in which he was hewing, would take him two years to finish the cutting. She instructed him to take a rupee and engage the assistance of ten or twelve labourers, who would cut the tree down, divide the branches into small logs, and bring the wood home on two or three carts. This being done, the logs were piled up near their hut, and with that stock in hand, they commenced a successful trade. It then occurred to the wife that it was the practice of some men to bury their wealth at the root of such trees. She told her husband, therefore, to go and dig at the roots. Doing so, he was surprised to find four jars containing money. This enriched the humble dwellers of the hut, who felt no longer the pangs of poverty, or the bitterness of want. With the riches they now possessed, they began to trade on a larger scale than before, and thus, after two or three years of prosperous business, they became people of some consequence. In the locality where the hut stood, a beautiful, stately edifice sprung up, the sole occupiers and owners of which were the woodman and his faithful, intelligent, prudent wife. Arriving at this stage of comfort and independence, they prepared a sumptuous entertainment, to which they invited the men of two or three neighbouring villages. A large number came and partook of the grand repast, and enjoyed all the amusements which were prepared for their diversion. Some of the guests, in conversing with the host and hostess, mentioned casually that the *Badshaw*, who was once so opulent, had come by adverse circumstances

14

to great poverty and want; indeed, such was his indigence that
he was compelled to undertake menial offices. The hostess
heard the narration with surprise and grief, and tears were
forced from her eyes, but though they ran down her cheeks in
copious streams, she studied to conceal her emotion from
her guests.

The woodman's visitors, while retiring from the entertainment,
spoke of their hostess in terms of high laudation, observing that
it was the ability and prudence of the woman, and not the man,
that had raised them from a humble position to one of respect-
ability, affluence, and comfort. To carry out her secret design,
the wife ordered the excavation of a large tank, and for its con-
struction, she desired her men to bring only such as were really
in want, and without anything to eat. Many poor men of the
village were supported by this work, and several came from the
neighbourhood, among whom was the *Badshaw*, but so much
changed in his aspect as scarcely to be recognised by any body.
The sircar who had the supervision of the excavation, saw that
a certain labourer was not at all qualified for the work, for he
could neither dig well, nor bear heavy loads. He felt it to be his
duty to represent this to his mistress. Having done so, she
desired him to bring the man before her. When the poor man
presented himself before her, he could not recognise her as his
daughter, but she was not slow to discover that he was the
Badshaw, her father. She made herself known to him, and informed him by what means their circumstances had improved.
They were soon locked in each other's arms, and over his ample
shoulder where her head rested, she wept at the memory of the
past, comparing it with his present altered condition. She
invited her father and sisters to reside with her, telling the
father to employ his time in conducting her profitable business.
She reminded him that what she had asserted before, was not
untrue, for in reality every man lived according to the destiny
prescribed by an all-wise God.

THE STORY OF A FAKIR AND AN IGNO-RANT MAN.

An ignorant man asked a fakir, " Who are you, why are you seated here, and what are you doing ?"

The fakir replied, " I am a beggar in God's service. I have abandoned the world that I might walk with God, though to do so I may have to endure pain, and suffer privation and sorrow. I am studying human nature, and the two classes of men of whom the world is composed—the one given to the pleasures of life, the other engaged in the service of holiness and God. In man's opinion there are several classes of individuals ; but in God's infallible judgment there exist only two—the good and the bad."

The ignorant man observed, " You say that you are in God's service, and that you know him, and are acquainted with man's nature, then, pray, allow me to put you three questions, which, if you fail to answer, I will esteem you not only a liar but a deceitful, wicked person, deluding others to earn for yourself a dishonest livelihood. If it happen to be as I surmise, I will beat you away from hence, and take all that you possess."

The fakir replied, " By this inconsiderate speech, you disclose the shallowness of your intellect and your want of prudence. Well, I am satisfied with your proposal. Pray, tell me in what matter you desire my opinion ?"

The ignorant man said, " Father ! the first question is this : Show God to me and tell me of what colour He is ? The second is : Satan is formed of fire, and hell is composed of the same element, how then can fire make any impression on Satan ? The third is : Whatever is being done in the world, is executed by God himself, and not man, for man is impotent and can do nothing by his own power. Is it so or not ?"

The fakir began to muse for a while on the subject, then, after a short time, laughed and looked at the ignorant man, and asked if those three were all the questions he had to ask. " Yes, father,"—he replied—" and their answer I have to request."

The fakir, looking here and there, took up a ball of clay, which he aimed at the ignorant man's head with a force that stunned him. The ignorant man began to make a great noise, and to call out for help, crying and telling the village men that the treacherous fakir had hit his forehead so hard a blow with a stone, that he was quite faint.

When the men had heard his complaint, they began to call the fakir all sorts of ill names, and to address him thus: " You say that you are God's beggar, but your action which is so culpable, shows that you have come from the kingdom of Satan. We will take you away to the *Cazi* or Judge, and then we will see who protects such a pretender." So the men beat and dragged him before the *Cazi* of the place. The *Cazi* inquired why they had offered insult and violence to the poor fakir. The people said in their justification,—"*Cazi Saheb*, this fakir is a pretender. He is of so violent a temper that he has struck this poor fellow a severe blow with a stone on his forehead which had nearly killed him, and all this cruel usage he has perpetrated, too, without the least provocation."

Hearing this explanation, the *Cazi* was highly enraged at his audacity, and inquired in a boisterous manner, why the fakir had inflicted pain without any reason for it. The fakir, seeing and hearing things not quite consonant with the character of a *Cazi*, told him that he too appeared to lack discretion. The *Cazi Saheb* became more irritated at what he considered the fakir's insolence. He remarked, " You, father, appear in sheep's clothing, but the wolf is seen through the flimsy coverlet. For what reason, and by what indications, do you recognise me to be a man of perverted judgment ?"

The fakir said, Be not angry, for anger is the symbol of weakness. Pray, consider the truth strictly and reflect on the subject of that man's three questions to me."

The *Cazi* calling the ignorant man, inquired what were the questions which being put to the fakir, gave him offence, and led him to retort so rudely. Hearing the three questions, the the *Cazi* turning towards the fakir, asked: "*Fakir Saheb*, was it proper for you to strike the man instead of answering him?" .

The fakir laughing said, "I have by that deed answered his three questions already. His first question was—show God to me and tell me of what colour he is? My answer is,—show me your pain and tell me of its colour, and I will show you God and tell you of what colour He is. His second question was, Satan is formed of fire, and hell is composed of the same element, how then can fire make any impression on Satan? My answer is, man is admitted to have clay for his origin. This man asserts that fire makes no impression on fire; if so, a ball of clay cannot hurt a body of clay. I did not use any stick or sword to strike him, but a lump of clay. According to his argument, therefore, I am justified, for I could not have hurt him. His third question was, whatever is being done in the world, is executed by God himself and not man, for man is impotent and can do nothing by his own power. My answer is, if nothing is done by man, then I have not struck him, but God, according to his showing, and I am therefore guiltless of his accusation."

AN OLD MAN AND WOMAN.

A DECREPID old man and his wife who were residing in a dense jungle, received a supply of their wants from God, for he mysteriously furnished them daily with a cake of bread. This gift from his bounty they divided between themselves ; one-half the husband enjoyed, and the wife partook of the other, satisfying their thirst from the water of a pellucid brook which stood in their neighbourhood. One day as the couple were seated conversing in their little hut, the old man heard the voice of a young boy, who called out, "Father, may I come in." The old man hearing this familiar address, was not only surprised but also annoyed, thinking that they were provided with just that quantity of bread which sufficed for their own wants, and what then could be done for their unexpected intruder, who had come to diminish their small allowance by claiming a share. He took no notice of the call, but the heart of the old woman was touched with sympathy. "Old man," she said, "we get the cake without our own labour and seeking. What we obtain so freely and generously, let us not grudge to share with the little boy. He might be a comfort to us in our isolation from society, and prove to be greatly useful in the hour of our highest need. Pray, invite him in ; my half share of cake I will joyfully divide with the lad, for in this forest he must starve, and die without our assistance." The boy was invited to go in, and the inquiry was instituted how he had come into such a desolate place. He said,—"I was led by some unknown person up to the gate, when he left me, and vanished from my sight. I do not know who he is. I rather think God sent me here." Thus the boy was fed every day with a quarter of the cake and some fruits from the woods, until he grew up to years of discretion, and became thoughtful and reflective.

One day, the boy told his foster parents that he could not remain any longer idle and dependent on them, nor take a share of the cake which was their portion, and which was barely sufficient for their own sustenance. Now that he was strong and big, he should be permitted to go to God himself, and ask Him to grant him his portion of a cake such as they were allowed. "Do not prevent me," said he, "from seeking out God and presenting my request personally." "Why will you leave us," they said, "and expose yourself to danger and privation. Why leave us to endure the agitation of mind which a constant apprehension that you may be in want and suffering would create, and why, alas! are you not satisfied with the little we receive from God, when we get it so easily? However small the supply, he has supported us so long, and with such regularity, that we have never been under any apprehension that He will fail us. Be content and give up all thoughts of your perilous journey." Their persuasive eloquence was lost upon him, for he was determined to seek God, and make his wants known to him personally. The old couple, at his departure, gave him their benediction that he might be guarded from harm, meet with a prosperous journey and success in his undertaking.

For three whole days he was trudging through the woods. On the fourth day when he had traversed the entire length of the forest, on its skirts he saw a tree withered down to the very root and fit only for fuel. The tree asked the youth where he was going to. The youth replied that he was going to God to ask Him to give him his portion of cake. The tree hereupon said, "If you are going to God, pray take this petition from me. Tell him, if you please, that I bear neither blossom nor fruit, and I am stripped of my garment of leaves. I am become useless and hateful to men, beasts, and birds. I afford no refreshment to any being, nor does the most despicable reptile seek shelter, as I have none to offer." Promising to make the complaint of the tree known to God when the youth met Him, he continued his journey through the tangled creepers and bushy herbage. He had not proceeded far when he beheld a tiger lying on his path in the helpless condition of a cripple. The tiger asked whither he was going. The youth answered that he was going to meet God and to ask Him to send his share of cake for support. " Go, my son," rejoined the tiger, "and lay my distress before Him, and bring me the relief I need, when you return again. I have lain here these twelve years, unable to stir or walk about, and rendered helpless from the loss of the use of my legs. There is no other path but this near me; pass this way." The youth hesitated, and evinced some symptoms of fear at his friendly request, but the tiger, to allay his needless alarm, added, " When I call you my godson, I can do you no harm. Pass near me without any apprehension, but do not fail to remember my miserable situation, and speak on my behalf." The youth consenting to remember his case, proceeded in his search after God. On quitting the forest, he beheld lawns carpeted with the verdure of a vivid green, on which calves and lambs sported with the buoyancy and hilarity of young life, while ewes and cows lay ruminating with eyes half closed, perfectly indifferent to the sport carried on by some crows which hopped and pecked about their backs and ears. He was delighted to see men moving here and there over the ample fields, some cultivating the land with high anticipations of a future golden harvest, some hopeful in sowing the seed, and some active and joyous in reaping the products of a their labour. He was glad to have arrived in the vicinity of habitable place. In passing near the house of the chief man of the village, he was asked, where he was going to, and he replied, as before that he was going to meet God and to ask Him to help him. " If you are going to Him," said the rich man, " pray, take my petition with you. I have erected a temple for His worship, but the dome tumbles down every night regularly, and every day I am compelled to build it up again." Consenting to be the bearer of the rich man's complaint, he departed from the habitations of men, and entered another forest of primeval grandeur, but still gloomier than the one he had traversed before. After a few strides into the woods, he came suddenly before an object which was revolting to his feelings. He saw a man covered with leprosy, with eruptions breaking out in all parts of his body, and bleeding in different places. The heart of the youth was moved with feelings of sympathy and compassion. He asked the man why he was lying in such an uncongenial place. The sick man replied, " Where else can I go ? Wherever I show myself, I am loathed for my sickness, and people pass me at a distance to avoid contact and contamination. Whose help can I therefore calculate upon ?" The youth collected a large heap of leaves and wild flowers, and desiring the man to seat himself upon it, hurried away in the direction of the nearest village. From thence he brought a pot, some water, and a burning coal, after which he set the water boiling, and when it had acquired the temperature he desired, he tore out a fragment of his garment, and commenced to sponge the ulcers. Under this operation, the sores began to heal and a gold-like complexion to appear. The sick man then asked the youth whither he was bound. The youth replied that he was going to God to ask Him for his portion of cake. The person who had assumed the form of a leper, told him that his prayer was heard, and his request granted. " Who are you to say so ? I am going to see God and ask Him that favour myself." " I am His messenger sent to meet you, and to try you." " I cannot believe unless you reveal yourself." Upon this he disclosed a refulgent form, which satisfied the desire of the youth and confirmed his belief. Being advised to return to his foster parents, the youth humbly laid before him the perplexity of the rich man, the infirmity of the tiger, and the barrenness of the tree. With regard to the chief man of the village, he was informed—" Tell the chief that he has a grown up daughter, who, after the amusements of the day, retiring to her dormitory at night, heaves a long deep sigh of sorrow and anguish, at which

15

time the dome falls. Desire him to marry his daughter to a worthy man, and the accident will cease the day her sigh ceases. The tiger is suffering from the lodgement of some thorns of the cactus in his paws. Have the thorns extracted, and the animal will recover the use of his limbs. The tree is a wicked sinner who is standing over a mass of wealth, which he cannot use himself, nor will he permit others to appropriate it to legitimate objects and useful purposes, so that by its wide circulation, thousands of indigent people might be benefited. As he has grasped the whole under the embrace of his avaricious roots, his own life has become barren, his leaves withered, his branches unfruitful,—a despicable object in himself, and a useless thing in the company of his numerous companions of the forest. Desire him to remove himself to a short distance from the spot, and to allow some one to take away that money, and the tree will then thrive with a greater luxuriance, and flourish with a higher degree of fecundity." Having obtained these instructions and received an answer to his petition, he returned homeward with sentiments of gratitude welling up in his heart towards the divine bestower of all good. He met the wealthy man on his return to the village. After being entertained by the chief, he enquired what was said about his peculiar case. The youth told him, the answer received was, that he had a daughter who had arrived at years of womanhood, and who by her nocturnal sighs, caused the fall of the dome. " Give her in marriage to a worthy man, and as her sighs cease, so will the falling down of the pinnacle be stayed." The rich man observed to the youth, that he knew very few persons of that character, and none among them worthier than he, for he who sought God diligently, must ever after walk in the path of life with integrity of heart, simplicity of manners, and honesty of purpose. The rich man marrying his daughter to him, gave his son-in-law wealth, elephants, horses, and a body-guard. The period of six months was spent agreeably and happily under his roof; after which the youth asked leave to go to his foster parents, and his wife not willing to remain even a few months behind, joined him in his journey. While his camp was directed to take the main road, he continued his walk through the forest. The disabled tiger was seen at the same spot, who with eagerness desired to be informed what the result was of his visit. The youth desired him to hold out his paws, and in examining them, he found some thorns of the cactus festering in them, which he extracted carefully. The tiger being relieved from the pain, stood erect, and, with an elastic spring, fell on a calf and bore away the prize into the nearest thicket to enjoy a feast. Continuing his journey, he approached the tree, and communicated what he had heard was the reason of its decadence. The tree proposed that, as none was worthier to receive the wealth, while he moved away from the spot, the youth should order his men to remove the money. When the tree had given up its hold of the mass of silver which lay below, by withdrawing its fibrous entanglements, it put forth a vigorous growth of foliage. The youth now sent for his guards who could be seen through a vista in the forest, encamped on the neighbouring plain. They dug up a large quantity of money, and with his wealth and attendants, he went to meet the old couple; they were bewildered at all they saw and heard. The youth addressed his foster parents thus: "It is no longer necessary for us to inhabit this wilderness; let us go and build a house in the next village." A fine mansion being rapidly erected, which money only could achieve, they lived in it, surrounded with comfort, and enjoying every happiness this world could bestow. The old man and woman often reflected in their quiet musings, that to befriend one in utter destitution, and to be a father to an orphan, was an act with which God was well pleased, and testified His pleasure by the communication of His blessings.

[This tale appears to me to have been derived from the monks, or priests, who had in their early intercourse with the natives, or the first Christian converts, communicated it to them,—they in their turn to others. I am of this opinion, not only from the structure of the story, but from the use and adoption of the term god-son.]

THE STORY OF A BRAHMIN AND BRAHMINEE.

A RAJAH who had established a large bazar, ordered his men, saying—" Whatever may remain unsold in the market until the evening, purchase the whole up from the venders on my account, that the poor may not suffer from loss and disappointment."

There was a Brahmin and Brahminee living in the town, who were in great destitution, so much so, that if by any means they had obtained sufficient food one day, they went starving the two following days. The Brahminee, who was skilful in devices when pushed to extremity, desired her husband to procure her some branches of the broad leafed plantain, and a new pot. Taking the leaves, she tied them into small bundles, these she placed in the new pot, then she covered the pot with a leaf, and fastened the lid by a string. After this operation, she instructed the Brahmin to take it to the Rajah's bazar, taking care never to uncover the lid, but to sell it as it was. Should any purchasers inquire what article it contained, he was to tell them that he had collected his misfortunes and taken them for sale. Hearing this, some laughed, and others wondered at his singular conduct, telling him that he must be an idiot to believe that he could find any customers in the market to purchase such a ware; that they would rather flee from its very presence; and that every one had his own share of misfortune from which they would, if they could, extricate themselves, rather than bear the burden of another man's ill-luck; for every man's burden was more than sufficient for his own back.

The Brahmin could make no reply to these just assertions. He remained silent, but when any new customer approached him and his pot to learn what it contained, he told them that he had come to dispose of his misfortune. In this manner the day declined, and his singular article remained unsold, and he was almost the only man sitting in the bazar, when the sircar of the bazar, agreeably to the Rajah's orders, came to see if there was any tradesman in the place who had not disposed of his goods. Finding the Brahmin seated quietly with his pot, he enquired what that was which he had brought for sale, how much he had sold, and what quantity remained unsold. The Brahmin answered that he had sold nothing, and had brought that for sale, of which he had more than enough at home, and would gladly part with all. "What is that?" asked the bazar sircar. "Misfortune," was the Brahmin's rejoinder. Such a novelty for sale, puzzled the sircar not a little. He felt it to be his duty to inform the Rajah of this unusual incident, as without it he deemed he was not at liberty to purchase misfortune for the Rajah, and to hoard it up with his other stores. He told the Rajah that a poor Brahmin had taken a pot to the bazar which he said contained a stock of misfortune; but not effecting a sale, he was still in the bazar with it. What the sircar should do in this particular case, was what he was desirous of learning. The Rajah told him, "Never mind, take it, for I have passed the order that whatever is brought to my bazar for sale, if not sold, I would be the purchaser. I cannot, therefore, violate this order without incurring censure for prevarication." The sircar went back to the Brahmin, and asked him what he would take for his ware. He demanded one thousand rupees. The sircar was surprised to hear so exorbitant and preposterous a demand. "What is this that you ask!" remarked the sircar, adding, "Do you think you could readily find a customer to purchase your poverty, or gladly take distress upon their own shoulders." The Brahmin, not at all disconcerted, replied: "If I sell at all, it must be for that sum, and not a cowree less, otherwise the object for which I have brought it for disposal, will be defeated. If I sell, I intend thereby to divest myself of a weight too insupportable for me to sustain. By selling for less, I would consent to take back a portion of my misfortune to my house and family, which I do not purpose to do." The sircar, finding that he could not bring the Brahmin to his terms, had need to go to the Rajah again, and communicate his difficulties and his failure in making reasonable arrangements with the Brahmin. The Rajah desired his sircar to pay the amount asked by the Brahmin for his ware, and to deposit it among his other articles. One night, when the sky was clear and serene, and the stars shone brightly from the vault of heaven, bathing the whole country in a soft flood of bewitching radiance, the Rajah finding all his efforts to court sleep ineffectual, got up and seated himself in one of the balconies of the palace, to contemplate the beauty of so fine a night. He then beheld the figure of a stately female, majestic in motion, lovely in aspect, attired in a flowing garb, proceeding from the palace in a direction away from it. Her countenance was illumined with the lustre of benevolence and joy. The Rajah called and asked her who she was, and whither she was going? "My name," she said, "is *Luckee*—Fortune. I am departing from your palace because you have admitted and are sheltering Misfortune. Our characters are antagonistic to each other. Beneath the same roof we can never dwell together." After some days the Rajah met *Dhormo*—Piety, going out of the palace after the same manner as *Luckee* did. He enquired where she was going? Piety answered, "I am going away from your palace because you have sheltered Misfortune." The Rajah was very sad at these occurrences. He addressed the form which personified Piety—" Pray, tell me—he said—what evil I have been guilty of, that you are departing from my house after a period of so long a residence? I am conscious of having done nothing to upbraid myself with, on the contrary by keeping my word and fulfilling my promise, I have done that which is laudable and esteemed pious." After his explanation, Piety, finding that she had no just reason to abandon the Rajah's house, went back and remained in her hallowed retirement. As Fortune generally resides in places where **Piety** puts up, *Luckee* returned to the palace and remained in the society of Piety, being as they were inseparable companions. Seeing *Luckee* back again, the Rajah asked the reason of her returning. She replied that she was one of *Dhormo's* connections, and therefore in whatever place she took up her abode, *Luckee* must also reside. Thus the Rajah in no way came to suffer on account of his just, truthful, and benevolent conduct, but on the contrary, prospered more and more by the benign influence of his heavenly guests.

RAJAH NUL.

A PIOUS Rajah lived in the southern provinces of India, who governed his country with equity, and who dispensed charity with a liberal hand, in order that his benevolence might ameliorate the sufferings of the poor and the destitute. He had a daughter who was celebrated for her personal charms, praised for her good conduct, and who was married to a Rajah of a neighbouring country. Rajah Nul, while at his *durbar*, saw a strange looking person one day, who was having an altercation with the guards in his attempt to obtain an interview with somebody of the court. He commanded his men who were near his person, to bring the man up to him. On his coming before the *guddy*, he was asked what was the motive of his visit, and what complaint he had to offer? The stranger replied, that he was weary with wandering from country to country for the purpose of selling his misfortune, but he could meet with no purchaser any where, and as a last resource, having heard of the Rajah's generous disposition and pious habits, he was encouraged to come to him. Being questioned for what sum he would sell his misfortune, the man replied that he wanted three lacs of rupees.

The Rajah ordered his Dewan to weigh out that sum and give it to the man. The man receiving the money with many *salaams*, quitted the *durbar*, repeating a long string of eulogistic phrases. Rajah Nul, on waking up next morning, received intelligence from a servant, that all his elephants, camels, horses, and cattle, had died during the night. It was reported to him a short time after, that his Khazanchi on opening the treasures, found to his alarm and grief, that all the wealth of the Rajah was turned into coal and ashes. The Rajah reflected for a while; then, addressing the Ranee, " I have little reason," said he, " to complain against these calamities which have come upon me. To help another man in trouble, I willingly purchased his misfortune. But all things are at the disposal of Him who rules the universe. We have long enjoyed prosperity, and therefore ought not to repine if the wheel of fortune has turned against us. We have lost all that we possessed in this place, and it has become painful to me to remain here any longer to see the wreck of our property, and needlessly sigh over our losses ; let us depart hence. and seek our livelihood in other countries." The Rajah and Ranee got out one night under secresy and cover of darkness, and commenced their journey in the garb of mendicants. The first place they arrived at in their aimless journey, was the residence of their daughter who had married a Rajah. Some men, more shrewd than others, recognizing Rajah Nul, ran and announced to the Ranee, that her parents were coming to her on a visit, and that they were already in the avenue of the road leading to the palace. The daughter went out to the balcony to see if the announcement was true. She was surprised to discover two travellers, dressed in very humble clothing, advancing towards the palace. Being told that they had fallen from their former affluence, and were now reduced to trouble and want, she went rapidly into her apartments, where she placed a heap of gold-mohurs on a large rich salver, and covering them up with some confections, sent them as a present to the travellers. Rajah

Nul, on receiving the gift from his daughter, uncovered it, and found nothing but a mass of coals. He buried the contents of the salver under the nearest tree, and then dismissing the man with thanks, remarked to the Ranee, that as their fate had undergone a change, they would meet with a succession of misfortunes, and would find all things prove adverse to their wishes. " Do what we may," said the Rajah, " if God's blessing is not upon us, all that we touch will dissolve, and all we attempt to taste will slip from our lips, or turn into gall. In our altered circumstances, our reception might not be all that we could desire from our daughter ; let us, therefore, not obtrude our society on her." They got away from the palace, therefore, and took the road to the fields. By a rivulet that glided noiselessly under weedy aquatic plants, some men sat angling They had caught a few fishes, and as the travellers were not only weary of their long tedious trudge, but hungry, the Rajah made himself bold to ask for a couple to roast, in order to appease the cravings of their empty stomach. But they declined to be liberal with that which was inadequate for the wants of their own families. " I have failed in my attempt to move their compassion," said the Rajah ; " will you try and ask them now ; it may be that they may be more propitious to your solicitation." The Ranee, screwing up her courage, asked the favour. They were not so ungallant as to refuse her, but their assent was given conditionally, that is, that they would give her the next two that they caught. On receiving the two they took them to a short distance, and while the Ranee was lighting a fire, the Rajah said that he was going for a short stroll into the fields, and would come back when the repast got ready. As soon as the Ranee had finished her culinary operation, and had left the fishes on a plantain leaf to cool, they vanished from the leafy plate in an unaccountable manner. She was at a loss what to tell the Rajah when he came back for dinner. On returning from his short walk, he requested that their breakfast table should be spread. The Ranee begged that he would not be

16

displeased, as, feeling unusually hungry, she could not refrain
from eating both the fishes. The Rajah knew too well that she
could never have done that, but that some accident must have
occurred, and her story was but an excuse. He said nothing,
but after resting for a short time, they rose up to pursue their
journey. After a walk of a few miles, they met with some
fowlers who were entrapping partridges, and who had succeeded
in bagging several. The Rajah again asked for some partridges, but he met with the same disappointment as before.
The Ranee however succeeded in obtaining a brace. When
they were being roasted on a slow fire, the Ranee proposed
that she should go and take a turn in the fields until the time
the game was dressed. The Rajah took them up from the
fire when they were sufficiently roasted, and placed them on
some leaves to cool. They had not rested on the leaves for two
seconds, when they vanished away as the fish did before. Now
the Rajah understood what had happened to the fish. He
mused on the variableness of human affairs, and moralised on
the vicissitudes of life. Misfortunes, he thought, never approach singly, but ever bring a prolific progeny of ills ; they
descend not by drops, but pour down as copiously as the rattling
showers on a summer day. They were destined now to meet
with disappointment from every quarter, even from what in
happier days would have tended to usher in success, where success
was little expected, or calculated upon or desired. The Ranee
coming back from her walk, sat in silent expectation of dinner,
but the husband resorted to the same excuse, and the Ranee
remained mute on the subject, being confirmed in her surmise,
that the game had taken wing and disappeared, as the fish had
done, all owing to their fortune being reversed.

Traversing through the grass plain, the Rajah visited one of
his best friends, whose mental and social merits he was eloquent
in praising. The friend received them with sincere cordiality,
lamented over the recital of their misfortune, and made them
a generous offer of his house. When the Rajah and Ranee had

retired for the night into one of the spacious rooms, and while the former was lying wakeful a good portion of the night, how great was his admiration in beholding an artificial peacock, decorated with real or mock gems, that glistened with the reflection of the light in the apartment with a meteoric refulgence. It stood on a pedestal, and had a costly garland suspended round its neck. The peacock began, after a while, to move and rustle its gorgeous plumage, and then to swallow the garland. This novel vision quite bewildered the senses of the Rajah. He courted sleep, but the coy visitor fled from his longing lids. As the morning began to dawn, he related to the Ranee the strange things that had transpired during the night. The necklace was missing from the neck of the peacock in the morning, and none but they were responsible. "If I mention this curious occurrence to my friend, he will scarcely believe that which is so preposterous; we had therefore better get away, and let time clear up the mystery." They therefore stole away quietly like people who had perpetrated a crime.

They strolled about for some time till they saw a shop, where a man prepared and sold parched rice, peas, and corn. The seller of these light refreshments called out to them, and asked if they were seeking employment, or for what purpose were they loitering about the place. The Rajah was glad to get an engagement, and he therefore accepted the offer of the pea-man gladly, residing with him, and holding his situation for some months. The reflections of the Rajah now became more cheerful and hopeful. "I think, Ranee," said the Rajah one day," that now that we have descended to the last step of the declining ladder, our prospect seems to be improving. The first indication that the cloud over our head is dispersing is, that unsought I have obtained an employment; the next token is, that we have succeeded in getting our meals, and they have not taken their flight on our approach. Let us now pay a visit to our friend, and watch the signs of our present destiny by what may happen to us there." As they were leaving his house,

they thanked the pea-seller for his kindness with a promise
that if their circumstances should ever improve, they would
express their gratitude in a more substantial manner than by
mere words. Visiting his friend, the Rajah was gratified to
find his reception as cordial as before, and as if nothing had
transpired from the time of their first visit. His friend was
desirous of learning the reason of their abrupt departure, but
refrained from pressing them for an explanation just then,
saying that it would be ample time on the morrow for them to
satisfy his curiosity, after they had refreshed themselves, and rested for the night. Overcome with the fatigues of the journey, the
Rajah had a profound sleep of several hours, but when towards
morning he had unclosed his eyes, the first object on which
they rested, was the peacock, which was now seen to disgorge
the necklace, inch by inch. Before it had put out the entire
necklace, the Rajah went and awoke his friend to witness the
extraordinary feat of his peacock. The Rajah now explained
to his friend, that the disappearance of the necklace from the
room in which they slept, and for which he could assign no
rational and satisfactory solution, was his only reason for departing without inviting observation, leaving the affair in the custody
of time for its clearance and solution. His friend gently chided
him for his weakness and want of confidence in his friendship.

Several days were spent very pleasantly and profitably in
converse with his friend, after which, the Rajah, with some
difficulty, obtained the consent of his friend for their departure.
Passing the grass fields in which the partridges had been
roasted, they were astonished to see the vanished game lying
on the leaves just as they had been placed. The famished
travellers did not hesitate for a moment to appease their inward
craving, but enjoyed the refreshment with a high zest. Further on, as they reached the place near the rivulet where the
fishes were broiled, they were found untouched on the plantain
leaf. Partaking of such fare on the road, they came to the tree
near which the goldmohurs, which the Rajah's daughter had

sent, were buried. They dug the place, and found the gold coins glittering on the salver. Placing the whole in their knapsacks, they went and furnished themselves with dresses which suited their rank and station. Being equiped from head to feet with becoming apparel, they visited the Rajah who was married to their daughter. Things having taken a propitious turn, their reception was warm, affectionate, and dutiful. Rajah Nul now no longer doubted that he would find affairs prosperous in his domain. After their visit to their daughter, where a fortnight was spent very pleasantly, they left her for their own kingdom. Arriving at their palace late one evening, the servants who had lingered about the place, recognised the Rajah and Ranee, and manifested great joy on their return. It was discovered in the morning that the Rajah's wealth and the valuables contained in the *Khazána-Khana* had undergone another transmutation, by which their property had acquired its original quality and value. The Rajah's latter condition became in a few years more prosperous than it had ever been at any previous time. The promise he had made to the pea-seller, was fulfilled in the grant of a pension to him for life. The Rajah lived a wiser and a better man for the trials through which he had passed, and the experience he had gained. His fame for benevolence, unselfishness, and many other virtuous qualities, obtained for him a world-wide reputation, and won him the regard and respect of all his subjects.

THE STORY OF A PRINCE AND THE SON OF A VIZIER.

A BADSHA had a son, who, being his only child, was loved by the father with strong affection. This feeling so obscured his judgment, that he became blind to his defects, and indulged the son in his follies and extravagances. It was the will of Providence that his Vizier had also an only child, a son. These youths, the Prince and the Vizier's son, daily attended the same place of instruction, and by this means their friendship became so closely cemented, that they did nothing without doing it together—walking, eating, sitting, or sleeping. It is most frequently the case that the son of a wealthy parent, having nothing to aspire after, becomes perfectly indifferent to studies that exalt the mind and rectify the conduct; while the son of a man of moderate fortune, or no fortune, under the apprehension of want, and with an ambition to ascend up to distinction and independence, puts forth an effort which seldom fails to procure him that for which he aspires and labours. While the young Prince gave indications of improvement in polished manners, and in the refinements of the Court, and had inherent good qualities of the heart, he was silly, and not so wise and prudent as it might have been expected considering his fair opportunities. His friend, on the other hand, neglected no opportunity of adding to his stock of general knowledge and experience, and thus, though young, manifested on all occasions a sound mind, a correct judgment, and a becoming demeanour.

In one of their private walks and familiar conversations, the Prince spoke to his companion in the following manner: "O Vizier's son! I wish you to make me a promise." The Vizier's son asked, "Tell me if you please what it is, for you can com-

mand my service and obedience at all times." The Prince said
that in the event of his being the first to get married, he would
send the princess to the abode of the Vizier's son on a visit; but
should the latter marry first, he must not fail to send his wife to
the Prince's residence soon after the celebration of his wedding.
Hearing this preposterous proposal, the son of the Vizier thought
in his own mind that the Prince was not only obtuse, but thoroughly void of understanding, and was without a grain of reflection. It was never the custom that the Vizier's son ever married before the son of the *Badsha*. The Prince becoming angry,
said to his friend, " Hear, O son of the Vizier why have you not
made me a reply yet. If you will not make me the promise
on oath, then our friendship must cease, and I will annoy you
in every way." The Vizier's son laughing replied, " Take
my advice and banish this desire from your heart, because whatever oath or promise a man makes, it becomes imperative in
him to fulfil." The Prince getting irritated said to his friend,
" Why do you multiply words unnecessarily, and invent excuses. Will you, or will you not make me the promise?"
His friend finding him persistent on the subject, addressed
him in a tone of displeasure, " Sir, give me time to consider
the subject, and I will make you the desired reply on the morrow." In the mean time, however, they passed the night in
their usual congenial conversation, and with friendly attentions
towards each other. Both the friends in the morning were
proceeding to the place of instruction. The Prince reminded
his friend on the way about his promise. " Pray, what
is your determination?" The Vizier's son, to divert him
from his object, said, " Come let us be going to school." Arriving at the institution, the Prince said, " We have come to
school, now fulfil your promise." The Vizier's son observed,
" Sir, Prince, you will deeply regret this circumstance." After
this he meditated on the just remarks of the sages who have said,
'women cannot be shaken from their resolution, children are
headstrong, hogs are not diverted from their course, and kings

are not thwarted in their wishes.' Having thought thus, he took pen, ink, and paper, and placing them before the Prince, desired him to write the agreement, he doing the same; then they exchanged papers. After this transaction, both the young men continued for months and years in friendly intercourse, nothing transpiring to mar their intimacy. It so happened afterwards that a neighbouring *Badsha* began negociations with the father of the Prince, the object of which was to solicit his son in marraige with his daughter. The *Badsha* one day invited his son into his presence and informed him about the letter. The Prince was alarmed to hear of it, and insisted that his father should get his Vizier's son married first, and then, he said, he would follow his example. The *Badsha* remonstrated against the folly and imprudence of the Prince, saying that such a thing was never heard of;-it was so unusual and reflected disrespect, should a Vizier's son marry before the son of the *Badsha*. " In that case," added the Prince, " I am in no haste to marry." The *Badsha* permitted his son the period of two months to consider the proposal of the king his friend, and then to inform him of his resolution, that he might answer the letter. After this conversation with his father, the Prince met his friend. The Vizier's son seeing the Prince in a melancholy mood, questioned him as to its cause, and the reason why he was summoned by the *Badsha*. The Prince to conceal what had transpired, observed that he had heard that the Vizier's son was about to marry. His friend guessed what had actually happened, and therefore remarked sarcastically, " Friend, I hope you have not forgotten your agreement." The Prince made no reply, but hung down his head. The *shazadas*, or noblemen of the court and country, after repeated explanations and wise counsels as to the propriety and policy of accepting the overtures of the neighbouring *Badsha*, prevailed upon the Prince to consent to the marriage, but the very thought marred his peace, and drove sleep from his eyes for many nights. After a *chundroz*, or few days, the wedding was celebrated with great pomp, festivity, and merriment. The Prince on returning with his bride to the palace, and on alighting from his conveyance, ordered his bearers to take the palkee and bride to the Vizier's son. The servants were amazed at this singular order, but as they could not disobey their master's injunction, they carried the conveyance to the Vizier's house in silent wonderment. The Princess was thinking within the curtained enclosure, of the reason for this strange conduct on the part of the Prince. That there was some stringent reason for such a procedure she could not doubt, but what that was she could by no means discover. On arriving at the door of the house of the friend of the Prince, the palkee was set down. The Vizier's son hearing that the Princess had arrived, came forth from his apartment with alacrity, to salute and welcome her. Coming before the conveyance, he folding his hands as a token of respect, solicited the Princess to favour him with her visit. She said with dignified displeasure, " Who are you that you should request me to come into your house. Should you again repeat the request, I will put an end to your speech, and fill your skin with bran; or should you touch my palkee, I will have nails driven into your fingers." Hearing this threatening language, the Vizier's son lost courage and was confounded. He began to reflect how he should proceed with this affair, when thinking of the agreement, he placed it in the hands of her retainers, and they conveyed it to the Princess. The Princess read the contents of the paper, laughed, and thought within herself that the duration of her trial was only for one night, it was a small matter to manage. She summoned her attendants and several of them appeared before the palkee to wait on her instructions. She desired them to go to the Vizier's son, and to request him to take off all the old plaster from the walls of his house, and to replaster them over again as soon as practicable. Hearing of this command of the Princess, the Vizier's son was overjoyed. He quickly sent for a large number of masons, and got the work finished as soon as possible, and then sent a message to

17

the Princess that it was executed. She sent her men to
inquire what hour of the night it was. They returned
saying that it was nine o'clock. Then the Princess again desired
her men to tell the Vizier's son to put a new roof to the
house, to wash the floors clean, and get them to dry soon, or that
she would have his head blown away by a cannon. The Vizier's son, quite glad, sent for numerous workmen, and ordered
the work to be completed with the utmost expedition. When
this order was accomplished, he sent word to the Princess. She
commanded her attendants to go again and enquire of the
Vizier's son what hour of the night it was. He informed her
that it was midnight. She then desired that he would have all
his chandeliers and all the lamps of the house, together with
the chair on which she was to sit, to be done up again with
fresh gilt and polish. This was also done. She then desired to know what time it was. He said it was three o'clock.
The Princess once more ordered that the bed-steads should be
newly done up, the mattrasses, pillows and cushions, washed
and dried, and the furniture of the dormitory newly fitted up
expeditiously, otherwise she would have his face blackened, seat
him on an ass, and exhibit him in the morning, in a humiliating procession through the city. The Vizier's son thinking
that the affair was now coming to a favourable termination,
became happy, and very cheerfully ordered the things to be
done up as instructed. On the completion of the work, he
went to announce it. The Princess inquiring what o'clock it
was, heard the gun fire and announce the dawn of day. Just
then she commanded her attendants to lift up the palkee and to
proceed to the palace. The Vizier's son looking surprized,
asked her what she meant by it. The Princess said that the
night, which was his, according to the Prince's agreement, had
expired, and the day which had dawned, was the Prince's, therefore he must not stop her conveyance, but allow her to depart.
The Princess, going to the palace and not having slept for
some nights, soon fell into a sound slumber. The Prince hear-

ing that she had come back, and seeing her fast asleep, thought that she had diverted herself with many amusements, and was therefore now weary and fast asleep. From inconsideration and want of reflection and asking no questions, nor ascertaining the facts from the Princess, or her attendants, he put her into a chest in which there were holes in the lid, locked it up, and sent it floating on the stream. In the mean time the fame of the Princess for her virtuous conduct, and skilful device, spread far and wide during the day, and it was also reported everywhere that she had ably defeated the Vizier's son, and taken herself back a virtuous, spotless person to the palace, while the Prince was reproached for his imprudence and want of judgment. The Prince hearing of his wife's laudable acts and her good principles, regretted very much for his rashness; tearing his dress in his grief, he put on humbler garments, and thus equipped, he left the palace privately, following the course of the meandering river, set out in search of his worthy wife.

The chest floated down with the rapid current, and driven by the wind, went on till its progress was impeded by a *ghat* at which a Prince of another country was beguiling his time in the amusements of angling and playing upon his *seetar*. He was surprised to see the chest, which he ordered his men to convey to his residence. Half a dozen of his servants bore it tottering under its weight, for the chest itself was ponderous, leaving alone the cargo with which it was freighted. The Prince was surprised, on opening it, to see what it contained. By the costliness of her dress, and the peculiar ornaments of wedding jewellery she had on her, he discovered that she was a person of no mean station, and that she must have been not many days ago a bride of some noble family. Without asking her any questions, he supplied her with several kinds of delectable viands that she might refresh herself, attended to all her comforts, and permitted her an undisturbed repose of several hours. When this was done he visited her and enquired of her history. The Princess said "All that I can at present recall to my mind, is, that I was married a few days ago, and while sleeping, was placed in a chest, and thrown into the river. How I am come here, and why I was sent away, I do not know; these are mysteries." The Prince could not long affect indifference to her uncommon beauty. He was charmed with her intelligent conversation, delighted with her winning manners, and amiable disposition. Being inspired by her with sentiments of holy affection, he desired to marry her; but the Princess, like another Penelope, contrived to keep him pacified by telling him—"At present suffer me to call you brother, and look upon me as your sister. After the period of six months, should my husband not appear, and I get no intelligence of him, I will then consent to be the wife of the man who has rescued me from a watery grave." The Prince who, from the moment of this strange landing of the beautiful Princess, had ordered the erection of a superb mansion for her residence, and which he called, "The house of the River Nymph," employed himself in directing the building of the new palace, that in busy occupation, the hours which now hung on him with a leaden weight, might glide away swiftly, ushering in the time on which was suspended all his future happiness. In prosecuting this work, conducted upon a large scale, artizans of several grades and different skill were employed, together with a large number of operatives. One of the workmen, meeting with a beggar on the road as he was returning home from his day's vocation, was vexed to see a robust, healthy young fellow sauntering about in the idle and disgraceful employment of asking for alms, who, if he could do no better, might easily employ himself as a labourer in the Prince's service. "You idle fellow," thus he accosted the beggar, "do you not feel ashamed to beg while you have those strong limbs and possess health and a vigorous youth, when the whole country is ringing with the report of the grand works, for which there is a constant demand for able-bodied men. Were your senses fast locked up by the fumes of *gunjah* that you have not yet heard of the River Nymph's house!" When he heard all this, the fakir meditated in sadness and sorrow, and imagined that she might perhaps be his own lost wife, in whose search he had wandered so far away from his country and home. Most joyfully he promised to be present at the spot on the following morning, hoping thereby to obtain some information about her, or even seeing her personally. Buoyed up with this hope, the fakir, or Prince in disguise, commenced his work with the labourers in supplying the masons with bricks. He took care to locate himself near a spot from whence he might see the Prince and Princess, playing some games in the verandah, and superintending the work.

The Prince, while bearing the load of bricks, repeated the following words in rhyme to himself, but which in reality was applicable to the Princess, and the mason whom he was assisting : " I have searched you through many lands but had sought in vain—take this load for your erection," saying which he threw the bricks near the workman. The Princess, hearing the words, was not slow to comprehend the meaning, nor to discover who was the labourer. In this manner the Prince, whilst carrying the bricks, repeated the couplet for three days. The Princess playing the game, responded, " By skill delivered from dishonor, shut up and flung away; why is any search made now ? This is my move in the game." The workmen daily heard the labourer muttering strange things, but they could not comprehend their import, nor could the Prince understand the enigmatical words which the Princess repeated each day when playing the game, so he got nettled, and closing the game abruptly, requested her to clear the mystery. She informed him in a respectful and grateful manner that she spoke to her husband, in answer to his words, and that the labourer in disguise was the Prince to whom she was married. The Prince invited him to his house, ordered a bath for him, and furnishing him with robes of royalty, remarried him to the Princess with great pomp and pageantry, merriment and festivity, for several days. After which tho Prince and Princess took leave of their generous friend with tears of gratitude, and professions of lasting frendship. They went back to their own country, the Prince more matured in understanding, and reformed from the frailties of unthinking youth, by the lessons which bitter experience and severe trial had taught him, and the Princess cheerful in spirit and tranquil in mind, inspired by a sense of conscious rectitude and fidelity.

A GRASS-CUTTER.

A GRASS-CUTTER, with a net bag under his arm, who was going to cut grass in a field with his sickle, meeting with a few men seated by the road side, engaged in earnest conversation, and hearing them mention "that the man who trusts in God never fails to receive his share of food daily," thought in his own mind that there was no longer any necessity for him to go and cut grass. So, abandoning his work, he sat quietly for two days, in the expectation that God would send him his food. But though he did not find that his trust in God was rewarded, he was not discouraged, but made up his mind to continue in that place, and sat expectant for a few days longer, believing that what he had heard from the lips of several honest men, could not be wholly false, but that many of them must have experiencéd the truth of it in their own lives. While he was thus seated, silently meditating, an angel was seen to descend and ask him what he was doing there. "I am trying if what I have heard, be true or not. I have heard that God sends food to those who place their trust in Him." "I am commissioned to inquire what you want." "I want nothing more than a loaf and a cup of water." The angel requested him to suspend his net and sickle to the branch of a tree, under which he was seated, promising to supply him with his requirements; and the bread and water was found ready, placed for him regularly as each day revolved in its course.

A *Badsha*, who had gone out for an evening promenade, seeing a dead camel lying in his path, asked the men who surrounded him, why it was lying so helplessly? They answered it was dead. When the *Badsha* asked why it did not move and go about, they told him that the life which had animated the animal and caused his movement and actions, had departed; hence the body was brought to that state of helplessness. The *Badsha* reflected that, if this was the condition to which life was finally reduced, his wealth and kingdom were not worth keeping. With this idea he dressed himself as a fakir, and went away from his country wandering about in sadness and recklessness. Approaching the spot where the grass-cutter was seated beneath a tree, from the branch of which his net and sickle were suspended, the *Badsha* thought of resting himself for a while; but the grass-cutter, seeing a stranger approaching him, just at the hour when he was expecting his loaf and water, looked on him with displeasure. He requested that the stranger would go to a distance and rest himself under the next tree, as the one to which he had come, was previously occupied. The *Badsha*, not willing to dispute such small matters with a person who lacked courtesy and did not possess a grain of sense, quitted it as he was bid. When the supernatural visitor came who had brought the grass-cutter his usual diet, he furnished the *Badsha* with rich and varied viands. Witnessing this distinction made between them, the grass-cutter murmured, saying to himself, " I have trusted in God so long, and am receiving only a loaf and a cup of water, while that fellow, who has for the first day commenced to place his confidence in Him, is treated so sumptuously." The angel being acquainted with his thoughts, observed that the *Badsha* had abdicated his throne, wealth, and kingdom, for the service of God, and having made such large sacrifices, was treated according to his position in life. There was no injustice done to him, for what he had asked he received, and he was not more sparingly fed than he did before in his former position in the world. There was no reason, the angel added, for his murmuring aud envying the prosperity of others. If he were dissatisfied with his portion, all he had to do was to take down his net and sickle from the tree, and resume his former labour.

THE STORY OF A LION.

THERE was a lion and lioness who had a beautiful cub that pranced and played before his fond parents, delighting them with his innocent, graceful gambols. The lion, feeling that the infirmities of age were creeping gradually on him, and that he must follow the course of all things, pay the debt of nature, and be no more prowling with the tenants of the forest, felt a paternal wish to leave some useful advice to his progeny before he departed and was no more.

The lion, in his excursions with his mate and cub, addressed the young one in these words : " We, my son, are lords of the desert, and there is no one to dispute our right, or question our supremacy. You have none to fear among the inhabitants of this forest domain, but you have every reason to dread the wickedness and prolific skill of human beings, and therefore study to avoid them."

The cub grew up into vigorous maturity. Though his parents died some months ago, he had not yet encountered a single human being whom his parent lion had taught him to look upon with fear. He became very anxious to see this strange animal called a human being, and for this purpose he began to make a long journey through the forest, resolving not to go back to his lair until his burning curiosity was fully satisfied. Jogging on for miles, he saw a huge elephant coming towards him with a seemingly heavy tramp munching branches of trees, and stripping smaller plants bare of their bark and foliage. He stood looking at him for some time intently, with fear in his aspect, thinking that this monster with his legs as thick as trunks of trees, might be a human being of whom his father with good reason had cautioned him. The elephant, on approaching the lion, evinced symptoms of anxiety, and was about to turn into another direction, but the lion hailed him and inquired if he was a human being. "Ah! no, I am but an elephant. Human beings are very wicked and ingenious. They have captured me and hundreds and thousands like myself from the *jungles*; they beat us with rods of iron whenever they wish, mount our necks, and burthen us with heavy loads at their pleasure." The lion's curiosity was still more excited by this relation of man's acts, and as this huge monster was not a human being, what like might then a human being be? With these thoughts in his cranium he proceeded on his journey with rapid strides, desirous that he might quickly accomplish his design, then return to his den, after having gained a knowledge of things, and made acquaintance with all created beings. The next object that presented itself to his anxious view was a stately camel. This, thought the lion, may after all be a human being. He began to look to the right and left as if wishing to secure a safe retreat in case of danger, but these symptoms of apprehension abated in some degree when he saw the animal hesitating to approach. He called out to the camel and enquired if he was a human being? The camel answered, "Not I, for I am but a servant of human beings, and my whole race are slaves in their service. They bore our noses, fasten us with a string, and a boy may lead a hundred of us at his pleasure in any direction he pleases." The wondering lion went on his search after a human being, and being now about a mile from the verge of the *jungle* where a carpenter had penetrated to procure some logs of timber for his use, he saw him

18

advancing in his direction, and instead of testifying any alarm as he did when he met with the elephant and camel, he was emboldened to present himself before the carpenter with an air of supreme contempt. The carpenter was not at all disposed to court his familiar approximation, and was therefore looking up the tree near him to ascertain if it were feasible to mount it in case of need. He was, however, encouraged to remain where he was by the unrepulsive tones and waggish speech of the lion. "Are you, you spindle-legged little fellow, a human being or not? If you are not, pray tell me where I may see one of them?" "Most certainly, friend! I will show you a human being." Telling him this, he took up his axe, and with a few strokes at the root of a tree, felled it to the ground. Seeing this operation, the lion began to admire the insignificant fellow's prowess in bringing the tree down with a thundering crash. The carpenter then employed himself in making an ingenious trap with two logs, and when the snare was completed, he informed the lion that if he desired to see a human being, he was ready to show him one. The lion was delighted with the idea. The carpenter told him to put his neck through the two logs and to look straight before him, when he would see a true human being. The lord of the forest doing as he was bid, gave the carpenter a fair opportunity to lock him up by his neck. The lion in this sad fix had ample time to reflect on the advice of his parent with a heavy and bitter sigh. Man, though a diminutive being, has, by his wisdom and ingenuity, a wide sway of mighty power. He saw that what strength could not accomplish, skill could execute, and on that account a human being was to be dreaded and avoided.

A SIMPLETON.

IN the busy bustling bazar of a populous town, a simpleton was seen to saunter about the place, evidently intent upon the execution of no particular object. A woman of middling age, but cunning looks, and possessing much shrewdness and penetration, was seen watching at the time his motions and actions. She was acquainted with the private history of the man, that is, his possessing some property, and his easy belief in any fiction that might be framed to dupe him. She began to cogitate by what scheme she might extract some money from his hoard, and just as a taking device was planned in her own mind, the simpleton wended his course in the direction of his residence. She slided behind him with quiet stealthy steps, and finding the street not thronged, she addressed him— "Where are you going, my son? Have you purchased any thing from the bazar?" "No, I could not find anything to suit my taste or answer my purpose." The artful woman asked why he did not marry, when ugly fellows, with crooked backs, and bandy legs, were married, and had happy families. The simpleton answered that he never thought on the subject, not knowing where to find a wife, and whom to ask to marry him. She promptly answered that she could get him a wife from a good respectable house. The simpleton rejoiced to receive such good news, and asked her, therefore, what preliminary steps were necessary to be taken. She said it was necessary to spend a hundred rupees, if he had that amount. Intending to be the bearer of the overture of marriage, it would be indispensable for her to put on a rich new suit of clothes, and take some presents with her. He gave her the sum that was needed, and told her to be expeditious with her negociation. She brought the tidings after a few days, that his proposal was accepted.

After two months, the woman again paid him a visit, and mentioned to him that his wedding would be celebrated on the morrow. He was highly delighted to hear of it. He desired to know what sum of money was required for its performance. The artful woman told the green-horn that one hundred rupees would suffice for dress, a few trinkets, and other contingent expenses. He gave her that sum with pleasure, and she went away exulting in her success. On her next visit she announced that his wedding had been solemnized in a respectable manner, and that as he was now married, she expected some reward for having brought it to a happy conclusion. Highly gratified to hear that he was married, he readily placed two *mohurs* in her hand. Nine months had quietly waned away without affording the cunning hag an opportunity for exercising her tricks, but in the tenth, she visited the dupe, to announce that he had a nice son, the wife having given birth to a boy, a day before. The joy of the man was boundless. He was anxious to know what he was to do on such an occasion. She said that he must provide her with one hundred rupees to meet expenses, paying the midwife, nurse, and providing baby-linen. This sum he handed to her with instructions that great care must be taken of his wife and child.

The employer of the simpleton called him one day and gave him instruction to go to a certain country, and execute a commission for him there. Before his departure, therefore, he called ed the woman who brought about his marriage, and told her, that as he was going on a long journey and might be away for a protracted period, he was desirous of seeing his wife and child before he set out. The artful woman requested him to buy some fruit and sweetmeats for his wife and son, and when he was ready to start, to inform her. He did so ; she conducted him some part of the way, when, seeing a fine boy near a respectable looking house, she pointed to the lad, and said that

that boy was his son, and his wife was in the same house. Leaving him to meet his son, she slipped away from his society, and disappeared into one of the bye-lanes. The father greeted the boy, supposed to be his son, with true parental warmth, hugging, caressing, kissing him for some time. The boy was tractable and docile under the influence of the fruits and sweets which were showered into his lap, otherwise he might have resisted such unceremonious encroachment, and immoderate liberty, particularly from a person with whom he was not familiar. When the lad was released from the lap and embrace of the simpleton, he ran to his mother, and with a gleesome spirit poured out before her the contents of his frock. The mother, seeing the things, thought that some friend of her husband's had perhaps come on a visit. She called her maid, whom she desired to take and offer a pipe to the man who was seated in the verandah, and also to serve him with a bowl of milk and a pack of cards to divert himself with until the return of her husband from his morning walk. The simpleton was gratified with the attentions of his wife, as he believed. He eyed the milk and cards with much self-gratulation. When the pipe had been released from his mouth, he drew the milk near, and thinking the fine cards to be some rare kind of edible, intended to be used with milk, he took the pack, and tearing them up into bits, put them to soak in the bowl. While conducting this pleasant operation, the master of the house came home. He saw the strange man, but so intent was he on his own business, and absorbed with his own thoughts, that he passed him on his way into the inner apartments without any notice. The master of the house inquired of his wife who the man was who was seen by him seated in one of the outer rooms. She informed him that she was unacquainted with the man ; but believing that he might be a friend of his, from the presents he had brought for their son, she had ordered him a seat, and sent him some refreshment. The master of the house then went and had an interview with the simpleton, and asked, " Whose house are you in search of, and who are you?" The simpleton, not at all daunted with this, to him, strange query, made a counter inquiry, " Pray, who are you, and what do you want here?" " I am the owner of the house." " You, the owner! This is my house, my wife is inside, and my child was just this moment with me." The master of the house, being a prudent man, soon discovered that he was a simpleton who was imposed upon by some artful person. " My good fellow," said the owner in explanation, " this house is my property, and my wife and children are within. This is a world of deceit and deception. Some wicked person has no doubt played you a trick, but have they cheated you of any money?" The simpleton related how an artful woman had deceived and drawn from him at intervals of time, some four hundred rupees or more. The man pitied his simplicity and loss, gave him that sum, and cautioned him never more to listen to the flattering tales of old women.

THE STORY OF A PRINCE.

IN a country that is well watered by numerous streams and their tributaries, is fruitful in every product of the field, and thickly studded with luscious fruit trees in the vicinity of pasture lands, a Rajah of ancient times chose for its being a pleasant situation for residence. His son, after his death, inherited his paternal estates, but by misfortune or mismanagement, the property which had descended to him, began to dimimish gradually until the Prince came into very straitened circumstances. As he was grieving over his destiny late one evening, and was cogitating what he should do to retrieve his fortune, he heard the voice of a fakir, who was at the time passing near his residence. The words of the fakir were these:—" Act according to circumstance; never forsake ready food; clothe the naked; be the road strait or crooked, even or rugged, never proceed without premeditation." The Prince, hearing these four wholesome maxims from the fakir, called the Princess, and told her that it would be best that they abandoned the country, because it was overcast with murky clouds, and there was no ray of sunshine to illumine the darkness of their hearts; that the prospect before them was gloomy, but perhaps in another country, the beams of Fortune might once again reflect on them more benignantly and cheer their sinking spirits." " In this country," remarked the Prince, " we have nothing to hope for; we are known to the inhabitants of every house and hut, and should we seek any employment for our support, we will meet with disappointment on account of our very rank, and thus starve in it; but in a strange kingdom, both you and I could work to provide ourselves with our daily wants, besides, it would be carrying out the precept of the fakir, ' Act according to circumstance.' " The Princess consented readily to this reasonable proposal, and so they set out with buoyant hope on their journey, unperceive by any one about the place.

Arriving in another country, they met with a few men of the village, who inquired from whence they had come, whither they were journeying, if they intended to remain in the village permanently, and what they were going to do? The Prince replied, that they had come from a distant country in quest of some employment, and be it of whatever description it might, he was not too fastidious about it. One of the villagers offered him a place in his house, saying that he could assist in the operations of the field, while his wife might help the women in bearing water for their use. The Prince and Princess became reconciled to their new situation and its drudgeries, by remembering the incidental instruction which the fakir had comunicated, " act according to circumstance."

Continuing their honest labours for several months in the

village, the Prince saw a *joghee* who never associated with
any of the villagers on account, as it was reported, of their
perverse conduct and for not listening to his good counsels,
whenever he proffered them, on suitable seasons. The *joghee* had
lived retired, and at a distance from the motley dwellings
of the villagers. He was found one day lying dead in his
cabin. As there was little congeniality, and no sympathy between the villagers and the *joghee*, they commanded a low-cast
man, a sweeper, to tie his legs up with a string, and in that
manner to drag him out of his shed, and fling him into the
river. As the *joghee* was floating down the stream, the Prince
and Princess were, at near sun set, returning from their daily
toil by the border of the bank. Seeing that the *joghee's* head
had sunk deep in the water, he observed that there must be
some reason why the head had gone down so low. It was an
unusual circumstance, and on that account he was anxious to
ascertain the cause, but in which way to execute his design he
was at loss to think. The Princess recommended his fetching
a tender shoot of the bamboo, and tying a hook to its extremity
to draw the corpse ashore. This being done, the Prince
unfastened the knots of his shaggy hair, and, to his surprise,
discovered a ball of pure gold weighing about a pound, and
round that ball the *joghee* had twined his long knotted hair
for concealing his treasure. They consulted together regarding
the disposal of the body, saying, that it was not proper to see
the *joghee* floating on the river when it was the custom to bury
such men ; they therefore took him up, made an excavation,
and interred him at a short distance from the water. Going
to their humble dwelling and conversing together, the Prince
mentioned to his companion in trouble, that now, by the will
of Providence, as they were furnished with a small property,
they should provide themselves with better dresses, and then
apply to the Rajah of the country for employment. The
Prince met the Rajah, who, seeing him, told him that he
seemed to be no person of a servile extraction, or poor ; what

was he seeking therefore? The Prince replied that had he been affluent, he would not have sought employment. The Rajah was pleased with his appearance and manners, and liked him much. He was kept about the palace without holding any particular appointment for some time, till the Dewan's death made a vacancy, to which the Rajah appointed him: and he filled it with honor, conducting himself with so much prudence, talent, and fidelity in his new office, that it won for him the good opinion of the Rajah and the regard of all with whom he had business intercourse. The Rajah permitted him to lodge in the lower apartments of the Palace, while he occupied the upper floor. As the Prince was in the lower floor, he saw the Rajah descending very early every morning to the ghât of the river for ablution and prayer, and the Queen a short time after following him, but whither, he at first did not know. By some accident, as the Prince was proceeding from the house, he saw the Queen in an improper state in the room of the gate keeper, when recalling the words of the fakir "to clothe the naked," he flung his own garment over her with inverted face, and walking away, continued his morning exercise.

The perfidious Queen, finding what was done, and by whom, and the likelihood of a disclosure, rose up hastily. To screen herself from crime, she cried out that the Rajah's Dewan had attempted to stain her character, and in trying to capture him, he had fled, leaving his garment behind in her grasp. The Queen made a complaint against the Dewan to the Rajah on his return from the ghât. Seeing and recognizing his dress, the Rajah had no doubt in his own mind as to the truth of the accusation.

The Rajah, though grieved with the ingratitude of his Dewan, was not willing to destroy him with his own hand; he therefore resolved upon sending him with a letter to his brother, detailing the particulars of his crime, and asking him to behead the Dewan on receiving the letter. The Prince, being about to carry the letter to the brother of the Rajah, the

Princess asked him where he was going so early, and in such hurry. He communicated to her his business. She desired him to stop and breakfast, as the food was ready. Remembering the words of the fakir, "never forsake ready food," he postponed his journey, requesting the Princess to serve out the edibles quickly. At this time the profligate ward of the Palace door, who had called on the Dewan on some business, asked, " What is it, Sir ? " The Prince told him he was entrusted with a letter from the Rajah to his brother, but as his food was ready he was thinking of partaking of it before setting out on his errand. The *durwan* requested that he might take it, as he was going in that direction, and that at his leisure, the Dewan might follow him. The Dewan assented to his offer, but desired him to inform the nobleman that he was on his way, and wouuld soon be with him, and would wait on him for an answer to the letter. The *durwan* on presenting the communication to the nobleman, was ordered to be beheaded. The Dewan, arriving soon after this catastrophe, was kindly and civilly treated by the nobleman, knowing him to be the Prime Minister of his brother the Rajah. He communicated to the Dewan what was done to the *durwan* by his brother's order, and said that he was anxious to know all the particulars of the case. This event brought the fakir's saying to mind, " be the road strait or crooked, even or rugged, never proceed without premeditation." The nobleman, asking the Dewan very pressingly on the subject which appeared to him very enigmatical, he could not help narrating the whole subject from the beginning. The nobleman addressed a letter to his brother, in which he exonerated the Dewan for the crime he was charged with, disclosed the guilt of the Queen, and told him that the punishment of the *durwan* was the retributive justice of Providence. The Prince set out on his journey, meditating on the salutary lessons of the fakir, and the vicissitudes of the world. Arriving at the Palace, the Rajah was startled to see the Dewan back again, but on perusing the letter which the Dewan handed

him, he became acquainted with the real posture of affairs.
He banished his unfaithful perfidious wife from his domain
into another country, got disgusted with his kingdom and its
government, and on that account resigned it in favour of the
Prince, his Prime Minister, telling him that he required nothing from him but a morsel of bread, and that being all that
he actually needed, he would spend the rest of his days, free
from cares and anxiety, in prayer and praise, and in peace and
tranquillity.

A WASHERMAN AND HIS ASS.

A WASHERMAN, who was in the habit of taking bundles of dirty clothes on the back of an ass to a tank
daily to scour them, passing near a school kept by a Moulvie,
heard the man of letters scolding some of his pupils, and in his
irritation telling them that they were nothing but asses, although
he had taken so much pains to make them men. The washerman was glad on hearing that an ass could be made into a man.
He thought of the foal at home, and of getting his nature changed.
He reflected that, as a human being, he could be of greater value,
and render better service. With this idea, he went over one
day to the school-master, and falling on his knees, begged that
he would take charge of his foal, and be so good as to make
him a human being. The Moulvie having sounded the depth
of the man, and finding how shallow he was, agreed to execute
the work on his receiving a hundred rupees for his trouble.
The washerman ran to his house, unfastened the foal from the
peg to which it was tethered, and brought it to the Moulvie,
who received the fee, desired the animal to be fastened to a
post, and instructed the washerman to come punctually to him
on a certain day and hour, when it would be fully metamor-

phosed for delivery. The anxiety of the washerman led him before the time fixed upon, to call twice or thrice, and inquire how the foal was progressing. The Moulvie replied, that he was picking up the language fast enough, was learning good manners, and was giving early proofs of his becoming very soon a human being. Instead, however, of the washerman making his appearance on the precise day as he was strictly requested to do, he went a day later to receive his foal, now no longer with elongated ears, but made a man by the teaching of the school-master. The washerman asked to see him, but the Moulvie replied, " Alas ! why did you not come yesterday ? When I had made a man of him, he was no longer under my control. He is gone away from us, and has been appointed *Cazi* of Jounpore." The washerman could say nothing more after hearing so good news. He went home musing on the road, and thinking that it would be a source of much gain to them now that the ass was the *Cazi* of Jounpore. He communicated these glad tidings to his wife, who, together with himself, agreed to go in search of their stray property. By inquiring the road, they reached Jounpore. There was no difficulty in finding the *Cazi*. Being directed to the place, the washerman saw him seated on a high platform, surrounded by a multitude of suitors and plaintiffs, and as he could not approach, he stood at a respectable distance from whence he could see the *Cazi*, and the *Cazi* see him. He held the bridle in one hand, and showing with the other a bundle of hay, called out, *khoor, khoor, khoor,* to attract the *Cazi sahib* to him. After the Court broke up, the *Cazi* felt some curiosity to ascertain who this whimsical fellow was, who put on such a ridiculous air before the Court. The *Cázi*, therefore, asked who he was, and what it was he wanted. The washerman exclaimd, " *Wah, wah,* sir, you don't know me nor seem to be familiar with this cord and bridle, or this pad which went on your back so often. Were you not the foal of my ass whom I got made a man by giving a hundred rupees to a Moulvie, who makes men

of asses and educates them in language and manners? You
are oblivious of your primitive condition, and wish now to prove
ungrateful to your benefactor." The *Cazi* perceived that he
was fooled by his simplicity, and imposed upon by an artful
person. Unriddling the whole affair to the washerman, he in
pity presented him with a note of two hundred rupees, and sent
him away to his home, a wiser man for his troubles, and the
experience he had acquired thereby.

THE STORY OF A FAKIR.

THERE was a fakir whose name was Jellalee Shah, and
who never went abroad to ask alms, as his brethren of
the same profession were in the habit of doing generally. His
wife told him one day, if he did not support her, to permit
her to go away, and seek her fortune elsewhere. He replied,
that the wealth which he once possessed, would have sufficed to
maintain ten persons like herself in comfort, had she not squan-
dered it lavishly by her indiscretion and extravagance. " What
use," the fakir added, " will it be to go and beg ; the few pice
that I might obtain by begging, would not suffice to meet your
immoderate expenses." The wife begged of him to overlook
her past faults and remissness, and to go and solicit assistance
from the kind generous inhabitants, saying, that should he find
her again prodigal in the management of the house, he was to
discontinue asking charity.

The fakir, accordingly, got out one morning with his bamboo
cane and wallet, and a canonical cap of Moslem invention, but
in doing so he was accosted by the men on the road, who saw
him begging—" Khan Saheb, what can you reap in this little
unpopulous, unfertile place ? the most you may gather will be a
very few annas, and that for a short time only, for in that

period, you will have shaken all the fruitful trees bare, and shake you ever so hard or often after that as you please, they will yield no recompense for your labour. Go to a place which is but a short distance from this, there a Rajah resides, whose mother has recently departed from life, and whose funeral obsequies will be performed very soon, and at that time princely gifts will be distributed to the poor."

Quite glad as the fakir was, he lost no time in being present at the ceremony, regarding which the people had informed him. While the Rajah was engaged in dealing out presents to numerous applicants, he seeing the fakir, called him, and placing two rupees in his hands, desired him to come every day, and that he would be allowed that amount regularly. The fakir, with humility and supplicating looks, said that he could not come every day, because he was living at a good distance, but if permitted, he would call and receive his gift on every third or fourth day. The Rajah consented. The fakir went home with much joy and satisfaction, and he took out and gave the two rupees to his wife. She managed her expenses with that sum so carefully, that it went a long way, and lasted about a month. The fakir went to the Rajah regularly, and received punctually his two rupees. In this manner, after the expiration of several months, he had saved a tolerable amount. One day, when the fakir, as usual, presented himself before the Rajah, the calculation as to what he was to receive being duly performed, and the money about to be handed over to him, the Rajah's Guru, who was present, inquired on what account the man was receiving the money which was counted out to him? The Rajah told his Guru that the fakir was a fine fellow, and he had taken a liking to him, and was allowing him two rupees per day for his support. As the fakir, after receiving his share of allowance, was departing, the Guru also left the *durbar*, or Court, and overtook the fakir on the road with rapid strides, speaking to him thus—"You are a stupid, uncivilized, dirty fellow; when I was at the *durbar* to-day, I saw you, whilst speaking to the Rajah, doing it so carelessly with your face near him, as to spirt your spittle on his person. When you call again, take good care to speak to his honor with your face averted."

Having communicated this malicious advice to the fakir, he ran back to the Rajah, and told him : " Maharaj, you are too credulous, and are therefore easily duped by every vagabond who comes to you with a plausible story of want and distress. The fakir that was here just now, is a great drunkard. I saw him go into one of the drinking houses and spend his money." The Rajah was sorry to hear this of the fakir, and regretted much that he had helped him to carry on a course of intemperance, yet he could hardly believe it. The fakir came again to the Rajah, but as he was warned by the Guru, he stood at a distance, and spoke to the Rajah with his face in an opposite direction. It now occurred to the Rajah, that what his Guru had intimated, was true, and there was satisfactory proof of it in the conduct of the fakir. To get him punished for his trick, he wrote a letter to his brother, in which he desired him to tie the fakir to a pole, serve him out some impressive lashes, and then send him away. With this intention, the Rajah handed a letter, which he desired him to convey to his brother. The Guru, thinking that his stratagem had failed totally in its design, and that the fakir's bearing the letter to the Rajah's brother, might be intended to promote his welfare, went up hastily and joined the fakir on the road, to whom he spoke thus : " The Rajah has written to his brother to pay you the sum due to you for the last three days. Why need you go so far. Here take the six rupees and depart. I am going that way, and will deliver the letter myself." The Guru, on taking the letter to the Rajah's brother, was treated kindly, received water to wash his hands and feet, got a bath, and then some refreshments. But soon after these tokens of civility, the brother, opening and perusing the letter, was surprised to learn from the contents the actual state of things. He was compelled to order the execution of the treatment which the Rajah had prescribed, but reconsidering the subject, he thought that it could not be a small crime for which punishment to a Guru was intended; he ordered therefore, that the ordeal through which he ought to pass, should be to mark one of his cheeks with chunam, the other with pot black, and have his neck ornamented with a necklace of old shoes, and thus adorned, to parade him about the most thronged parts of the city and markets with beat of drum. When the Guru was thus being made a humiliating spectacle in the town, the Ranee, seeing him from her lattice, exclaimed with astonishment to her attendants, that the man who was being punished, did not look like the fakir as it was reported, but rather like their own Guru. She ran and acquainted the Rajah with the circumstance, chiding him for his severity in thus insulting the Guru, telling him at the same time, that such a crime might bring down disaster on his *raj*, or kingdom, and some bad luck on himself. The Rajah observed, that he had sanctioned the punishment of a fakir who had deceived him by false pretences, and who had taken away a good deal of money to be wasted in debasing drinks, regarding which he had been informed by the Guru.

The Rajah was sorry for what had happened by a sad mistake. He hastened to ascertain if the statement he heard was true, and finding that the man punished was no other than the identical Guru, he apologised for the accident, and had him washed and dressed, while he issued strict orders for the apprehension of the fakir, and his immediate presence at Court. The Rajah's injunction was promptly executed, and the fakir was apprehended. The Rajah questioned him as to the manner in which the letter had passed from his hands into that of his Guru. "Sire,"—he said, "I am a simple man whose profession is begging. I am not an adept in deep artifice, or in complex scheming. I visited you not to obtain your charity by force or deceit. You freely settled that sum on me out of your own benevolent disposition. One day, as I was going

away after receiving your bounty, your Gurú came and met me
on the road. He asked me,—' In what manner, you worthless
fellow, do you speak to the Rajah, that in doing so, your
spittle falls on his person ? Take care when you next present
yourself before him, that you do not dare to look at him when
you speak.' When I heard this, I thought it might be true,
for I could never believe that your Guru could ever be guilty
of so mean an act as a lie. When, therefore, I last called for my
stipend, I took good care to turn my face round when speaking, in case my spittle might fall on you. When I did so,
and you gave me the letter addressed to your brother, the
Guru, who overtook me on the way, told me that it was no
business of mine to meddle with writing, being illiterate, and
therefore unable to decipher characters, and ignorant of their
import; saying which, he snatched the letter, and carried it himself, promising that I should continue to enjoy the allowance
of two rupees which I had hitherto received." The Rajah
here turning round to the Guru, interrogated him as to
the truth or falsehood of the fakir's representations. The Guru
could not deny them. The Rajah then acquainted the Ranee
with the transaction, and the culpable conduct of their spiritual guide. They agreed, on consulting together, that he should
be dismissed from the .service of the palace, but the fakir was
invited to leave the unwholesome village in which he was
residing, and to take up his quarters in the garden of the
Rajah. This pleasing invitation he joyfully accepted, living
with his wife, free from care and anxiety, and taught in the
school of want, to be careful of God's gifts.

THE TWO BEGGARS.

THERE were two beggars who, having a regard for each other, strolled about the streets asking alms. They often passed close to the palace of a *Badsha*. In passing it, one of them was heard to repeat—" May the Lord give ;" the other—" May the *Badsha* give." The *Badsha*, hearing this petition for several days, felt some pity for the man who called on his name, and put his trust in him for support. The beggar being called in, the Vizier was instructed to furnish him every morning with a loaf, in which he was told to conceal a gold-mohur. The *Badsha*, when giving him the loaf, desired that he would not go and beg again. The beggar accepted the loaf with grateful sentiments, and retiring from his presence, went and seated himself beneath the shade of a banian tree which was a place of assignation, where, after their labours, the two beggars rested and conversed on the subject of their respective gains and acquisitions. The two beggars on meeting together again beneath the tree, inquired of each other what was the result of their morning labour. The one, who would always repeat, " May God send," related that he had received pice, couries, fruit, grain, and dholl ; the other, with a mournful countenance, told his own tale. " Friend," said he, " the *Badsha* has ordered me the gift of a loaf every day, with an injunction that I should not beg any more after receiving it. I am puzzled to think how I can satisfy the hunger of my wife, my seven children, and myself, with this single loaf. When I used to beg and obtain rice, I made a simple gruel which answered our purpose better." "Well, friend, I will buy it of you for four pice," said the other. The man accepted of his offer, and with it he procured some broken rice, with which he prepared some gruel, and fed his family. **In this manner,** for a period of six months, as he got **the loaf, he** sold it to the other beggar. Within this time the other beggar, who exclaimed, " May God give," was seen to thrive **in body and** prosper in his affairs, while the beggar, who had put his confidence in the *Badsha*, was reduced to a skeleton, and had on dirty tattered clothes. The *Badsha*, seeing through his window the two **beg- gars** passing one morning, **observed the** difference **of their** respective **appearance—the one hale and hearty, the other a** walking shadow. **He desired his Vizier to call the beggar up** to him. **When he appeared before the** *Badsha*, **the** *Badsha* **asked him** with surprise how it was that he wore dirty **tattered** clothes, and looked famished, and if he did not regularly re- ceive his allowance **of a** loaf. **The beggar related about the insufficiency of the single loaf to appease the hunger of nine** persons, **and that on that account, he had sold his loaf to his** friend **for four pice daily. The** *Badsha* **told him that he was an** unfortunate man to lose the loaf, for **with the loaf he had** given him sixteen rupees every day, and had therefore expected to see him in a better condition of **body, purse,** and clothing. **The** *Badsha* told **his Vizier to send for a cart, and loading the cart with as much money as it could hold, to see it safely** deposited **in the** house of the poor man, lest so much wealth might tempt the cupidity of some wicked men to rob the man on the lonely road to his abode. The Vizier escorted the treasure safely to the door of the beggar, **who, leaping down with** elated hope, ran **into the house with an erect gait, instead of** entering **with a stoop as before,** to avoid contact with the **low** frame of the **door ; the** consequence was, that the beggar's **head** struck **violently** against it, and he fell down dead **on the spot. The** Vizier, after leaving his men to watch the cart, went and informed the *Badsha* of the sad catastrophe. The *Badsha* was surprised and sorrowful on receiving the tidings. He went to see and to ascertain how the **misfortune** had happened. Going to the beggar's house, he saw **him prostrate on** the ground, his forehead skinned nearly to the crown of his head. Stooping to examine if the cranium had sustained a fracture, he discovered some faint characters on the forehead, which on being deciphered, the following words were found inscribed : " As none can change man's destiny, so no one can give life to the dead." The *Badsha* became thoughtful and reflective after this accident, and as he could not help the man, do what he might, he told his Vizier to help his family with a regular supply of all their wants, and to attend to their comfort.

STORY OF ANOTHER FAKIR.

THERE was a fakir whose practice was never to reside more than one night at any village, but like a bird of passage to change place every day of his abode. It happened that, on arriving at a certain village, he was saluted by the villagers, thus,—" Father, you are wandering throughout this wide domain for your daily bread, but without our going a mile from our own country or home, God provides for our wants, and we receive, seated at home, whatever we ask for." The fakir replied—" I am surprised to hear that you get whatever you ask from God. If he gives you all you ask, he will not refuse giving me also." He went on in his journey, but when he came to a desolate place near the bank of a river, he gave utterance to this prayer: " As thou, God, givest others, so give me, a child first, then wealth, and last of all a wife." When this strange prayer was offered, a heavy fall of rain descended, that flooded the whole country, and it reached up to the neck of the fakir. He began to reflect, that it might be indicative of the displeasure of God for the petition he had offered, still he resolved in his own mind, that as he had already asked for the gifts, until his request was granted, he would not stir from the place, though he got drowned by the flood. Standing in that position, he began to feel thirsty, but for some time he found no means of allaying his thirst, the surrounding water being muddy and impure ; but a cocoanut was seen very opportunely to float by where he stood ; he took it up and drank half of its milky fluid. That the remaining juice which it contained might not run out, or the external water of the disturbed stream might not get mixed with it, he closed the aperture of the nut with a stick, after which he sent it down the river. The cocoanut went dancing and whirling on the water, and as it was passing, a Princess, who had gone to the river for ablution, seeing it, desired her maid to get within its reach by throwing her flowing garment over, and drawing the nut close to the bank. Obtaining what she desired, she drank the water it contained, and took the cocoanut home to enjoy the inner substance. She began very soon after to show symptoms of pregnancy, and as the time for her accouchement approached, her situation could not long remain concealed. Her condition began to be known to the inmates of the palace, and by them the circumstance was brought to the knowledge of her parents. The Rajah could not suffer his child, who had brought, as he was led to think, so much dishonor and disgrace on herself and her parents, to remain any longer in the palace ; he therefore commanded that a palkee, with a female attendant, should be speedily provided, and the Princess taken and left by the bearers in the heart of some gloomy forest. The Princess being awoke in the morning from her disturbed dreamy slumber, by the early songs of forest birds, and the light of dawning day, called her maid and inquired why the bearers had set down the conveyance, and where they had gone ? When the Princess and her maid found that they were abandoned by the attendants, their grief knew no bounds. But the emotion of sorrow soon gave place to another feeling—apprehension of danger,—this roused them to action. The Palkee was placed under the trunk of a wide spread banian. **They** enclosed from the two poles of the conveyance to the tree, the space with stout branches of thorny plants, **for** protection from wild animals; the palkee itself being like a trap, was a sufficient scarecrow for them. The conveyance had been provided with a store of provisions sufficient to last them for several days, so they were under no fear of immediate starvation, nor **any** necessity just then to ramble in quest of such fruits and succulent herbs as **might afford** sustenance. The Princess after a few days was confined of a beautiful boy. This occurrence, which **in any** other circumstances would have **been a** copious source of pure delight to the maternal bosom, **was joy not unmixed with regret to** her guileless heart. She **reflected that, if not** destroyed by the denizens of the forest, **they might waste and pine away for want** of food; **and the** same appalling disaster might **fall** on her lovely **child.** With these thoughts in her mind, she told her maid that, as soon as the fountain of nourishment with which nature had provided her for the support of the child failed, it was her intention to **launch him on** the bosom of the river, that some humane person might see and adopt him, and by this means free her innocent progeny from a cruel banishment in a repulsive wilderness. **Agreeably to this** design, when the child grew up, and was not wholly dependent on the mother for his supply of food, but **could subsist by** means of artificial **diet, she** prepared an oblong basket **of** wicker work, lined it **with bark and the leaves** of the lotus, covered the top with light rush, and placed the little vessel on the stream with its precious cargo, and then offered many tearful prayers for its safety. The little artificial boat glided down to the spot near which the fakir's hut stood on the bank, when it swung **round by** the eddy, and stuck at the shore where the man stood in silent contemplation of nature, or perhaps nature's God. He looked at the object with mute wonder, **and** thinking with much satisfaction and delight that his first prayer had been granted, lifted the tiny ark with the child, and bore it to his **humble** residence. High was his gratifica-

tion too, and great his joy, when he beheld the little innocent
being whose face was radiant with a smile, throwing out his
playful hands, as if they sought the shelter and protection of
the fakir's stronger arms. The fakir now released the innocent
prisoner from his unconscious bondage, and dandled him with
parental fondness. He discovered a small bag in the basket
which had been placed near the child; opening which to satisfy
his curiosity, he discovered that it contained jewellery and
gems of considerable value. In this occurrence, he found that
his second prayer too was in a very signal way answered.

Days and months passed by in their rapid course, when one
day, the Rajah, weary of his protracted labours in the constant
administration of justice, thought of unbending himself by
some recreative indulgences; to carry out this pleasant
project, he commanded his painted boats to be fitted up, with
a sufficient complement of men, to be provided with necessaries
for the cruise, and to be got ready by the first of the month.
With his numerous retinue, the Rajah dropped down the stream,
and descending occasionally into the woods where deer, rabbits,
and hares were shot, and game of several kinds bagged by the
sportsmen. The Rajah, who was seated smoking his pipe,
saw a very fine boy playing at the door of a mean hut further
down the stream. Ordering his barge to be fastened to the
shore, he descended, and with sentiments of pity and surprise,
beheld the boy, for he could see no one in the hut, whilst the
boy was amusing himself with the pretty flowers of spontane-
ous growth. Where the lad had come from, was a puzzle which
he could not easily solve. Playing with the boy for some time,
he felt an inexplicable fondness for him. When the fakir
came back from his short excursion, the King asked him how
he came to possess the boy in such an uncongenial place. The
fakir replied that he had offered three petitions to God, of which
two, which regarded a son and wealth, had been very remarkably fulfilled, and he was now waiting for the accomplishment
of his last wish—the gift of a wife.

The fakir related to the Rajah the manner in which his prayer had been heard and answered. The Rajah, who had become so much attached to the child, that the thought of parting with him became truly painful, invited the fakir to leave his desolate retirement, and to return with him to the city in which, as he had several houses, he might take up his quarters with the child in any one of them he fancied. The fakir, considering that it would be highly injudicious to reject so advantageous an offer, and thinking too that it would secure not only the safety of the child, but might advance his welfare and promote his future prospects, willingly and thankfully acepted the proposal. When the exiles were in the Rajah's country, there was not a day that passed by without his sending his men for the boy, who beguiled the hours of the Rajah's sorrow, anxiety, and care, by his winning manners, and his bewitching playfulness. After the expiration of some months, the Rajah again proceeded by land on a shooting expedition. When he had gone about a day or two day's journey, he entered the very forest where his daughter was left by the bearers. In one direction in the chase, and another, beating the bush in all quarters, he came up to the spot in which the palkee was placed. With much surprise he questioned the sportsmen how such a thing could come there, and what such a conveyance had to do in the dense jungle,—for no one in his senses would travel there,—and to ascertain if there might be any whimsical traveller in it. In lifting the shutters of the conveyance, they discovered a female fast asleep, of attenuated form, pallid complexion, but possessing handsome features. The Rajah could see her also, as the doors were set ajar. He could not forget easily the features of his own daughter, and without hesitation, pronounced this miserable being to be his own child. He regretted deeply that in his haste he had banished his child without satisfying himself of the truth of the report of his daughter's guilt. He embraced her fondly, wept over her bitterly, and bore her away from the spot giving up the chase which had now no attraction for him. Remaining a few days in the palace, in which, in the enjoyment of comforts and nutricious viands, she recovered her health and strength, and with it all the other blessings of life ; still her heart was sad and heavy, and sick with love for her child, whose destiny was unknown to her.

As the fakir's child was daily brought to the palace to be caressed and toyed with by the Rajah and the inmates of the palace, his daughter saw him on one occasion, so pleasing in his innocent gambols, so beautiful in face and form, and with such attractive lustrous eyes, that she ran up, lifted him, and folded to her bosom with affectionate warmth. This she did every day with increasing intensity of love, but though all were amused and happy in their intercourse with the child, the Rajah's own daughter's spirits became ever after depressed. One day, when the Ranee was in her own private apartments with none of her attendants present save her daughter, she communicated her suspicions to her, telling her that the child must be her own son. The Ranee prevailed on her daughter to disclose her secret, promising not to abuse her confidence, but to aid her if there should arise any injury to her character by its publicity. The daughter, with genuine innocence recounted, what had happened ; relating how she went out to bathe with one of her maids in the river, and whilst doing so, saw a cocoanut floating, with a stick used as a cork in the aperture ;—that, being thirsty, she drank the sweet water it contained, and intending to eat the inner kernel, brought the nut home and placed it in a corner of the wall, where, if not removed, she said it ought still to be. If there was any fault which she had ever committed, it was that, and no other, for she could not accuse herself of any impropriety. This was all that she did, and the symptoms which had appeared subsequently were the result of her partaking of the water of that cocoanut. This strange confession being made to the Rajah, he went and met the fakir ; and to sift the matter to the bottom,

21

he made minute inquiries. "Sire, your many perplexing questions," observed the fakir, "evince a tendency to entangle and involve me in some guilt, and perhaps to deprive me of my child. It was for this reason that I did not wish to resign my liberty and happiness where I could enjoy both undisturbed in my solitary cell. I have told your highness that I had asked three gifts from God ; first, that I might have a child, then that I might obtain wealth, and lastly, that he would grant me a wife. When the inundation was high, and I was up to the neck in water, a cocoanut passed where I stood. Feeling thirsty, I took the cocoanut, and with a stick made a passage for the water. When I had drank the half, I closed the aperture with a stick, and as I dropped it into the river, my prayer was that whoever drank that water might give birth to a child. I have told you already how God was pleased to send me a child, and with him wealth, and that my last prayer has not yet been answered."

All these circumstances being well weighed in the Rajah's mind, he narrated the whole subject to his wife, the Ranee, when they came to the conclusion that their daughter was fated to be the wife of the fakir, and that on that account they ought to do nothing to impede their nuptials, or oppose the workings of providence. The Rajah then took the cocoanut to the fakir, and before showing it to him, asked if he could identify the nut out of which he had drank ? He affirmed that he could. Hereupon the cocoanut was produced, and by its marks and the identical stick, the branch of a certain tree, he pronounced it to be the very one used by him. The Rajah now disclosed the other incidents mentioned before, and concluded by saying that the child was his, and she who had drank the water of the cocoanut, was his own daughter, and he would therefore give her to be the wife of the fakir. That what God had done so wonderfully in his mysterious providence, should be confirmed by a public marriage. This was done shortly after with the pomp and festivity which generally attend such occasions.

The fakir, though raised to affluence and a position of honor in the Court, never forgot that it was possible to get all things by prayer.

THE TWO SISTERS—DOOKHEE AND SOOKHEE.

A N independent chief who held sway over a large territory covered with wide-spread undulating hills, was celebrated for his peaceful tendencies, his love and care of his subjects, fondness for field sports, and his active benevolence. He had two daughters, whose respective names were *Dookhee* and *Sookhee*, or Distress and Comfort. On account of the isolated situation of his country, and his own natural love of peace, he was induced to marry his daughters to worthy and high born men of his Court. After a few years, the chief died, as also the husband of Dookhee, who departed leaving a young daughter behind him. Dookhee was living with her daughter in great want; so reduced was she in her circumstances, that she had a small bungalow built on a mound formed by the ruins of some houses. Here she passed her days, being occasionally helped by the *Mundul*, or head man of the village, and the *Gomasta*, or writer's family, with a small quantity of rice, vegetables, and greens. These faithful men were once in the service of her father, and they therefore, in gratitude to his memory, paid some attention to the wants of his bereaved daughter. Dookhee one day communicated to the *Gomasta* and the *Mundul* her desire to visit her sister Sookhee, who was in a prosperous condition, and might render her some help. They advised her to go, saying, that the interview might tend to her benefit. With this advice, they gave her,—the one a two anna piece, and the other a four anna coin, to help her to prosecute her intended journey. On arriving at the house of her sister, she was announced, but Sookhee repudiated all connection with her, exclaiming, "Who is my sister, that *chandal dhangur*, that witch my sister? Send that low person away." After a short time, however, she commanded her servants to call her back. On her going in, Dookhee saw her sister seated on a costly chair, her feet resting on a stool, and her unfastened hair flowing down and covering the back of the chair, while two maids were employed in combing, oiling, and dressing it. She was desired to occupy herself with the same performance. Engaged in this manner for full three hours, her child crying from hunger, herself feeling weary after her journey, and yet not finding her sister offer any refreshment to herself or her child, poor Dookhee felt deeply grieved to think that her sister's heart had grown so callous, and she had become quite a different person to what she was before. After the tedious work of playing with her hair idly for several hours, Sookhee ordered her maids to give this woman and her child a seer of broken rice. When Dookhee was departing, after the receipt of this beggarly donation, she was called back, and told that she had not dressed her hair properly; therefore she must do the work over again. After the expiration of another hour, on dismissing Dookhee, her sister told her servant to take back half the quantity of rice from the woman, on account of her slovenly work. Going away from her sister's, Dookhee wept bitter tears on the road, reflecting sadly and mournfully on her reception. The Nazir, who was in her father's service, seeing her pass his house, called out to her, "Who is that, is it Dookhee? Come here my child. Where have you been?" Poor Dookhee, with a heart rent with grief, obeyed the summons, and in doing so, told her sister's treatment of her, and the help she had obtained for herself and her daughter. The Nazir, who was a man of tender sensibilities, was moved on hearing her sad story. The kind man and his wife paid her all attention, tenderly alleviating her sorrow, fed her with the choicest viands their larder contained, and gave her and her child a suit of decent clothes, with some money at parting. She went back to her house, and seeing her kind well-wishers, the *Gomasta* and *Mundul*, ready to greet and welcome her home, she, on being questioned, repeated her short tale of disappointment. They were stunned to hear it, and felt sincerely for her troubles. The daughter, now growing up to years of maturity, would assist her mother by various little helps which, according to her capacity, she gave cheerfully. She went one day far into the fields and forest, to gather withered branches, and pick up greens which grow luxuriantly on the surface of tanks. Having collected a sufficiency of sticks for fuel, and gathered several kinds of greens, she made them into a large bundle; but how was she to lift it up on her head, for without that she could not carry it away! At this time, her guardian angel, disguised as a very old man, was seen approaching her, supported by a walking cane. He saluted her, " What do you want my child?" She told him, she was powerless to lift the heavy load. He entered into conversation with her, regarding what relations she had, and what were the circumstances in which they were placed, asking if she were desirous of marrying, for he was able to provide her with a good man for her husband. She informed the old man of what he was desirous of learning, and consented to his proposal, believing it would be the means of relieving her mother. The man asked her to come again after two days to the forest, then lifting the bundle, and saying she would feel it light as a feather, he disappeared. Her mother was all this time in great anguish of mind, seeing that evening was deepening, and her child had not come back. She paced the compound, going in and out of the house full of anxiety and apprehension for the safety of her daughter, until she faintly discerned a figure at a considerable distance, coming toward the house. When the figure, advancing nearer, became more distinct, and the mother recognising her daughter, ran up to her and said—" My poor child, why were you so late in the forest? Had you no fear of wild animals? What a load you have on your head. Come, I will relieve you." Saying which, she lifted the bundle and placed it on her own head, remarking that it was heavy for her to bear, and must consequently have been much more so for her poor child. The daughter said, she did not find it heavy at all. Going home, she boiled a little rice, fried the greens, and made a supper upon that, which, if not dainty, appeased their hunger and invited sleep. As she had promised, the daughter went again to the forest on the third day, and having collected a bundle of twigs, and picked up some greens from the surface of the tanks, she halted to see if her old friend would again help her. Just then she saw the old man approaching by the same path as before. When he had come up to her, he told her to leave her bundle where it was, and follow him. Going through the forest by his side, she passed many wild animals, and the girl shrunk with fear at their savage looks and fearful howl, but the old man pacified her, saying that for her they were harmless as lambs. After a two hours' journey, the old man conducted her into a superb house, furnished with the costliest articles; moreover, passing through one of the rooms, she saw a man of uncommon beauty, sleeping on a silver bedstead. After she had noticed these things in thoughtful silence, he took her back to the forest, where her bundle lay. Helping her to lift it, the mysterious old man inserted in it a bag of money, saying her mother must employ it in erecting a house, and on preparations for the wedding. Everything being ready, Dookhee invited her friends, and at the proper time the forest friend brought with him a prince of remarkable beauty, gorgeously dressed, and with a splendid retinue. The wedding was kept up in a style of grandeur, and with a prodigality of entertainment befitting the rank and reputed wealth of the prince. Sookhee began during the festival to enquire after her sister. Just then, Dookhee made her appearance, and saluted her thus; "Sister, why do you enquire after me? I am neither worthy of your regard **nor your** notice, for I am she **whom** you called by every **opprobrious** epithet, and **to** relieve whose distress you gave her **some** broken rice." Sookhee hung **down** her head **in** shame **and** sorrow. **Her** unsisterly conduct was sufficiently rebuked before a large **company of respectable** people, who witnessed her humiliation and **contrition.** The friends who **were** entertained so sumptuously, **had for** a week or two no **other subject of** conversation but the **splendid preparations for the wedding, the** rich treat, and **the excellent music ; while the unnatural conduct** of Sookhee towards Dookhee was **commented upon, and** abundant reproaches **were showered upon the delinquent, but** the mead of praise was lavished on Dookhee, **for the amiable** traits of her character, **her forbearance and patience, and her** charitable disposition.

Several **years** elapsed, **during which the circumstances of** Dookhee **improved,** but the **increase of wealth and comfort did** not corrupt the heart of Dookhee nor render it callous. **She** had an ear for every tale of sorrow, and while relieving distress **with alacrity, she** sympathised with the **sufferers, nor** withal was **she given to slander, but spoke words of comfort and** kindly greeting. **On the other hand, time wrought a painful** revolution **in the condition of Sookhee and her** husband. They **were so reduced by poverty, that their** houses and estates, **with** everything **they** possessed, were sold to support them. They were now in rags and without shoes, and in this distress her husband told Sookhee, **that if she could give him a clean suit** of dress, **he would go and seek assistance from Dook hee, for she** was above want ; **and might** pity **their** destitution. He went **with slow faltering steps to the** house of Dookhee, not knowing **what his reception might be ; and** with scarcely courage enough **to lift up his head and** announce to the servant **that he** wished **an interview with the** mistress of the house. Some of the old servants, recognising him, though **so sadly** changed in face **and** dress, hastened into the **house, and** informed Dookhee that the husband **of her sister** was at the gate in poor clothes, barefooted, and with a haggard look. She desired her servants to bring him in immediately. Dookhee, seeing the affecting change both in his looks and condition, was moved to copious tears of sorrow. She upbraided him, not for the treatment she had received from her sister, (for the hand of God was heavy upon them,) but for his delay in coming to her, and informing her of their ill-fortune. She ordered some clothes to be given him, gave some for her sister, and when he had eaten, desired that they would not scruple to come and make her house and fortune their own. They were grieved and mortified, but as sorrow and regret for past errors often have a beneficial effect in curing bad habits, they felt happier than ever for being better persons.

A FOX AND AN ELEPHANT.

A SHREWD fox having motives of self interest, became very intimate with an elephant. In their frequent meetings, the fox diligently informed the elephant of the fields where he might obtain the best fodder, and revel among the most luxuriant crops. The fox having matured his plans, had an audience one day with the prince of the foxes, urging that his lank body and decayed strength, required the flesh of a living elephant for their restoration. The prince was annoyed to hear of this impracticable request, but as he could not, without sacrificing his dignity as chief, remain indifferent to the complaint preferred, he convened a meeting of foxes, at which he demanded if there was any among them bold and valorous enough to sally forth and procure the flesh of a living elephant. The artful fox, hearing this order, came forward, and with an erect gait and a proud bearing, signified by a prolonged howl, his willingness to execute the undertaking. Before proceeding however, to accomplish his task, he told the prince of the foxes, that he should keep his subjects under strict control during the time he was occupied in hunting, nor even after he had secured his game, should any fox, unless he heard the previously concerted sign, make the least noise.

Leaving these instructions behind him, the fox, with sly looks, and cunning steps, marched out in the direction where he was sure to meet with his friend, the elephant. Saluting the elephant with winning smiles and flattering speeches, he told him he had seen that morning a fine field thickly planted with large sugar-canes, and that if he desired it, he would conduct him to the spot. The elephant was very much pleased with this news. He placed himself willingly under the guidance of his friend. The fox marched onwards till he came within sight of a *jheel*, or swamp, beyond which the sugar-canes grew temptingly. To show the sincerity of his friendship, the fox desired the elephant to wait on the firm ground where he stood, and that he would advance and try the softness of the ground where a path led through the *jheel* to the cane field. The fox traversed the swamp, and coming back, told his friend that it was practicable to cross. The fox led the way, but the great weight of the elephant could not be sustained by the flimsy layer of earth, which encrusted the soft clay below, and his feet began to sink. He called out to the fox, telling him the ground would not do, and that he must go back, but the fox encouraged him to go on, saying that the ground where he was standing was particularly marshy and soft, but he would find firmer footing if he stepped a little further on to the place where he stood. The elephant struggled and waded through his difficult journey, but instead of finding the ground improve, he was inextricably buried up to his hips in the marsh. The fox ran to his assistance, and began to pull him by the tail and ears alternately, but finding all his powers of no avail, he asked him if he might call for his

22

fellows to assist him. Having obtained the sanction of the elephant, he gave many loud preconcerted *hoahs*, and in a short time, scores of foxes arrived, and surrounded the helpless animal, who was soon overpowered and eaten. The elephant made these reflections before expiring : " It is always unwise and unsafe to form improper acquaintances, and cultivate friendship with people between whose nature and our own there is great disparity, nor to give easy credence to the advice of our enemies, who flatter but to destroy."

A PEA-SELLER AND HIS WIFE.

A PEA-SELLER, to whom nature had given no grace of person, nor bestowed any mental endowments, made up for these deficiencies by a large share of physical strength and energy. His wife, too, if not gifted by nature with personal attractions, had, by constant companionship and intercourse with her husband, acquired his shrewdness and penetration. Though their trade was humble, and yielded but a small profit, the pea-seller had, by skill and economy, saved a small amount, and investing it in some other speculations, and more especially in loans of money, he became in time noted as a small capitalist in the place where he was conducting business. He had a comfortable house to live in, a well from which to draw water for culinary purposes, and near the well stood a large tamarind tree, on a branch of which some hornets had made a large hive. One night, a thief got into the house, and whilst trying to open a latch of the door, was observed by the pea-seller and his wife, who were awake at the time, and guessed that some one had entered their dwelling. Shrewdly guessing his purpose, the wife spoke in a whisper, which, however, was sufficiently audible to her husband and the robber, asking where the money box was concealed, the husband replied that the box was fastened to a branch of the tamarind tree near the well. The robber, obtaining by chance this information which he was so desirous of learning, abandoned the thought of getting into the house. He went under the tamarind tree, and looking up, discovered by the reflection of the moonbeams, that something like a box was hanging to one of the branches. He climbed the tree with agility, and just as he had put out his hand and seized the hive, the hornets who were disturbed in their night's repose, flew in numbers to resist the wanton attack. They alighted on his face, hands, and back, inflicting a hundred wounds at once, against the torture of which the robber who could not stand, let go his hold of the tree, and fell with a loud splash into the well beneath, smarting. There smarting from the stings, he began to kick and buffet the water for some time. The pea-seller, knowing that the robber was safe, let the night pass away quietly, only now and then inquiring who could be bathing at that hour in his well. The next morning the robber was taken up and consigned to the stocks. By his shrewdness and penetration, the pea-seller saved his own and the life of his wife and preserved his property, showing us that every talent has its use, and that our gifts, of whatever degree and quality they may be, are adapted to our special wants.

A CROCODILE AND FOX.

A STRONG friendship, by mutual kind offices and attention, was contracted between a crocodile and a fox. Their intimacy was not, however, of long duration, for the crocodile capriciously took offence at the remissness of the fox, in rendering him some service upon which he had fully calculated. The crocodile resolved on the destruction of the fox, and to execute his design, waited near the ghât to which the fox resorted for the purpose of bathing, or drinking. The fox, descending the ghât with a secret presentiment of harm, went down cautiously, and when near the water's brink, he began to lap it with erect ears and vigilant eyes. The crocodile, though himself invisible in the muddy water, could discern every object near the bank. He laid hold of one leg of the fox with a spring, and was dragging him away, when the fox exclaimed—" I was prudent to put my cane first into the water, to ascertain its depth, or my leg might have been caught by the fellow. Let him take away my cane; it is of small consequence." Hearing this, the crocodile felt disappointed and vexed, and in his annoyance, let go his hold of the leg of the fox. The fox, on being extricated from the sharp jaws of his foe, ran up the flight of steps, and called out to the crocodile, " You fool, does a fox ever walk with a cane ?"

The crocodile watched diligently for an opportunity of revenging himself on the fox for his deception and taunts. He therefore crept slowly along, one day, and went quietly into the house of the fox, where he remained silently in the corner, expecting that as soon as the fox returned home after his ramble, he would pounce upon him, and show him the strength of his jaws. The fox, going back to his residence, merrily wagging his tail, stood still as soon as he smelt a fishy odour, and beginning to snuff the air and cock his ears, spoke thus : " House, house, why do you not welcome me home this evening ? I believe there must be somebody within." The crocodile listened for some time, and then thought that he might make a response for the house. He called out to the fox in a disguised voice, asking him to come into his own house as he was wont to do every evening. The fox replied, " Thou fool, does a house ever speak ? I know thy treacherous voice, and thy evil design ; so adieu."

Baffled in this scheme also, the crocodile thought of another plan to catch the fox. In a field where the bones of dead animals lay strewed bleaching in the sun, and which the fox visited for the purpose of feeding on carrion, the crocodile went and stretched himself down, remaining there for hours showing no signs of life and animation, waiting for the fox. The fox, seeing the crocodile, exclaimed, "This fellow is surely feigning, for dead crocodiles generally turn on their back, and shake their toes." The crocodile heard this speech, and reasoned, that he might as well turn over and confirm the belief of the fox by dispelling his doubts. No sooner had he began to give indications of extinct life as he thought, than the fox sung out, "Thou fool, does a dead animal ever move, or has it the power of turning over?" Saying which he trotted away.

The crocodile was very much mortified with his repeated failures, but still he would not abandon his malicious design, and knowing the familiar haunts of the fox, he went to a field covered with tall grass not very far from the banks of the river, where he thought of lying concealed and waiting for the fox to pass. He did so, and watching him from sun-rise to noon, he grew weary, and sleep overtook him. The fox, in the mean time, as he travelled through the field, saw the crocodile taking a nap in the sun-shine, surrounded with a quantity of dry grass and weeds; so he went and procured some fire with which he ignited the grass, and presently the whole field began to burn. The crocodile, who was bent on the destruction of another, fell into the snare himself. The weapons of malice, and the shafts of injury which we aim at others, often rebound fatally upon ourselves.

THE TWO FRIENDS.

THERE were two persons who had a sincere attachment for each other; this sentiment time matured into ardent regard, and the two men were known to be inseparable companions and bosom friends. The one had, however, contracted a habit of intemperance, whilst the other made long and loud prayers in thronged places every day, from no sincerity of heart, but rather as an ostentatious display, and from motives of worldly aggrandisement. The praying man missed no opportunity of telling his friend of the evils of drunkenness, in order to dissuade him from a practice so fraught with harm to his health, injury to his reputation, and so detrimental to the comfort, peace, and the happiness of his family;—dwelling on the results which his indulgence in that vice was calculated to produce. He urged him to reflect on the subject, to abandon what was so great an evil, and to pursue the path of sobriety and righteousness. The unwearied and wholesome counsels of his friend, after some time, had a beneficial effect on the mind of the drunkard, and he reformed. He gave up the bad habit entirely, became a man of sincere prayer, and of unostentatious piety; but though the practice was abandoned, he was still seen to frequent the haunts of the devotees of Bacchus, but with what motive, that was a secret unknown to his associates. His friend still continued to remonstrate with him against his visiting public houses, thinking he had not entirely given up the habit of drinking.

These friends were going together a short journey on a certain day, when one of them, the man of long prayers, happening to find a bag of money on his path, was quite glad at his unexpected good fortune. Going still further on, the other man's foot hit against a **thorn** which **caused** severe pain. It **was** extracted, **but not** without some **difficulty** and suffering. Reflecting upon these favourable **and** adverse incidents **of the** journey, the man of long **prayers** co mmented upon **them,** drawing **the** conclusion, that **in God's** service, **his worshippers meet with** a reward even **in this** life and **receive** tokens of **his** generous favour and goodness, while the wicked-doe**rs** experience his displeasure, **meet with reverses, calamity, and** disappointment.

About this time **an angel** descended **with lightning** speed **and glowing with** radiant wings, enquired what they were disputing **about. This** inquiry **was** not instituted **from an** ignorance of what had actually **transpired**; for a spirit of a higher nature than man's is conversant with these things, some **of** their number being present on earth, while others receive **intelligence;** but **the question was put** with **a view to elicit conversation. The man of long prayers rehearsed all** the **circumstances that had transpired, giving a** short history of the past regarding his **friend and himself.** " I am the Angel Gabriel," said the ethereal visitant, **in a soft, rich, winning voice.** " I will explain to **you the true state of things. You, who make prayers** with a worldly **mind** and motive, **have** received **in that** bag a worldly reward, while this man's prayers, which **are sincere** and a real outpouring of the soul in humility and earnestness, have ascended to the paradise above, and been heard. The never-healing thorn of future **remorse** which would have rankled **in the bosom of this man** through eternity, has been averted **by this smaller measure** of punishment." Finishing **this short address, the angel** took his flight, wrapped **up in** the **folds of the clouds,** leaving the two **friends silent** and impressed.

[This story was recited **to me by a** person of **Sirdhana, the** province of **Begum** Shumroe, wife **of a French Officer. As** she was a Catholic, she invited some Italian priests who **settled in the country and were** supported by her. **This story, therefore, appears to have a Christian idea** for its origin.]

A BRAHMIN, A SANDAL WOOD, AND WILD TREES.

A BRAHMIN, being one of the principal persons, is never lost sight of, whatever festival, ceremony, or entertainment may be given in his district within the range of ten or twelve miles, be it the celebration of a marriage, a funeral dinner, or a *poojah*. A Brahmin was accordingly invited by a Prince to a sumptuous dinner. Going to the entertainment, he had an unpleasant interview with a formidable tiger that was dozing in a field on some soft tufts of grass, which grew plentifully on the spot, and where he lay as if reclining on a bed of ease and comfort. The Brahmin thought if he advanced any further, the rustling of the grass, or the decayed fallen leaves under his feet might rouse the terrible enemy; he began, therefore, to beat a retreat, facing the foe, but walking backwards with a tread as soft and light as fear could make it. With all his vigilance, however, the tiger was up, for though his eyes were closed, his nasal organs were at work, and the smell of a human being, wafted to him on the breeze, was so delectable to his senses that he awoke from his noon-day siesta, and stretching his body to shake off his drowsiness that he might be the better able to run in pursuit of his prize, he sprang forward. The Brahmin, shaking with terror, ran as well as he could to the nearest tree in the neighbourhood with a view to climb beyond the spring of the tiger, but finding the old tree had a cavity large enough to conceal him, he took shelter in the bosom of the tree. By good fortune it happened that it was a *sandal* tree, which diffused its odour through the air, and the tiger thereby lost all traces of the human being.

The Brahmin, who had remained concealed in the tree throughout the night, got out in the morning, and went to the **Rajah's** entertainment. Wherever he seated himself in the company of the Rajah's numerous guests, a strong smell of the sandal wood was emitted from his person. The visitors and the Rajah began to inquire from whom it came, because the perfume scented the whole palace. All denied, but the Brahmin came forward and recounted all that had happened to him the day before on his journey to the *Rajbari*. The Rajah was gratified to hear of the valuable tree, which stood not many miles from his residence. He ordered his sappers and miners to bring away every chip of the wood, together with the roots. While this was being done, the servants of the Rajah, knowing that the entertainment at the *Rajbari* would last for several days, cut down large numbers of wild flowering plants, wherewith to adorn the festive saloon.

There were two wild trees which grew in the vicinity of the sandal tree. They bore an inveterate antipathy to the sandal tree, the scented shrubs, and the richly coloured flowers of the underwood, on account of the commendation they received from every traveller who journeyed by that path, while none regarded the two wild trees, but passed them with contemptuous neglect. When such a fate overtook the flowering shrubs and the scented sandal, the two wild trees gave voice to their own reflections—" Brother," says the one wild tree to the other, " we had long envied the condition and prosperity of our neighbours, but we see that their beauty and attractions have proved a snare to them. The flowering shrubs have been robbed of their ornaments and left bleeding at every pore by the wounds inflicted by cruel men, and the proud sandal has been rooted out of the place, no longer to mock our humble birth and lonely condition. It is true that we could not bear to see the homage paid to the sandal and the flowers, by men and women who adorned their person and took away chips of the tree as a great treasure in their pockets, praising too and commending

23

them in our hearing, while we were considered insignificant. Would we now wish to have been in their situation ? Is it not rather better with all our imperfections to be enjoying health, life, and an undisturbed tranquillity ? Though we bear no external beauty, and our hearts send forth no fragrant sigh to enrich the breeze, or delight the hearts of human beings, we are crowned with luxuriant foliage, and bear flowers useful to the feathery tribes ; thousands of birds are fed by us ; and beneath our sheltering arms they pass the dark perilous hours of night in safety. In the morning and at noon, they repay us with a thousand mellow notes and thrilling melodies. At our feet, how often the weary tenants of the woods have rested protected from the noonday sun and the pelting rain ; have they not looked up to us with eyes expressive of gratitude ? We have not been, therefore, altogether useless in the sphere and condition in which our lot was cast."

A splinter of the sandal wood which had fallen on the ground and remained there, hearing this pompous speech of the wild tree, made this reproving answer : " Ye wave your branches proudly now that the noble and worthy ones of the forest have fallen. Before their presenc ye were humble and silent. Your base hearts cannot appreciate the nobility of theirs, nor are you taught to value the dignity there is in exhaling our very existence away, in doing good to others, in making others happy, and answering the object of our creation, and thereby leaving a fragrant memory behind us."

A GARDENER AND A WILD BRINJAL PLANT.

A PRINCE of Hindustan had a splendid garden, in which grew all sorts of fruit trees, indigenous as well as of foreign culture; with flower beds laid out with choice exotics, and some valuable plants of Indian growth; pretty parterres dividing the plots, and arbours, over which trailed creepers of a variety of forms and diverse foliage. The gardener who superintended the pleasure grounds, having gone one day to a distant market through the adjacent fields, saw a wild brinjal plant which had sprung up through a dense undergrowth of grass. The wild brinjal, seeing the head gardener of the Prince pass, humbly solicited that his generous heart, which had an affection for plants of all tribes, from the stately palmyra to the humble grass; from the wide-spread banian to the lotus, would compassionate his forlorn and destitute condition, for he was choked to death by the smothering embrace of the grass, and could not extract a drop of moisture for his sustenance, on the spot where he was growing, every particle of nutriment being approriated by the wild grass. The brinjal requested, therefore, that the gardener would be so good as to transplant him to a corner of the Prince's garden, that he might be able to breathe there more freely, and draw only such nourishment from the soil as was not needed by other families of the garden, not doubting that such a generous act would bring good fortune to the gardener, as good deeds were never lost. The gardener's heart was so softened by this speech of humility and flattery, that he transplanted the brinjal to a remote corner of the garden.

The garden, being well manured and properly irrigated, the wild brinjal grew and spread rapidly, covering a surface of fifty feet square with his progeny of children and grand-children, within the space of six months. In this rapid extension, the wild plant had destroyed several nursery plants, and a few other hardy ones too.

The prince, visiting the garden after some months, and going towards the nursery one evening, discovered the remissness and neglect of his gardener who permitted the growth of the wild brinjal, thereby causing the destruction of several valuable plants. Reproving the gardener for his carelessness, he dismissed him from the superintendence of the garden and his service. The gardener when dismissed from his post, passed the brinjal, and upbraided the plant for his ill advice, in tempting him to act against his own judgment, for he knew too well that no good could result from planting him in the garden. The plant replied, "Knowing my evil propensities were you wisely persuaded by my talk? My presence is never tolerated in any well kept garden. All wise gardeners know that where I flourish, there decay and destruction is wrought on all the plants, and a faithful man's duty is to exclude a baneful plant from those that are good and valuable."

A HERON AND A KINGFISHER.

A HERON, who had, for some time during the dry season, when the river was low, and tanks, jheels, and canals nearly dry, enjoyed an abundance of good fare, for he could then make use of his long legs and go hither and thither in pursuit of small fishes sporting in shallow water, found that the tide of good luck had ebbed as the tide of the river had risen with the rainy season. His aquariums had been so much inundated that he found it hard to get a living any where. The river, the jheels, and the tanks, became equally inaccessible to him, nor, from the depth of water which covered them, could he pick up even a single tiny fish to keep him from starvation. This misfortune made him thoughtful and unhappy, and he could see by the reflection on the water that his lank figure was getting every day still more attenuated. In this, distress, he thought of visiting the kingfisher, that he might cultivate his acquaintance, and beg assistance in the dark hour of his necessity. " Friend, we are of the same profession and pursuit, and I might say of almost the same lineage ; we ought to have more sympathy and regard for each other than we have hitherto shown, and this for a still more cogent reason, for should any misfortune happen to you, who could help you so well as I ? Were you to fall sick, and thereby be unable to fish, I would be the very person who could supply you with food every day. Again, in the dry season, when the water is too shallow and you cannot plunge and dive safely for your food, and can obtain by chance alone a scanty fare now and then, you would at such times know the value of my friendship, which could keep your larder replenished. As good and bad fortune alternately happen to all, so it is my turn to experience just now some difficulty in fishing when the country is submerged. Should you help me now and then with a little out of the abundant quantity you get, and thus save me from trouble and starvation, you may calculate on my friendship, and trust to my assistance in all times of need." The kingfisher, who had a generous heart, and who pitied the heron, desired him to live in his neighbourhood during the season of scarcity. Thus the kingfisher supplied food to the heron for three months, after which, as the water began to recede from the field, and the jheels, tanks, and canals, began to assume a definite outline of form, the heron bid his friend good-bye, with a promise of coming to his help so soon as the dry season would render it necessary. Though the kingfisher did not actually need the heron's assistance, still he waited for some months to ascertain if there could be found a single spark of gratitude warming the bosom of a heron. A fortnight after the kingfisher had indulged these thoughts, the heron by accident came and roosted for the night on the very cotton tree in which the kingfisher lived. Opening his eyes in the morning with some surprise at the proximity of the kingfisher, the heron exclaimed, "Friend, your legs are in ugly contrast with your body. Pray, why are they so black?" "You ungrateful being! every thing now appears black and ugly, because your design has been accomplished, and you have gained your object. You are a worthless being, with whom I will not deign to hold any further conversation, so fly away and conceal your mean person in stagnant pools and among putrid weeds."

THE JUNGLE FEVER AND THE COBWEB.

A POOR wood-cutter, who supported himself and his family with much toil and difficulty by hewing trees, went into the Sunderbuns for the prosecution of his work. The jungle fever and his friend the cobweb, happening to travel through that forest together, the fever told the cobweb that he was going to fasten himself on the wood-cutter, because his poverty could not provide the means of repelling him, for he could not afford to call in a doctor. He advised his friend the cobweb not to enter humble dwellings, for his situation in such a house would be so low as to be within the reach of every man's arm, whose caprice might place him in constant jeopardy. He advised the cobweb to go therefore to the house of a Prince. The jungle fever went and perched himself on the wood-cutter, who felt a shivering and pains over his body, and with many heavy *hos* and *hás*, he was forced to give up his occupation and descend from the tree. The wood-cutter going home, took nothing to provide for the wants of his family. He suffered the whole night from fever, but the cries of his children for food induced him in the morning, though still indisposed, to take up his tools and go out to work. Though shivering under the influence of the fever, the thought of his starving family forced him into vigorous exertion. He worked hard and sweated profusely under the operation. The fever could not any longer stand this effort to throw him off. His incessant wrestling with the fever subdued him completely, and he was obliged to leave the wood-cutter. The cobweb, who calculated upon remaining undisturbed in the residence of the prince, was disappointed, for the first thing which a *mehter*, or sweeper did in the morning, was to strike the cobweb with a broom several times till it was dislodged from the roof and flung out of the window. The two friends, meeting each other again afterwards, related about their want of success, coming to a unanimous conclusion that it was a great error to think that fever could remain undisturbed on the person of poor man, or that the cobweb's most tranquil residence was the house of a prince. The cobweb now addressed his friend and tendered this advice—" Friend, I think you ought to visit the house of a Prince, where you will be highly honored with rich covering and receive the respectful attentions of doctors, noblemen, and ladies of rank. I will content myself by going into the house of this poor wood-cutter, whose poverty will give him no time to think of me and little leisure to occupy himself with the labour of hunting me out from his residence." Being thus resolved, the fever went and settled on the person of a Prince. The Prince, shivering with the fever, covered himself with rich shawls, and called for several doctors, who made much of the sickness and paid great attention to the patient. The cobweb visited the house of the wood-cutter, and not content with lodging in one corner of the roof, spread his domain all over the ceiling with boldness, fully assured that the poor were so occupied as to take no notice of his presence, and if his intrusion was discovered, the poor man had scarcely sufficient time to drive him out from his net-works which he had spread widely through every nook and corner of the ceiling.

THE SON OF **AN** HONEST MAN.

AN honest *gresto*, or family **man,** who on his deathbed left a son and **a wife** behind, advised his son about the small sum which he had honestly acquired, and which he had hitherto spent prudently, saying that though he might **be compelled to** take **service, and his** wages might be very small, he should take employment under no one except an honest man. **The son** and mother lived **with** the strictest economy for some months, but as the money **diminished, the son was** forced to look **out for a** situation. Knowing that there **was** scarcely a single honest man **in the village in w**hich he was residing, **he** thought of visiting the adjacent town, in order to secure the success of his intentions.

He called at a respectable man's house, asking for employment, and telling him **that** he did not mind what pay he **might obtain, as that was not of any** great consideration to **him,** but he was anxious to secure a place under a man of probity. The great man told the youngster that he was a merchant, **and that** there **was not much** honesty in a profession like his, desiring him at the **same** time to visit his younger brother, who was in another **country, and who was** the most likely person to engage his services. The young man **journey-**ed in search of the house, and was not long in finding out the place, but he was surprised to find the occupant of the house **not as** he **had** expected, a younger, but an older man in appearance, though he was the younger brother of the person to whom he **had at first applied** for situation. The young man stated the terms on which he was desirous of engaging himself. The rich man told him his vocation was that of an usurer, and **on** that account he could not undertake to be honest. The rich **man desired him to** go to a certain country, where his youngest **brother was residing, as** he would be the most suitable person, and with him the young man might take service and **find a** congenial master. The honest man's son travelled, and discovered the residence of a very old man, although he was the youngest of the three brothers. He found the man occupied in counting *cowries*, or shells. Making the purport of his **visit known** to him, the old man told him that he was **not** in affluent circumstances to employ more than one **person, but** the young man solicited and **prayed hard for** service in his house, **telling him that it was the** dying **request** of his father to decline **serving a man who** had got rich by dishonest means, however tempting the wages might be, but to serve an honest man, though the salary might be very small. The old man, finding it was not easy to send him away, agreed to employ him for a few quadruple of *cowries* per month. After the young **man** had **served him** for three months, **he asked the honest man to be permitted to** take leave for three days to go **and see how** his mother was doing. Before leaving the old man, **he** received all the *cowries* which became due to him on the day **of** his departure. After he had gone a day's journey, and come to a market which was half way from his village, **and** consider-**ed that the entire journey would occupy four days,** and he **could** not be punctual to his promise, he gave up the thought of **going to** see his mother just then, but resolved upon doing so after the servitude of six months, when he would be entitled to six days' leave. **Finding a** woman from his village in the market, he purchased **a lime** for his mother, and sending it by her, he spent **the rest** of his *cowries* in getting a dinner for himself and a clean shave of his chin. Going back to his employer on the second day, and before his leave had expired, the old man was surprised to see him return so soon, but the young man explained the reason of his speedy arrival. He continued in his service for six months, faithfully discharging his duties, **but** within that period, a Prince of the place where his mother resided, being laid up with an obstinate disease, a *hakim*, or doctor,

24

prescribed certain remedies to be administered with the juice of lemon; but as the Prince's recovery depended on that draught, and it was not obtainable throughout the country, the Prince by beat of a drum made his want known to the public, and offered a very handsome reward to the person who would furnish it. The neighbours of the woman who had a lime from her son, ran and communicated the intelligence to her, desiring her to be expeditious in tendering the fruit to the Prince. She had stuck it into the roof of her hut, and taking it out, she bore it to the palace. The medicine being duly administered according to prescription, the Prince's recovery was rapid. When quite well, he made her a present of a house, land, and a large sum of money. She began to live in comfort, and was surrounded with all that her heart could desire, yet these could not make up for the absence of her son, for whom she sighed daily, longing to know where he was, and how he was employed, but all inquiries on that head terminated in disappointment, and her heart remained weighed down with sorrow. The young man was equally desirous of seeing his mother. Now that six months had expired, and he was privileged to obtain six days' leave, he asked and obtained his employer's permission to visit her.

The old man counted out the shells which were due to him for the six months he had served. With his earnings he got himself shaved, bought some light refreshment for the journey, and purchased a fish for his mother, to pickle and preserve which from taint, he procured a small quantity of salt. Travelling on his way with the fish and salt, he thought that it was a pity he had no knife with which to salt the fish. He went to some neighbouring cottages and asked for the loan of a knife. Some refused the loan, being too lazy to find out one, but a woman whose heart was full of the milk of kindness, drew one from the reed mat partition, and offered it. He divided the fish, and inserted the salt to preserve it, and while curing it, he discovered in the head of the fish, a gem of inestimable value which, by accident,

touching the iron knife lent him by the woman, transmuted it
into pure gold.

The instrument being returned to the owner, she was surprised to find it changed into gold. She hastened with joy to show
it to her neighbours, who, with herself, believed her strange
visitant to be a saint, to honor whom would be a privilege and
a meritorious work, they ran therefore to find him, but he had
gone beyond their reach and sight.

The honest youth met no other adventure or molestation in
his journey. In due time he arrived at his native village, and
not perceiving his maternal residence, inquired what had become of several matted cottages which existed not long ago in
that locality, and where the widow was who had an only son
who had gone out to work. To these queries the response
was that great changes had taken place in the village, by the
sudden elevation of the widow to affluence and comfort, for her
son had sent her an ordinary lemon as a present, which being
the means of saving the Prince from a dangerous indisposition,
he had rewarded her liberally, and had made her independent.
The son approached his mother's mansion with garments
which bespoke poverty and want; and fear made him feel
diffident in asking for admission of the warders, lest they should
disbelieve his assertion that he was the son of the owner. He
waited patiently for a short while, to see if he could discover
any familiar face coming forth from the house, to whom he
might confide his story and gain credence. A well known man
of the village who was employed by the widow, at length made
his appearance, and by him the glad tidings was borne to the
anxious mother. Being informed of his arrival, the widow ran
to meet the object of her only consolation on earth. The son
was soon locked in the mother's fond embrace. Streams of
tears ran down both their cheeks, but they were not the indications of sorrow, but of joy which had succeeded so suddenly to their late anxiety and apprehension. The mother
furnished him with all the necessaries of life which could add

to his happiness or comfort. Two days were spent joyously in recounting to each other the history of the past six months, after which, the time approached for him to return to the old man as he had promised; he accordingly left home after a few days, going to his employer in a comfortable boat. His employer welcomed him with cordiality, for he found him to be a truly faithful, diligent, and honest person, with whom he was well pleased, and with whose service he was satisfied. The young man informed him how the fortune of his mother was made by means of the honestly acquired *cowries* which had come to him from the coffers of an honest man; and how he himself had bought a wonderful fish with an invaluable jewel in its head. He was desirous of touching with the stone everything which the old man possessed, but his employer said that he was perfectly satisfied with his condition, and happy in it, knowing that God had placed him in that position. The young man warmly invited his employer to go and spend some weeks with them. He accepted the proposal with pleasure, intending to witness their happiness, and delight himself with the contemplation of the change wrought in their circumstances by an all-wise, beneficent, and gracious Providence. The mother was very glad to see and become acquainted with the good man who had taken care of her son, and who was always his wise counsellor. The honest man, after a residence of a few days, produced the gem with which he touched all their property and changed it into gold. He said it was their right to have the benefit of the stone, and not proper for him to aspire after, that which was not his property, for it would indicate his murmuring spirit, his dissatisfaction, and discontent. After spending a fortnight with them very happily, he took leave to go to his own country, promising to see them when business brought him again into their locality. By all that transpired in the life of the widow and her son, they learnt the lesson, that acting fairly and justly, in whatever sphere and condition of life we may be placed, meets with a reward in this world, either by an increase of property, or the pleasing self-satisfaction which it inspires, and which is of greater value still.

DHURM RAJAH.

A RAJAH'S father having died, it became imperative for him to give a dinner to one thousand and one persons, and to distribute alms among all classes of his guests. This circumstance being known to the bazar men, the confectioner, the cloth-merchant, the brazier, and the tyreman, they had all received their respective orders to furnish the *rajbari* with a large supply of their ware. Besides these men to whom instructions were communicated to furnish the necessaries in requisition for the obsequies, the Rajah's command was, that if any one brought any article expecting to earn a trifle on such an occasion, he would not disappoint them, but would purchase their goods. Tradesmen came flocking in during the whole course of the day with large quantities of their respective articles.

When all the guests had arrived, they were served with water to wash themselves, after which, a suit of clothes was given to each brahmin, with other necessary articles. The first course of the entertainment was rice and curry, after that, as a second course, tyre and rice were helped out to them. No sooner had the one thousand and one brahmin partaken of tyre and rice, then they fell down dead on the spot. The Rajah was very unhappy on account of this sad accident. He thought people would look upon him with abhorrence, as being the murderer of so many holy men, or at least, if not the actual perpetrator of such an atrocity, still as a man so profligate, that the performance of an act of piety was not permitted him, or that an audacious attempt was undertaken, and a fearful catastrophe betokened the displeasure of heaven.

This unfortunate event induced Dhurm Rajah to place the reins of his government in the hands of his Dewan, and to set out on a pilgrimage, and live secluded in some solitary forest, devoting himself to penance and prayer. He journeyed on for some days until he came in sight of a forest which had peculiar attractions for him, and there he resolved to spend the residue of his days in heavenly contemplation.

A sage resided in the forest, who was believed to go to paradise daily for the purpose of attending the court above. Dhurm Rajah wandered about the forest for two days, and on the third, he came in sight of the hut of this sage, on the back of which he remained concealed for the purpose of ascertaining the character of the person who resided therein. The sage's last visit to paradise being rather protracted, his wife asked him the reason why he stayed two days away from home. He replied, that "a pious Rajah who had recently given an entertainment to some brahmins, performing his duty as a son to his deceased father should, and doing an act of charity and piety, had met with a lamentable misfortune. The one thousand and one brahmins who had partaken of the tyre which Dhurm Rajah ordered to be served out to them, had fallen down dead the moment they had tasted it. "We have been very busy," —he said—" these two days in investigating the subject. We have been thinking who would be the right person on whom to lay the sin. When the tyre was being taken to the *rajbaree*, a vulture was flying with a putrid snake for his food over the head of the tyreman. The putrescent matter which dripped from the carcase, fell into a pot of tyre, and that tyre being poured out and mixed with other pots, envenomed the whole fluid, and caused the destruction of the brahmins. Were we to charge the snake, vulture, tyreman, or Rajah with the crime of their death? This question has engaged our thoughts for some time." The Rajah was gratified in obtaining a solution of what appeared to him very mysterious and inexplicable. He now thought of remaining a day longer in his concealment, that the further disclosure of the decisions of the ethereal court, which the sage might make to his wife, would enable him to learn to whom the crime had been imputed.

The Rajah enjoyed greater peace of mind and more satisfaction of heart, now that he knew that he was exonerated from the sin, and having more joy in his bosom, he felt a desire to ramble about the forest, as no one there was familiar with his person, and none therefore could lift up the finger of reproach against him. But he was not left long undisturbed even in such a retired spot, for a man issued out of the forest, having a vessel in his hand, who recognised the Rajah at a glance. The man exclaimed with surprise, and some fear, "Ha! what have I done to see this sinner's face in the morning; the man who has been the murderer of a thousand and one brahmins! What misfortune may befall me to-day!" Just as the man had spoken these words, and articulated these unjust accusations against the Rajah, the sin was recorded in the archives of heaven against that man. The Rajah went and hid himself again behind the house of the sage, waiting his return. The sage came back earlier than before, when he was asked by his wife the reason of his speedy reappearance. He replied that for three days and nights they were employed in discovering whose sin it was, when the Rajah going out one morning for a walk, met with a worthless reprobate, who was also sauntering about in the forest. On seeing Dhurm Rajah, he ejaculated that it was a misfortune to have beheld that morning the face of a great sinner who had slain more than one thousand brahmins. For this wicked speech, and presumptuous charge against the Rajah, on whom none of the judges of the heavenly court could place the smallest stigma, it was adjudged that the sin should be recorded in that man's name. "The reason why I have come back," he added, "earlier than before, is because the investigation has closed. Dhurm Rajah should now go back to his own kingdom, and execute the other rites and ceremonies as prescribed in the *shasters*, and then rule his subjects with equity and kindness, as he has hitherto done." Dhurm Rajah, hearing this from the place of his concealment, glided away from the forest silently but thoughtfully. He went to his own realm, where he resumed his station and office as before, pacified in his own mind that the sad catastrophe had happened by no sin of his, and which might have been intended to teach him lessons of wisdom and caution, not to judge others hastily, nor arrogate to himself the prerogatives of the Supreme Ruler of the Universe.

THE STORY OF A BADSHA.

THERE was a *Badsha*, who sat one evening in his verandah, and saw the wide sea extending before him in all directions, in the majesty of an interminable expanse, when a small craft came sailing from some island, and anchored at his very ghat. A *joghee*, or religious mendicant, issued from the craft and wended his way to the residence of the *Badsha*. The *Badsha* desired his Prime Minister, or Vizier, to inquire what business the *joghee* had with him. The man replied that he had come to sell three adages, which might, some time or other, be of great importance and use to His Highness. Being invited to the presence of the *Badsha*, after saluting him respectfully, he repeated the purport of his visit, and was asked what sum he desired for selling his three sayings. The *joghee* asked three thousand Rupees. The *Badsha* consenting to his terms, requested him to communicate them—" The first," he said, " is that to be awake is better than to sleep ; the second, that to be seated is better than to stand ; thirdly, it is better to walk than to sit." The *Badsha* asked if these were all that he had to communicate. The *joghee* said that his three adages were told, and that he had nothing to mention besides. The *Badsha* felt disappointed and chagrined that for these three simple sayings he would have to pay that high sum ; so out of vexation he pulled off a ring of that value from one of his fingers and flung it to the *joghee*. He, receiving the costly gem, retired from the durbar with expressions of thankfulness. The *Badsha*, in the mean time, going to his chamber, inscribed the words on the walls of his apartment, just before his bedstead. When he had gone to his dormitory for the night, and awoke in the morning, his eyes fell on the words, " to be awake is better than to sleep," he thought, that having spent so much on the maxims, it would be proper that he should test their value, and so he kept himself awake. Being awake, he read " to be seated is better than to stand ;" he accordingly seated himself. Again, as his eyes rested on the third inscription on the wall, " that it is better to walk than to sit," he got out of his room and began to stride about in the hall right earnestly. In this employment, he saw a gigantic African on a wall of the palace, who, having scaled it, brought the ladder over to the opposite side, and began to descend into the inner court. He then went on to the quarter where the *Shazadee*, or Princess, resided, and awaking her from sleep, they removed the cot, by doing which a secret door was opened, leading to another apartment which they entered. The *Badsha* followed them unperceived. Having gone after them, he found a superb palace and a pleasant garden which were much finer and costlier than those which he had erected. He now began to perceive that this structure was built by money which came out of his own purse, and done by his daughter who, being an only child, was indulged and gratified with all that she needed, or which her whim and fancy solicited. He then saw the African and the Princess, after spreading a carpet of the highest value, seat themselves to play a game of chess. Seeing their familiar intercourse, he went behind with his scimitar and decapitated both with one fell stroke. With his open sword he went on walking in the garden, when he discovered another African, brother to the former, of a still more stalwart

25

and Herculean build. The fellow, seeing the *Badsha* approaching with his naked sword, still reeking with gore, thought no doubt that he had slain his brother, and was now coming from that act of retribution to execute farther vengeance; so he grappled with him in a deadly contest. They wrestled and struggled from midnight till near dawn, neither succeeding in subduing his antagonist. Adam and Eve were passing about this time in the air above their heads, when Eve said to Adam, "See, the *Badsha's* life is in jeopardy, and he will in all probability lose it; his adversary is more powerful than he." Then Adam spoke to Eve in an audible voice that the *Badsha* might hear and follow the advice. He remarked that the *Badsha* was very forgetful in not remembering that the gallows stood not far from the spot, and all therefore which he had to do was to push his adversary forward till he brought him beneath the gallows, when he might fling its pendant rope over the neck of his foe. Having taken the hint, the *Badsha* wrestled with his adversary until he dragged him below the gallows, when he succeeded in placing the rope round his neck. After this performance, he discerned a woman coming to meet the African. She was found to be the daughter of the Vizier, who had come to keep her assignation with him. She coming up to the scaffold asked her expiring lover who it was that had hung him. He answered that for their sake, meaning her and the Princess, both he and his brother were brought to suffering and death. He desired her to put her little finger in his mouth to allay his pain. When she did so, he bit it off and then expired with it in his mouth. The wily daughter of the Vizier, having spied the *Badsha* at a distance retiring to his palace, and to conceal the cause of the loss of her finger, ran back to her house, where, throwing herself on her bed, she began to scream out, crying that the officer of the watch had entered her apartment with an intention to rob, but failing to execute his nefarious design, from her vigilance, he had cut off one of her fingers. This uproar brought her parents to her room, who, learning the cause of the tumult, ordered the immediate execution of the officer. When the officer was taken before the scaffold, the noise and bustle, consequent on such scenes, awoke the *Badsha*, who, having ascertained the reason, sent a message upbraiding the Vizier for his rashness in ordering the execution without first apprising him of his intention. The Vizier excused himself by saying, that when the finger of his child was destroyed by such a villain without reason or provocation, his ungovernable passion urged him to take an instant satisfaction.

The *Badsha*, who desired his Vizier to follow him, told him, that he would have found cause to regret the step which he was about to take, had he not prevented it. They went on together till they came to the quarters where the Vizier's daughter was residing. There he desired the Vizier to help him in lifting the cot on which his daughter slept, when they discovered a secret door into which the *Badsha* entered first, and then the Vizier followed. The Vizier began to be surprised how the *Badsha* came to know the privacies of his house. They continued the walk up to the garden, when the superb palace was visited, and the carpet of uncommon beauty and value was seen, with the bodies of the Princess and the African. The *Badsha* then conducted the silent, wondering minister up to the gallows, where he gave him his cane which had a curved handle. With that he desired him to open the mouth of the African, and the finger of the Vizier's daughter, with a ring on it, fell out. The *Badsha* now gave his sword to him, telling him to destroy and remove the object of his disgrace, and then to bury the two heads, but to bring back their bodies to him. The bodies being taken to the *Badsha* according to instruction, they were ordered to be exposed at the *chowk*, or the principal square of a bazar, and a person was set to watch if any one should say anything regarding the bodies, and to report on it.

A merchant who possessed great wealth, and carried on an extensive trade, had come to the country where the *Badsha* presided with his court. He had three daughters; they took a fancy to go out one evening in disguise as men, with a view to stroll about without restraint. They walked up to the spot where the bodies were exposed, when one of the sisters remarked before the corpses, that the men used to wear platted hair ; the second sister observed, that the men were in the habit of chewing beetle and of putting antimony to their eyes ; the youngest sister's remark was, that if she were the Africans, she might have shown some better fun. The man who watched the bodies, followed the three sisters to ascertain their residence. Having done so, he apprised the *Badsha* of what had transpired. The *Badsha* summoned the three daughters of the merchant that they might come and give the reason of their remarks. The merchant inquired of his daughters if they had been out on the previous day, and in what costume. They told their father of the disguise assumed by them, and what they had spoken about the two bodies exposed at the *chowk*. They assured their father that they were under no fear to appear before the *Badsha*, and to tell him the reason of those remarks. They were conveyed in covered palkees and placed before the durbar. The *Badsha* asked the first daughter how she had acquired the information that the Africans used to wear platted hair ? She answered that she had discovered some marks on their backs which clearly indicated that they had worn their hair after that fashion. The second daughter was asked how she came to know that they were in the habit of chewing beetle, and tinging their eyes with some black powder ? She replied their fingers bore marks of the beetle which they had frequently used, and the skirts of their garments which had been used to wipe the superabundance of the powder from the eyelids, indubitably proved the habit they had of colouring their eyelids. The third daughter was asked what fun it was which she would have shown if she were the Africans. She replied that she was willing to communicate the secret if the *Badsha* would first draw up twenty-one pitchers of water from a well, and pour their contents round the spring. The *Badsha* being pleased

with her wit and spirit, desired that the other two conveyances
might be taken back to the merchant's, while he sent his
Vizier with overtures of marriage to the father. The merchant's
consent being obtained, he was married to Farcoonda. Being
again interrogated about the interpretation of what she had expressed, she urged the condition on which she was willing to
disclose her secret. The *Badsha* felt annoyed that she persisted
in imposing a task which was beneath his dignity to perform.
Seeing him so headstrong on the point, she too became obstinate.
From vexation, he ordered the erection of a tower on one of the
rocks of the sea, which should possess a single aperture for venti-
lation, and be the medium of communication with the interior
for the purpose of supplying daily food to the inmate. Into this
tower Farcoonda was sent and confined. Three months had passed
without anything of interest occurring to break and diversify
the monotony of her dull existence in the tower. On the fourth
month, early in the evening, she heard the splash of innumerable oars, and being herself the daughter of a merchant, she
knew at once that a fleet of some merchant vessels were passing
the place ; she, therefore, having inscribed some words on a
thin brick slab, flung it through the aperture, and it fell on the
seventh and last vessel on which the merchant was. The inscription was to this effect : " I am a handsome woman whom
you may possess by releasing." The plate descended just at the
feet of the merchant who, reading the engraving, ordered the
inmate to be released. When a gap had been effected, the handsome prisoner was seen and admired by the merchant, but the
moment Farcoonda saw him, she saluted him with the appellation of father, saying that her reason for doing so was that she
was the wife of a *Badsha* who would be thankful to him for his
parental care of her. The merchant's vessels were all moored
in the very country where the husband of Farcoonda was the
reigning *Badsha*. The merchant, at her request, engaged a
magnificent house right opposite to the palace. She desired
him to spare no expense in procuring twenty-one girls for her,

who might bear the closest resemblance to her in person, figure, and appearance ; and when they were procured, then to expose his goods for public inspection, and especially to invite the *Badsha* to come and make his first choice. When the girls were brought to the merchant's, Farcoonda had each of them dressed with an apparel differing from the others, and all bedecked with a profusion of costly jewellery. On the morning when the *Badsha* was expected, one of the maids with a blue garb, was sent to offer some folds of beetle, and otto of roses, on a salver of elaborate workmanship. Just as the maid had offered them he, seeing her so like his own wife, exclaimed with pleasure and surprise, " Ah, Farcoonda, how have you come here ?" and as with this ejaculation he was about to embrace her, the maid, being prepared to make an appropriate answer, replied : " *Badsha*, it is beneath your dignity to stoop to a servant, and regard her with so much familiarity." Another girl was sent on the following day with a scarlet robe, on a similar office, when the *wadsha* had come on another visit. The *Badsha* was again deceived with the likeness between his wife and these waiting maids. He was again about to embrace her ; when the second maid remarked, " *Badsha*, your taste must be low, and your habits not strictly moral, otherwise you would not evince such familiarity with a menial." In this manner all the twenty-one girls were paraded before him, and he mistook all of them for his own wife, Farcoonda. Last of all, Farcoonda presented herself one morning, when he was about to repeat the same thing. Farcoonda observed, " *Wah, Badsha*, the twenty-one waiting maids of the merchant were all supposed to be Farcoondas in your estimation. How low a value you must set on your wife." With this prelude, Farcoonda entered into intelligent and agreeable conversation with the *Badsha* on that and several following days. He was charmed with her wit, good sense, and conversational ability ; nor did the attractions of her person lessen by frequent sight and familiarity, but they rather heightened as her valuable qualities were daily developed. To divert the evenness of their daily intercourse, Far-coonda proposed to ride on a fine day, and for this purpose, ordered a handsome pony, accoutred with rich trappings for him, and for herself, a noble charger of lank anatomy, but orna-mented with grand housings. Before riding, it was proposed to the *Badsha* that whoever should arrive first at the house, after going round the course, should be the slave of the other. Knowing that the pony would go in a peculiar sort of amble, which, though graceful and easy, was not of any speed, she proffered it to the *Badsha*, but he declined, saying that an animal so prettily ornamented was better suited to her riding than his. Farcoonda would on no account assent, but prevailed on him to ride it. When mounted, she applied the gentle stroke of her whip to the charger, and it bounded forward, leaving the *Badsha* far behind. He began to chafe with vexation, lashed the poor animal furiously, fearing to loose the race, but his beating could not augment the natural speed of the pony. Farcoonda had, in the mean while, gone far round the ring, and halted near a well, at which she descended, and having exchanged her costume with a farmer's wife, and tethered her horse at an adjacent copse, went and sat near the well with that common dress. Resting her head on her knees, she began to cry and wail, louder and more piteously, the nearer she saw the *Badsha* approach. Hearing the cry of a lonely woman at the well, he commiserated her distress, and felt for her sad situation. Descending from the pony, he inquired the reason of her sorrow, and as she lifted her reclining head, by that act her beauty was partially revealed to the admiring eyes of the *Badsha*. She in-formed him that she had a rite to perform, and there was no one to help her, for she was weak of strength to perform it ; that she had an imperative duty in fulfilment a certain vow, and that to lift twenty-one pitchers of water from that deep well. Saying this, she essayed to lift the water-pot, and to commence her work, but the gallant *Badsha* offered to help her, as she was letting down her pot. He had thus lifted the water, and poured round the spring for the twentieth time, when Farcoonda slided away, and mounting the charger, was soon out of sight, and at home before he could remount the pony. The *Badsha* was again annoyed that he lost time and the race, and on this account he felt no disposition to go to the merchant's, but proceeded on slowly and moodily to his own palace.

For several days, Farcoonda found the *Badsha* not disposed to visit her from his disappointment, vexation, and shame. She therefore thought of another device. She dressed herself like a respectable native officer, and mounting a highly mettlesome steed, went every morning and galloped and curvetted before the palace windows, for several consecutive days. The *Badsha* seeing this singular equestrian every day, capering and prancing, became desirous of knowing who he was; for this purpose he was invited to the palace. He inquired who the rider was, what was his name, and what was it that he was seeking. She replied that she was a soldier of fortune, her name was Farcoonda Khan, and that she was in quest of employment. He was so pleased with the handsome looks of the officer, that he willingly engaged his service for Rs. 100 per month, intending to have him always before his eyes, that he might look upon his beautiful person and graceful figure. The *Badsha* whiled away his unemployed hours in the agreeable and intelligent conversation of the officer, or in playing chess at night. In this manner, time glided on silently, when Farcoonda Khan thought of playing a game on a wager. In this game she won from him his signet ring, waistband, and his sword; having obtained these, Farcoonda Khan sought her cot, which was not far from the *Badsha's*, and going to rest for the night, her head dress fell off, and by it he discovered her luxuriant hair, and her sex. Now that Farcoonda Khan had obtained her wish, by getting those articles which belonged to the *Badsha*, to prove her skill and the guiltlessness of her intimacy, she rose up before dawn and went away to the merchant's. She acquainted the merchant that it was now her best time to go back to the tower, thanked him for his more than parental care of her, promising that some time or other, she might have the pleasing gratification of repaying him for his benevolent action. When she had got within the tower, she desired the workman to build up the gap. When nine months had expired after her self-imposed confinement, she had a son born in the tower. The man who brought her food daily, was surprised to hear the cry of a baby within the building. When he went back after furnishing her allowance of bread and water, he duly informed the *Badsha* of the strange incident. The *Badsha* was greatly incensed on hearing what he thought would tend to his perpetual dishonor, so he proceeded to the tower with the intention of cutting her down with his sword after having satisfied himself of the truth of the report. Going and ordering an aperture to be made in the tower, and when an opening was effected sufficiently wide for the admission of a person, Farcoonda sent down the unconscious baby with a looking-glass for the *Badsha* to consult his own physiognomy, and compare it with that of the child; and also his belt, sword, and the signet ring. The *Badsha* became now fully sensible that the child was his own progeny, and the ingeniousness of Farcoonda, her innocence and virtuous disposition, were disclosed and made apparent by all that transpired. He took her home, acknowledging his rashness and hasty disposition, and doating on her much more for the perfection of her character which these circumstances had brought to light; the injustice which he had done her previously, and the severity he had exercised, these he admitted were culpable.*

---

* The story of Adam and Eve, after the fashion in which it is given here, leads me to think that this tale has a Moslem origin.

THE STORY OF A MERCHANT.

THERE was a merchant who was not only famous for his smartness and skill in his occupation, but was known for a good and benevolent man in the country in which he lived. It was indispensable from the nature of his calling, that he should leave his country on long journies at times, in order to prosecute his trade with distant nations. Thus he had prepared to set out for a period of twelve years; but before doing so, he deemed it proper to leave strict instructions with his mother, regarding her care and watchfulness over his wife, whose want of experience and mature judgment might lead her, though unwittingly, into acts of impropriety in the absence of the restraining influence of moral example, or wise precept. But there existed, unfortunately, a perpetual disagreement between the mother-in-law and her daughter-in-law. The merchant's mother was glad to have this authority delegated to her, and thought in her own mind that it was now her opportunity to revenge herself upon her untractable, headstrong daughter-in-law; for the very first fault which she might find her commit, she would endeavour to pack her off from the house. Being constantly on the watch, she saw that her daughter-in-law's maid-servant, on getting out early one morning, left the gate open. Upon this pretence, she met her, and rebuking for opening the gate at an unseasonable hour and leaving it ajar, desired her daughter-in-law to quit the house instantly. The innocent creature made solemn protestations as to her not being guilty of any improper act, but the old woman, who was determined upon sending her away from the house, would not listen to any asseverations which she made.

Nine months after the departure of her son, on his trading expedition, she sent his wife away, and acquainted him of the circumstance by letter in an exaggerated form. At the time when the merchant's wife was quitting the house, she informed her mother-in-law that, as she was carrying, and was soon expecting to be confined, she might permit her to live in a hut in the neighbourhood, and after the birth of her child, she would then gladly go away and seek her fortune elsewhere. But determined as she was to revenge herself, she would not listen to any pleading which her daughter-in-law had offered. She was forced to go away, but whither, she could not determine upon, for want of the knowledge of the country and the roads. Her troubles and sorrows had almost driven her to the verge of insanity ; in short, people thought that she had gone crazy. As she was lying in a state of utter helplessness on the road-side, Masoom Mulna, passing that way and seeing her, asked her history, but she was, from prostration of strength, prevented from saying any more than disclosing the condition of her want and suffering. The Mulna invited her to his house, telling her that she might live with his family, who would provide for her wants, and assist her in her confinement. When she was conducted to the Mulna's residence, his wife, a shrewd and punctilious woman, was displeased that a woman was picked up from the streets, and admitted into the family without knowing who she was, and what character she had previously sustained in the world. "She is in great distress, and is near the time of her confinement," said the humane Mulna, " and this is sufficient reason for us to shelter her at present." The over-scrupulous wife would not so easily yield up her point. She rejoined, " For your probity and unblemished character, the people of the village compliment you by calling you Mulna. The presence of a handsome stranger in our habitation might give to scandalous men an excuse to stigmatise your reputation, and you would forfeit your good name thereby. I would, therefore, advise you to send her to live in yonder shed under the cocoanut tree." This proposition being acceded to by her husband, she was placed in possession of the hut.

A village road lay close by the hut, and by that road a zemindar was journeying, who seeing that the woman belonged to some respectable family, inquired after her circumstances, and finding that she was in actual destitution, sent her a few rupees to help her in her need. This small assistance was of great use, as she was soon confined of a very handsome son, such as is rarely born even in the house of a Prince. The midwife who attended on her, waited to be remunerated for her service. The merchant's wife related her distress, and informed her that she had lately received a present of twenty rupees, out of which she had spent some, but that she was willing to give her eight rupees, and to reserve a few to meet her own future wants. About this time, the wife of a Vizier was also in labour, and his servants were sent to invite the midwife over, but not finding her at home, they had come in search of her. As she was returning from the poor woman's house, they met her and conducted her to the Vizier.

The midwife, on arriving at the Vizier's house, desired to know on what terms he wished to engage her services. He being a wicked cunning man, said, that it was customary to pay four annas at the parturition of a boy, and if a girl, it ought to be but two annas. The midwife informed him that she had attended a short time ago on a poor woman who was dependent on the charity of a Mulna, and that she had given her eight rupees, and she was confined of a boy so handsome that even among the noble and affluent, she had never seen his like. The Vizier, who had a daughter, dismissed the woman after paying her four rupees for her assistance.

He could not forget what he heard about the child of this poor woman, for he was desirous of possessing him, and rearing the boy up as his son. In the court to which he attended, there were four men who were long known to him as being adepts in all sorts of trickery and villany. He invited them to a private conference, in which he promised them a handsome reward if they could bring him the child secretly. These men, who were quite up to any atrocious deed, and to any desperate

work, hesitated at this novel kind of tax put upon their skill.
The Vizier, seeing them somewhat reluctant to venture on this
sort of undertaking, promised them a higher reward. The love
of money tempted men of such black character to any work,
stifling their gentler feelings if they possessed any in the deep
and secret recesses of their hearts. They went on their errand,
consulting with each other as to the best and the most efficient
mode of executing the work, when finding very opportunely a
pumpkin which grew on a shed on the road which they were
pursuing, they took it, and substituting it for the child, brought
away the baby and made him over to the Vizier, who was highly
pleased with the success of his secret wish. He brought up
the child as his own, gave him a good education, and supplied
all his wants. The poor mother, after so great a loss as the
bereavement of her first-born, became distracted in mind. She
went about roving from place to place as an insane person, and in
doing so she happened to go to the country where her son was
with the Vizier. She saw there some fakirs, dervishes, with other
destitute classes of persons, going in crowds to a public treat
which was to be given by the Vizier. She inquired of her
fellow-travellers on what account the dinner was to be given.
They informed her that the Vizier had a handsome boy, and
as his marriage overtures were completed, the feast was intended in honour of the occasion. The poor woman, hearing of
this, had strong secret presentment that the lad might be
no other than her long lost son for whom she was grieving; so
she ventured to follow the tide of the crowd with the anxious
expectation of seeing the dear child by some propitious accident,
and that she might by that means ascertain if he were her son for
whom she was mourning so long in utter despondence. When
she had taken a quiet seat at a distance from the residence
of the Vizier, the boy, all life and hilarity, came out skipping
and playing with other young persons of his own age. The
moment that her eyes, in their searching glance, alighted on
him, she discovered him to be her own son. Unable to

suppress her maternal feelings and her emotions, she ran with tears and sobs, and embracing, kissed him fervently, saying that he was her own lost child. This turmoil and bustle which had collected a number of idle spectators, soon reached the acute ear of the Vizier, who suspecting the cause, and fearing the result, instructed the four ruffians, who aided him in the capture of the boy, to convey the mad woman away from the place to some distant field, where they might strangle her, and put her out of the reach of mischief; but the youth, who was at that time within audible distance from the Vizier, concealed by a cloth partition, hearing his cruel request to the men, met them as they were about to go forth on their errand, and threatened to bring them to punishment if they ever dared to imbue their hands in the blood of the poor innocent creature, being, as he was, in possession of the secret of their conspiracy. If they liked, they might conduct her to a distance from the country, where she might be left with a menace never to approach the place where the Vizier was, for in fact, she was guilty of no actual crime. He hastened also to have an interview with the woman ; he remonstrated against her imprudence for calling him her son, for a person like the Vizier, he added, whose influence was considerable, and whose authority extensive, had it in his power to inflict severe punishment. He warned her not to come to the country again if she valued her life. " You are my own son, how can I live without seeing you ?" she said—"let me rather die than be prevented from beholding what to me is more than life." She was taken away, however, and set at liberty in a field, at a considerable distance from the Vizier's locality, but she did not quit the country, and remained at the adjacent village, where she made daily minute inquiries where the school was to which the Vizier's son went to receive instruction, at what hour he left home, and the way by which he went there. Having ascertained these particulars, she went and seated herself patiently on the road by which the youngster was expected to return from the school.

As the Vizier's son was going home in a palkee, his sight
fell on the woman. After passing her a short distance, he
stopped, and going up to her, remonstrated against her being
seen in the country, and the danger to which she was ex-
posing herself indiscreetly. She wept, and told him how difficult it was for her to part from him, having found him after
the lapse of so many years. "Enquire, my son,"—she said—
"of the midwife who attended on me at your confinement, and
who is living in this very country, and she will corroborate the
fact and satisfy you if you are my child or not."

The Vizier's son, hearing all this, returned to his abode with
a head full of musings and a heavy heart. He could neither
relish his dinner, nor take any pleasure in his usual recreations,
until the mystery was solved to his own satisfaction. Going
one day for a walk, he took his course towards the house of the
midwife, from whom he learnt whose son he was, and the incidents of his past life. He became dissatisfied with his situation
at the Vizier's, having learnt by what means his poor mother
had been deprived of her child. He had a private interview
the next day with her, and advised her to institute a suit against
the Vizier in the *durbar* of the *Badsha*. She adopted his advice, but found many obstacles, and met with strong opposition
at Court, where the influence of the Vizier was considerable.
The poor woman was about to be driven out of the *durbar*, with
hisses and ridicule cast on her statements and for making invidious
charges against the man of rank and position. She could find
no sympathy from people whose sentiments were biassed in favour
of the man of wealth, but met rather with laughter and derision.
The youngster, making his appearance at the Court when the woman was being dismissed, spoke to the *Badsha* without the least
trepidation—"Great *Badsha!* you are considered to be the
father of your subjects. Your government is established in
the affection of your people by the impartial administration
of justice, and the exercise of equitable laws. Can you send
this poor woman away without investigating her case, and

not incurring the reproach of foreign Princes, and the Chiefs, your neighbours, or exciting no discontent among your own subjects, who possess common sense and a perception of right and wrong. Try her case, good *Badsha!* and if it should prove that her allegations are false, punish rather than set a deceitful person at liberty; but do not, I beseech you, let a woman, because poor, go away without receiving redress, nor let the innocent suffer wrong and injustice at the hands of a man who is surrounded with power, and screened by his station from punishment, while he continues unchecked in the perpetration of deeds of atrocity." After this public appeal was made to his justice, the *Badsha* was obliged to give a hearing to her complaint. The midwife gave her deposition at the *durbar*, and the poor woman substantiated her claim by producing the Mulna as witness, in whose ground she was residing at the time of her confinement, and from whence she lost her offspring in so tragical a manner; nor could the Vizier give a satisfactory explanation how he had obtained possession of the boy. The weight of these combined evidences inclined the balance of justice in her favour, and so the case was decided to her entire satisfaction. The son, to show that he was not unmindful of the favour and kindness he had received from the Vizier, interceded for him with the *Badsha* with tears and a glowing eloquence, and on his account the Vizier was taken back into favour. The son was soon locked in the arms of his fond mother. They left the country together, and proceeded to the place where his father, the merchant, was expected to return from his protracted journey. They arrived at their own residence one evening. The meeting of the merchant with his wife and son was, though joyous, not unmixed with bitter regret on account of the many sad events which had transpired. Now that the mother-in-law, who was the cause of the wife's sufferings, was dead, the past was buried in oblivion. As a good, faithful, and prudent wife, she forbore to reproach him with the faults, not of his heart but his judgment. Having passed through the billows of tribulation, obtained her long lost child, and restored to the society of her husband for whom she had a deep and sincere regard, she, like a wise woman, studied to forget her sufferings, and to make the best use of the blessings with which she was now surrounded; and with this nice sense of propriety, she endeavoured to dissipate the gloom which at times flitted over the life of her husband, when memory held to his view the remorseful picture of the past.

HE THAT DIGGETH A PIT FOR ANOTHER, FALLETH INTO IT HIMSELF.

THERE was a Rajah who had a very valuable flower tree in his garden. He ordered his gardener not to permit anybody to pluck a single leaf, or to stand holding one of its branches, and to secure this object, he ordered a *sentry* to watch the tree, with power to shoot the culprit who violated his order.

It so happened, that a poor simple youth had strolled into the garden unperceived by the guard, and holding one of the branches of the interdicted tree, stood looking admiringly at the gorgeous flowers, and inhaling their redolent fragrance. The guard, approaching the youth, told him of the offence of which he was guilty, beat him soundly, and sent him away. The reason why he did not unscrupulously destroy his life was, that he was a simpleton, and that he did it from sheer ignorance. The youngster, smarting under the infliction, and hearing the relation of his offence which appeared to him very preposterous, exclaimed, " Ah! what wonderful tree is that for which there are such curious restrictions. I know a tree of incalculable value, called *assnee* tree, with *murtca* leaf, which bears pearls and yields coral, and on whose branches *lacs* of birds roost at

27

night, while the shadow of the tree falls over a circumference of eighty miles." The sentry, hearing this bold expression of the youth, caught and took him before the Rajah. He was interrogated regarding the tree. The youth related its virtues and wonderful properties, when the Badshá asked him to produce it.

The youth, having obtained three months' leave to find the tree, went on in his journey not knowing exactly whither. He came at last to the border of a *jungle*, entering which he saw a *joghee*, behind whom he went and stood in breathless silence. The religious mendicant, knowing that some one was standing behind, requested him to come before. In doing as the youngster was bid, he saluted the *joghee* with the conciliatory appellation of father. The *joghee* observed, " If you have come to serve me, my son, go and fill yonder pipe with *gunjah*." The youth did as he was requested. The *joghee*, enjoying his intoxicating pipe, waited the arrival of certain devotees who brought him every morning and evening a variety of edibles as offerings to be presented by him to the rural deities. After accepting these offerings, and going through the religious cere- monies, he gave the men back half of what they brought, and retained the residue for his own use. The youth shared daily with the *joghee* in the refreshments thus brought for their sus- tenance.

Living in this manner for some time, the *joghee* found the youth one day rather moody, and inquired the reason of his abstraction. The youth disclosed to him the reason of his visit to the jungle. The *joghee* advised him to travel in a certain direction of the forest, where he would come in sight of a tank, near the verge of which he would discover a bushy tree, climb- ing it he should remain concealed until he saw some one going to bathe in the tank. The youth did as he was advised. He saw three seraphic visitants from his concealment on the tree. Coming near they divested themselves of their outer bright garments, and went down to enjoy the refreshing liquid of the tank. While they were sporting in the pellucid water, the youth took up and concealed their garments. The celestial beings, coming up to dress themselves, and not finding their garments, were placed in a sad state of perplexity. They called out to any one who might have taken to restore them the articles, and that they were willing to accede to any terms, or requests which might be made for their restoration. The youth, in giving up the things, stipulated that they should consent to marry him. They were compelled to yield, but they intended to defeat his object by some of their many artifices. The eldest of the three sisters presented herself on the day fixed for the solemnization of marriage, in the revolting condition of a female covered all over with unsightly sores and ulcers. The *joghee*, who was deeply versed in the occult sciences, and who had a familiar knowledge of all things, perceiving the manœuvre that was about to be practised upon his *protegé*, winked at the youth not to evince any hesitation, or decline the marriage, but to accept her hand cheerfully and cordially. Having succeeded in gaining the hand of the eldest of the celestial *purrees*, her two younger sisters were easily subdued to his wishes. Taking his three wives to the country of his birth, he resided in their happy company, forgetful in the witchery of their charming conversation, of his engagement with the Badsha.

One day, when his wives' nails had grown beyond a decent length, and they had expressed a desire to have them pared, the barber who was sent for to execute the office, happened to be the Rajah's hair-dresser. When the first wife submitted her hand through the folds of a flowing drapery that answered the purpose of a screen, it was a sight of such dazzling beauty to the barber that he sank motionless to the floor. When the two other sisters presented their hands in their turn, it had the same effect on him. When on the following morning the barber was visiting the Rajah, he told him, in the glowing language of admiration and wonder, that he saw the hands of three very extraordinary beauties living with the plain poor youth who was under engagement to the Rajah to produce a very rare tree. The barber strongly urged the Rajah to destroy the worthless fellow, as he had not yet executed his commission, and to take two of his wives to himself, and to make him a present of the third. The Rajah informed him that the time appointed for accomplishing his promise was not up yet, and therefore to go and remind him of the tree. This the barber did with alacrity. Three days, however, before his contract with the Rajah would have terminated, the youth became sad and thoughtful, and in that depressed predicament showed little dispositon for the enjoyments of the table. One of the *purrees*, with winning and persuasive manners, extracted from him the reason of his dejection. He related to her all about the Rajah's famous tree, the rules which he had laid down for its preservation, and the stripes which he had endured on account of unwittingly violating his injunction, adding that, in his vexation and suffering, he had uttered the name of a tree of which he had not the remotest idea if it existed any where in the whole universe, and that it was this folly for which he was regretting and repining. The *purree* requested him to cheer up his spirits, saying that the thing was of easy accomplishment. " Go," she said, " and tell the Rajah to make a covered path from our residence to the plain before his palace, and to encircle the field with a wall of cloth and a canopy on the top, covering an area of eighty miles, when the tree will be produced and exhibited before the *Badsha*, his subjects, and such friends as he may wish to invite to the wonderful show."

The preparation being got ready with all expedition, and all the guests invited to the exhibition from neighbouring countries, the oldest *purree* went to the plain through the covered passage, stood at the centre of the field, and there shook her luxuriant raven tresses loose from their graceful confinement. In a moment she sprouted forth to the full dimensions of a magnificent tree, her hair forming leaves of gorgeous loveliness, while the entire form and outline was of exquisite beauty. All stood at first gazing at it with mute attention, wrapt up with thoughts of wondering admiration, and then burst forth into loud and exultant praise at such an uncommon sight.

The poor youth was heartily glad to have escaped from a dilemma into which his imprudence had thrown him, but the envious barber would not let him alone. He went to the Rajah, and again urged him to destroy the young man, take two of his wives, and bestow on him the third as a gift for his protracted faithful services. The Rajah told him that he could not do him an injustice. The barber advised him to send for the youth, order him to put out all the mustard seed from his godown, for the purpose of drying and airing in the sun, and after that to gather the whole, and store the seed in the same place by the evening, taking care that there should not be the smallest deficiency in the quantity, or delay in its execution, for in that case he should be beheaded. The command of the Rajah was speedily communicated by the officious barber to the youth. On receiving this unpleasant order, he was made thoughtful and reflective, not only on account of the arduous nature of the task imposed, but justly conjecturing that such a novel and whimsical injunction foreboded no good, but appeared rather to be a snare by which to entangle him. The second *purree* was made acquainted by him with this other secret grief which was rankling in his bosom. She recommended his banishing all apprehension from his mind, to go to work with alacrity, and after the mustard seed had been spread out, dried, and aired in the sun, according to his instructions, to tell her then, and she would send somebody to gather the seed into the barn without the loss of a single grain. She possessed some secret power and influence over all tribes and classes of pigeons; she, therefore, by supernatural means, commanded a large flock to appear. They came before her in dark clouds, and waited submissively to hear her commands. They were desired to go with all expedition and gather every particle of mustard grain which was drying in the sun, into the godown of the Rajah before sunset, and to take good care that not a single grain was lost in performing the work. This was executed with celerity, and the necessary care and attention which it needed.

The wicked barber, in the performance of his office on the following day, was informed by the Rajah that the youth could not be entrapped. The baffled barber set his diabolical genius to cogitate on some other plan to ensnare the youth, and before the day had closed, he presented himself before his royal employer with sinister advice, from which he deemed there would be small chance for the youngster to extricate himself. " May it please your highness," said the barber, " to command the youth to pay a visit to your honored parents in paradise, and to bring news from thence how the venerable couple are doing there." The youth was sent for, and the wishes of his sovereign was communicated. He was sore puzzled to know by what means a journey to heaven could be accomplished, but the barber, who was present at the conference, enlightened him on the subject, by informing him that the journey was to be performed after the same manner as it was done by a *Suttee*. The youth went home with a drooping head, and dejected countenance, and overwhelmed with fearful forebodings. His third wife, ascertaining the cause of his altered mood, told him to entertain no fear, for that she had the means in her power to preserve him from the destruction his enemies were aiming to execute. While the Rajah had ordered a funeral pyre of the scented sandal wood to be erected, and the wood was being piled for the morrow's immolation, the *purree*, who presided over all rats as their sovereign, invited them to appear before her, and they came tumbling, scratching, and crowding in large herds. She commanded all of them to start off immediately, and commence an excavation from her residence to the spot over which the pyre was being erected, taking care that the whole operation should terminate within the night. The youngster was advised how to act on the occasion, when the Rajah's officers came to take him away on the following morning. He mounted the logs of wood amidst the deafening roar of drums and other equally discordant instruments, and the cheering shouts of the spectators; but as soon as the pile was lighted, and the smoke had risen from the bottom and enshrouded him, he turned over and dropped into the excavation which led him on to the room of his own residence. The barber was highly gratified at the destruction of the youth, and the success of his treacherous scheme.

He took an early opportunity to visit the Rajah, and to remind him now that the fellow was despatched to the shades below, to take two of his incomparable wives to himself, and make him a royal present of the third. The Rajah reminded him that the stipulated time for his return, which was the fourth day, was not yet expired, and on that account, that he could not so soon set about making a division of his wives. On the morning of the fourth day, as the youth was proceeding from his house to the palace, such men as had been spectators of his immolation, seeing him resuscitated, ran away from him with fear. The Rajah, with whom was his flatterer, the barber, seeing the youth approaching, fell senseless on the floor, not knowing if he were a spirit, or the same person in his corporeal appearance. So soon as the Rajah revived, the youth, saluting him, said, that he had much pleasure in seeing his worthy parents; they were doing very well, except that his father's beard had grown inconveniently bushy, and his mother's nails had become too long, and that he was delegated to convey the wishes of his respected parents to him, which was to send them their old servant, the barber, to cut his hair, and to pare her nails. The Rajah, in the presence of his full Court, compelled the barber to pay a visit to his father, as it was, he observed, their united, urgent, and particular wish that he should be sent. The cursing and swearing, and debasing humiliations of the barber, could not avert his fate. He was forced to fall into the snare which he had thrice laid to destroy a harmless innocent person. He was burnt on the pyre the next day to be a warning to those who read his story.

A PARODY ON THE CASHMERIAN GIRL.

With Soorma tinge thy black eyes fringe.

L. V. DEROZIO.

LET thy eye's soft blue, shine on my view,
    That will gladden oft my weary day ;
Let virtue dress each modest tress,
And Lena love shall be my lay.

Lena ! there's many a glitt'ring gem,
Which the dark caves of ocean bind,
But none, thou dear, and sainted maid,
O none like thee I e'er shall find !

In Seraz walks many tints may glow,
Which many men may fondly seek ;
But who can find, so rare a kind,
Like that which shades thy brow so meek ?

By thy side to walk, with holy talk,
Pleasant the earth would be to me ;
Thy chasten'd look, calm as the brook,
Would bid the clouds of sorrow flee.

Nay, smile in love, for thou shouldst smile,
Though the fair world be not our home ;
Our hopes are bright, and the future light,
Illumes our path where'er we roam.

That light my love, is from above,
No sad'ning darkness we shall know ;
That ray was deign'd, with love unfeign'd,
Our hearts to gladden with its glow.

The worldly life is full of strife,
And all its scenes below are sad ;
Then I would haste, with my angel guest,
To that fair world where all are glad.

No shades of gloom, would be our doom,
In that love's ocean depths above,
Where the fair field, would ever yield,
Spontan'ous joy and lasting love.

In that verdant shore, where evermore,
No sorrow's tears would dare to flow ;
There we would live, no more to grieve,
Our hearts circl'd with a holy glow.

Then come on love, we'll wing like dove,
And mount up to that region of peace ;
We will there dwell, leaving this dark vale,
With bright seraphs in endless bliss.

THE TEARS OF SYMPATHY.

An imitation of " The Liquid Gem,"—adapted to the same air.

TINY drops of sparkling dew,
   Changeful in thy lovely hue;
Nature's shrine and earthly bower,
Cradles thee midst morning flower.
But the liquid gems that shine,
Ever truthful and divine,
Are the holy tears that lie,
Deep in hearts that ever sigh.
                       Tiny drops &c.

Humid orbs of heavenly love,
Born of feelings from above;
Priceless pearls from holier mine,
Glisten sweet o'er human shrine.
Pour thy soft'ning soothing ray,
O'er hearts that weep and fade away;
Thou soft gem of lasting light,
Shed thy rays o'er life's dark night.
                      Humid orbs &c.